# A FELLOWSHIP OF BAKERS & MAGIC

## J. PENNER

Poisoned Pen
PRESS

Copyright © 2023, 2025 by J. Penner
Cover and internal design © 2025 by Sourcebooks
Cover design by Erin Fitzsimmons/Sourcebooks
Cover art © Katie Daisy
Map art by Travis Hasenour
Internal design by Tara Jaggers/Sourcebooks
Internal tip-in art © Clara Fang
Internal images © Garsya/Getty Images, Daria Ustiugova/Getty Images,
Olga Shipilova/Getty Images, Kseniya Ozornina/Getty Images, Ekaterina
Kudriavtseva/Getty Images, Tatyana Sidorova/Getty Images, Kyosi/
Getty Images, Lidia Rodkina/Getty Images, Mimomy/Getty Images

Published by Poisoned Pen Press, an imprint of Sourcebooks
P.O. Box 4410, Naperville, Illinois 60567-4410
(630) 961-3900
sourcebooks.com

Originally self-published in 2023 by J. Penner.

Cataloging-in-Publication Data is on file with the Library of Congress.

Printed and bound in the United States of America.
WOZ 10 9 8 7 6 5 4 3 2 1

*To all the kind people.*

DUNDES HEIGHTS
THE SEA OF THE SOMERDOWS
ADENASHIRE
Mount Blackdon
Stouling Forest
COLMORE MOUNTAINS
LANGHEIM

THE

NORTHERN

LANDS

RIDGELANDS

THE
PRESMAR
GULF

THE
SOUTHEAST SHORES

DRYWARD

THE SOUTHERN
DESERT

N

THE
LOWER
OCEAN

# 1

A thyme-infused raspberry tart sailed off Arleta Starstone's rickety old wagon as if it had sprouted wings and taken flight of its own accord. The pastry smacked into the ground, the sweet, red fruit exploding through the thin shell and splattering its sticky juice onto the earth with a horrible little squelch.

Wasted.

"Oh, stars in heaven," the young woman muttered under her breath, her wavy hair sticking to the back of her sweaty neck, making the entire situation another level of worse.

Arleta pulled her wagon over to the side of Adenashire's rocky dirt road, her nose wrinkling at the ruined tart's fruity scent as it mixed with musty earth. She quickly adjusted her pastries so no more might escape.

As she was sighing, her gaze flicked up to the oak trees stretching above, where a group of ebony-feathered crows sat cawing and hopping from branch to branch. They hungrily eyed the awaiting breakfast, which it would be shortly since she had no time to clean the mess she'd made outside the main street.

She was late. *Again.* The timepiece in her pocket had told her so before she'd even left her cottage.

Arleta quickly glanced around, checking if anyone had noticed her mishap.

Other than the crows, it seemed no one had.

Wishing she had tied back her long chestnut hair better before leaving home, Arleta hiked up her tan linen skirt and brushed the loose strands from her face. Determined, she yanked on the metal handle of her overloaded wagon and soldiered on. Heart quickening at the exertion, she surveyed the rocky terrain ahead of her, mentally calculating the best route through the jumble of stones littering the way. There would be no more lost bake stock that morning.

All the while, the aroma of fresh bread and sweet pastries wafted from the back of the wagon; her stomach gurgled in protest, reminding her that she'd forgotten to eat before she'd left her cottage.

*Again.*

Verdreth and Ervash, the too-kind orc couple who lived next door, would surely lay into her if they discovered she wasn't eating enough. They always tried to act like her fathers, but she was not a child anymore. She hadn't been for a long time.

Time. She just needed more time in the day.

But there was *never* enough time.

All the booths would be reserved if she didn't arrive at the market by half past, so she needed all the shortcuts she could take. Tonix Figlet, the stall renter, never held a spot for her. From the looks of him, the round, furry face and cute-as-a-button expression, one would think quokkans were a kind folk, but they had quite the sordid past in the Northern Lands—although who knew what was true and what wasn't. This one seemed to fulfill the rumors of their renown. Tonix, forever crabby, would have much rather rented the stalls to more *prestigious* merchants: elves, dwarves, even the rare ogre with goods to hock.

Magicless humans like Arleta were at the bottom of his list, along with anyone else with no magic.

No magic, no respect.

Even if she made it to the market on time, Tonix would surely relegate her to the back, where she'd need to sell her delights at a fraction of the price as those sellers who'd snapped up the premium spots.

"Despite everyone going on about how *good* the cardamom lemon bars are," she muttered under her breath.

As she rounded a corner into the village proper, Arleta's wagon wheels clattered against Adenashire's uneven cobblestones, the sound echoing through the narrow alleyway. The thick, pungent scent of refuse and decaying vegetables made her nose wrinkle. The smell was so strong that it completely blanketed the tempting aromas from her wagon.

She quickly approached the alley's entrance and the sounds of the opening market hit her ears. Tonix Figlet stood in the bustle in all his glory, his furry taupe paws firmly planted at his waist. His clothing, tailored wool pants and jacket over a freshly pressed cotton shirt, was simple but well-made, and of high quality, showing that he earned a good living as the market's owner. The marsupial's nut-brown eyes flicked over to her, and, for a moment, recognition sparked.

Then he plastered on a honeyed smile, turned on his heel,

and walked away in the opposite direction, toward the linen sellers.

Arleta cursed more than the stars.

She gritted her teeth and pulled her wagon forward, determined to find a spot to sell her pastries no matter what the quokkan thought about her. Arleta knew there would be a decent amount of groveling on her part in the next few minutes, but going back to the cottage with this much inventory was not an option. Not that morning. Not since she'd spent most of her weekly budget to buy and make what was in the wagon. She needed to sell it that day, or everything would go stale.

"Mr. Figlet!" she called after him. The wagon's handle was slick with sweat, and her arms trembled with the effort of pulling the heavy load forward. Her voice rang out, slicing through the market noise, more than one seller looking her way.

"Mr. Figlet!" she shouted again.

The quokkan's worn leather boots scuffed against the rough cobblestone street as he came to an abrupt halt. Arleta would simply continue acting as a thorn in his side if he didn't speak to her, her tenacity no secret. He turned.

"Yes, Miss Starstone?" As soon as the words left his mouth, he pursed his marsupial lips and sucked his teeth. From his pocket he pulled out a golden watch, glanced at it, and held out the timepiece. "You know what time it is?"

Contempt was written all over his deceptively adorable features, but Arleta refused to let it get to her. Instead, she squared her shoulders, ready to do whatever it took to get a spot.

Beg. Plead. Offer Tonix Figlet free pastries for life.

She slid to a stop and the wagon behind her bucked, nearly dumping more raspberry tarts. While the quokkan waited for her to speak, tapping his foot, Arleta cleared her throat.

She glanced over his shoulder and scanned the booths. Sure enough, the worst spot at the back was still available, and customers were only just starting to trickle in.

There was still time to set up.

"Yes, Mr. Figlet. I'm just a *little* late." With a small shrug of apology, Arleta made a pinching gesture with her fingers.

"Girl, you're *always* late. The vendor queue closes at eight sharp. It's now ten past. I'm sorry, Miss Starstone," he said, his voice drenched with false sympathy, tacking on a precious expression she felt was solely for the benefit of any onlookers.

Arleta winced. "Yes, I know." The quokkan was right, of course. She was always running behind, always struggling to keep up with life's demands, and she had given him all her excuses before.

She was the only person doing this work.

She had no magic to help her.

Time had gotten away from her when she was trying to perfect a new recipe.

The pastries needed to be sold somewhere, but Arleta couldn't afford a food cart or the license that accompanied it, or, stars forbid, save enough gold to actually buy a *bakery* in town. The market was her only option to sell her goods.

But Tonix Figlet didn't seem to care about any of those things, and especially not from Arleta. Now, if a local *elf* had fallen on hard times, he might have extended a small courtesy, although what Tonix *really* cared about was the reputation of his market. Everyone knew this.

And those without magic brought that reputation down.

"I'm afraid there are no spots left for today," the quokkan said and started to turn. "Perhaps you should try again next week."

Arleta was incredibly aware of this dance between her and Tonix, the one that kept her in her place.

"I have silver," Arleta said and quickly dug into her pocket to pull out the coins.

At the clinking of metal, Tonix twisted back, his demeanor changing in Arleta's favor, though just by a fraction.

Arleta took it as her in.

"You still have one booth open, and I can offer you...*six* coins for it." The booth was in the back *and* slightly blocked by a pole, so truly it was barely worth the usual four, but offering him more always seemed to soften the blow of renting to her.

A knot formed in Arleta's stomach as she thrust out the coins. The weight of them was heavy in her palm, a familiar, tangible reminder of the sacrifice she was making. Unless she sold out that day *and* generous customers filled her tip jar, paying the extra coins would mean choosing between not eating dinner for a few days and giving up some special ingredients for an upcoming test bake she was planning.

But right then, it didn't matter.

She *needed* that booth.

She had to stop living week to week.

Around her, the market continued to buzz with rising activity. Vendors preparing their wares mingled with friendly chatter and the occasional burst of laughter from a passing group of children. Fires were stoked, scenting the air with the roasting of all kinds of savory meats.

"Six coins," she proclaimed as if it were a fortune. Then she added, her tone dripping with honeyed sweetness, "You don't want the place to look *empty*, do you?"

Arleta was fully aware of how that last addition would knife

Tonix a little. He had a reputation to uphold, after all, and even filling that space with a magicless vendor's goods would be better than the eyesore of an open booth.

As she waited for his reply, tension rose between her and the marsupial. Every word she said was a gamble, a delicate dance, and she had to get them just right if she wanted to secure her day's sales.

"Fine." The quokkan grabbed the coins from Arleta's hand. "Now get out of my sight."

"Thank you, Mr. Figlet," she said, not waiting for him to change his mind. With a grunt, Arleta took hold of her wagon's handle and raced to the empty booth, just missing the pole with the corner of her wagon.

To her left was a minotaur woman selling costume jewelry, clad in a flowing dress that shimmered in the sunlight. Her jewelry also glinted in the light, reflecting sparkling rainbow patterns onto the surrounding stalls. Arleta couldn't help but admire the intricate designs, each piece more beautiful than the last, though nothing she could ever afford.

On her right, the bouquet of rich, golden honey wafted toward her from the booth worked by a stocky, bearded halfling. The stall was adorned with jars filled with thick liquids of different shades, ranging from pale gold to rich amber. Each container glowed in the sunlight, casting a golden hue onto everything around it.

Neither vendor said hello, but just the thought of the honey lit the baking part—which in fact took up more than an average percentage—of Arleta's brain on fire.

Fluffy honey buns with silky whipped frosting.

Flaky puff pastry laden with honey and walnuts.

Rose water and honey cakes.

Her stomach rumbled, and she knew she would have to pick up a jar or two before the day's end.

*If* she made enough to afford it.

"Focus," she muttered to herself while she pulled out a fine lace tablecloth that had belonged to her mother and spread it out on the display table. Every time she used this particular cloth, it transported her back to a time when the family kitchen was filled with the redolence of her mother's freshly baked goods.

Back to when things were right in the world.

Arleta gulped the sudden swell of emotion down and spread the cloth out, taking care to smooth out every crease and fold, wanting it to look perfect.

Her mother had been an avid amateur baker. It was where Arleta had inherited the "pastry passion," as well as her noteworthy jawline.

Her father had run an apothecary business. When she was younger, his shop had always been a mystery to her. Back then there were just strange bottles and jars lining the shelves, but as she aged, she'd appreciated the herbs and plants, and eventually this knowledge had helped her create unique and flavorful treats. Plus, the tasty ingredients also had healing properties. She believed that when her customers ate them, the pastries healed them from the inside out. If not the body, then the soul.

It was Arleta's own "little dash of magic," the way the ingredients came together and created something new and delicious. It was a kind of alchemy that she loved.

Even if she, or any human, *couldn't* use real magic, the only beings in the Northern Lands who the earth and stars guaranteed would not have it.

Over 50 percent of humans could be *affected* by magic, but

they were not gifted its use, not by having it flowing in their blood or by having the ability to channel it from the outside.

Arleta arranged her offerings. The thyme raspberry tarts were her newest creation. The earthiness of the fresh herbs and the raspberries' sweetness was almost intoxicating, and she knew how the tart's delicate, flaky crust melted in the mouth. Next to the tarts were soft and chewy wild blueberry cookies. Verdreth and Ervash had sampled a taste of them last night—though, because they were orcs, sometimes a "taste" equaled more of her product than Arleta expected.

There were also several loaves of rosemary sourdough bread, cinnamon rolls, and petite lemon lavender cakes, each one a small work of art. Last, she arranged the wooden price signs that Ervash had carved for her. She'd told him it wasn't necessary, but he'd made them anyway. The orc was quite an artist, with a fine eye for detail.

When she had finally unloaded her stock, Arleta forced on a necessary grin. Tonix eyed her from across the way, and Arleta spread her arms out wide to show off her fully stocked and ready booth.

She might only be human, but at least her baked goods tasted magical.

# 2

By the time the blistering midday sun beat over the top of the covered booth, everything at the market had slowed. The laughing children were gone, the scent of cooked meats and smoke had dissipated. Twice over the day she'd tried to chat with the halfling selling honey, but other than a grunt, he'd always been busy with something. The day *had* been busy, and Arleta didn't even have time to see what else was for sale that day.

It was nearly time to close up shop, and Arleta twisted around behind her to check the stock left in her wagon. Empty, which was great, but…

If she had judged by *sales*, her silver should have been set for the week, but there were always too many hagglers who talked her down on her prices.

"These are only human goods," they'd complain, or something of the like. "I can't pay nearly that much when I could get fairy-baked options right over there." Then the patron would point to one of the fancy, infinitely stocked booths near the front that, yes, was run by fairy folk, but Arleta knew for a fact that her offerings were always tastier.

But this didn't matter. She always ended up offering a discount, or she'd lose the sale.

Or twenty sales.

It was enough to give up on her dreams of owning a bakery in town. How could she make a profit *and* pay rent if no one respected her for something she couldn't even control?

"I'll take two," a gruff voice said from behind Arleta.

She spun toward the voice and looked up, and then up again at Ervash, her kindly, greenish-complected orc neighbor. His dark hair was pulled up into a messy bun on top of his head, and he stood grinning down at Arleta, holding several coins in his large hand. Just the slightest hint of densely tattooed skin peeked out from the cuffs of his rolled-up, wrinkled cotton shirt.

"Two of what?" Arleta asked as she plopped back onto her off-balance wooden stool, exhausted from the day. There wasn't a large assortment left to purchase on the platters. A few cookies remained, along with several broken and unbroken raspberry tarts and two loaves of bread, as well as the crumbs she hadn't yet gotten to.

Ervash squared his massive shoulders, making himself even more hulking. "What do you recommend?" Humor peppered his gruff tone.

Arleta crossed her arms over her chest and scanned over what was left, as if the decision would be incredibly difficult. "Well, a couple of my neighbors *really* enjoyed the blueberry cook—"

She barely got the words out before Ervash had plucked up

the cookies in one hand, dropping more than enough coins to pay for his order into Arleta's payment box. "Sold."

"You don't have to do that," she said.

The orc eyed her with a playful glint in his amber eyes. "Oh, I'm taking the lot." He then swept everything left on the table into a canvas bag he had slung over his arm that already looked heavy with purchases.

Crumbs and all.

Behind him the market had mostly cleared out, other vendors busy cleaning up their booths. Tonix was roaming. He caught her gaze and rolled his eyes, but Arleta shook it off.

"For you *and* Verdreth?" she asked the orc instead.

"Um." His expression became sheepish. "He's working late at the bookstore, and an orc needs a snack."

"Or five." Arleta chuckled.

Ervash straightened his shoulders again and puffed out his muscular chest. "Yes, *yes,* we do." His lips stretched wide, displaying his toothy grin, complete with two small tusks.

Despite the potentially terrifying look of it all, the expression was endearing to Arleta.

"Need help cleaning up?" he asked.

She pursed her lips and scanned over the table. "I think you did that already."

"Nonsense." He waved his massive hand in the air and in a flash was behind the table, fetching the wooden wagon. "We're headed in the same direction, and you don't want to make an orc *angry.*"

Ervash feigned a scowl. The orc would barely swat flies in his house.

He was strong though, since the earth had granted the orcs magic tied to their strength, which was nice when Arleta needed a little muscle for moving something heavy. Ervash and Verdreth always obliged.

Arleta pinched at the bridge of her nose. It was no use arguing with him. She'd told both Ervash and Verdreth that she wanted to prove herself, on her own, so many times that she'd lost count. They didn't listen, and there was a part of her that didn't mind, since hurting their feelings was never an option. They were too kind.

And, just maybe, she would miss them if they didn't come around.

"That's fine," Arleta said as she gathered the wooden price signs and platters. She gently folded her lace tablecloth while staring longingly at the honey vendor next door. The halfling had a few jars left.

"Of course it is." Ervash turned to the table as he ducked under the tarp covering the booth.

After he loaded the wagon, she handed him the tablecloth and he tucked the money box under it. "Sell okay today?"

She shrugged. "It'll do, especially with your tip." But she knew without looking that the profits were not enough to buy the honey. She'd have to make do with the stock she already had on hand for tomorrow's bakes.

Ervash grabbed the wagon handle and pulled it out from behind the booth. "I'm walking you home."

It wasn't a question, or a request.

The two of them strolled slowly through Adenashire. The heat of the day had slowed any of the earlier lingering activities to a crawl. A few patrons sat outside the Tricky Goat Inn and Pub, lazily enjoying their drinks and food.

Arleta's stomach growled as she caught sight of a bowl of beef stew brimming with meat and potatoes on one of the tables. In all the rush and business, she still hadn't gotten any-thing to eat that day.

Coming toward them on the other side of the street was a man with five sheep, probably either off to another pasture or to sell the lot. As he passed, a sign tacked to a pole she'd been avoiding for the last several weeks caught her hazel eyes. Arleta stared at it for a moment too long.

"Did you enter?" Ervash asked, snapping Arleta from her thoughts.

"Enter what?"

She knew exactly what he was talking about though. The Langheim Baking Battle. This year was the hundredth anni-versary of the baking competition, held in the Langheim realm of the Northern Lands by the woodland elves who lived there.

She scanned to the bottom of the announcement where last year's winner was named: Taenya Carralei, two-time baking champion. By the surname, Arleta knew Taenya was an elf. The winners were almost always elves, but she had no idea what Taenya looked like since Arleta had never traveled to Langheim, let alone much out of Adenashire.

All the other details were laid out on the large, thick wooden sign, inviting the best bakers in the Lands to submit their entry in a fancy elvish scrawl.

"Ervash, I'm not going to enter." Arleta picked up her pace slightly, but it didn't take much for the orc and his long, mus-cular legs to catch up with her. "What's the point?"

He caught Arleta's arm gently, and she stopped and turned his way.

"There are no rules against the magicless."

"But they *always* find a way to disqualify any who enter,"

she said quietly, realizing they were in front of the empty shop she'd been watching for ages. It was perfect for a bakery.

The orc eyed her, forcing out his bottom tusks. "And by *not* entering you find an easy way of disqualifying yourself every year. But if you *won*? You'd earn more than enough gold to buy this building and remodel it for your business."

They stood in the street, silent for a moment until a murder of crows, probably the same group from that morning hoping for more snacks, let out a series of caws from the edge of the rooftop to their left.

Arleta huffed and crossed her arms over her chest. "See? Bad omen."

The orc scoffed and waved his hand in the air. "The only bad omen is you not going for it."

Ervash was stubborn. At least as stubborn as Arleta.

She flicked her attention back to the sign. "The deadline is tomorrow. It's already too late. Plus, even if I received an invitation, how would I *get* to Langheim? It's at least a day by cart, and affording that rental? I can barely pay for my supplies, not to mention food to eat."

"Verdreth and I could help you." His eyebrows arched into an undoubtedly parental-esque scold. "The bookshop is doing very well, and my side jobs are really picking up."

*Side jobs.* Ervash was too modest about his art. His paintings had become the talk of the Adenashire upper class, and the news of them was traveling fast around the Northern Lands. Everyone who was anyone wanted a commission. But none of that nonsense would ever go to his head.

"My parents raised me to be self-sufficient." Arleta threw out her hip the slightest amount in defiance. She immediately regretted bringing them up. "I'm not a child anymore. I'm twenty-five, so I haven't *been* one for years."

Ervash held her gaze. "Verdreth and I have lived next door to your family for much longer than you've been alive. I can say for certain that your parents raised a happy child."

She opened her mouth to protest, but he cut her off.

"And not only children need support. I know you are a woman, and a businessperson." As he spoke, his voice became louder and louder. "Other than devaluing your work, you are *good* at it. You are the best baker in Adenashire, and possibly the Northern Lands. And I don't just say that because I care about you. I say that because it's *true*."

Arleta looked around to see if anyone had noticed the orc's burst of energy. And yes...they had. The crows had flown away, and a dwarf had stopped on the other side of the road just to listen to Ervash and his suddenly enthusiastic declaration. Back at the pub, those same patrons enjoying drinks and food were staring, also enjoying the show.

She let out a long breath and uncrossed her arms. "Possibly next year."

Ervash's gaze instantly softened. "Next year for sure." His eyes drew to the modest corner shop. "I have a good feeling about this place."

In a year, the shop surely would have been rented by someone else, but Arleta bobbed her head, then gestured for them to continue toward their homes. The walk wasn't far after they turned down the next street on the right, their two cottages laying just ahead.

Their twin homes were situated in a quiet section of Adenashire. The gray buildings looked the same, with tall, pointed roofs made of straw and windows with wooden shutters in a crisscross design. Ervash had hand-painted both front doors a forest green, and forever maintained the rose-bushes along the front of the homes, since Arleta had no time for this.

Soon, they reached the path to Arleta's cottage. Before she could unload the wagon, Ervash, with his giant arms, had already picked up everything, including his snack bag, ready to bring it inside.

Arleta pushed open the door for them both. The cottages were small, but Arleta's cottage was nicer than anything she could have afforded if her parents had not outright bought the home years before. The ceilings were high, one of the main reasons Ervash and Verdreth had bought theirs over thirty years before. Ceilings tall enough for orcs were not always easy to find in Adenashire.

Each cottage had two bedrooms. The orcs used their second as a study and painting space, while Arleta used hers as a pantry. Both had a large kitchen, which was also a rarity, but since Arleta's mother loved to bake and her father was always tinkering with apothecary goods, they had needed a substantial kitchen. On the wall were shelves of Arleta's herbs in glass jars and her father's books, which she loved studying when she had a free moment—which was almost never those days. The wooden countertops held large containers of flours, dried fruits, sugar, and other baking supplies, neatly organized along with all her bowls and tools, all of which had been her mother's.

"I remember installing that stove with Declan." Ervash eyed the stove, then put his load on the counter. The tablecloth kept the money box and other supplies out of sight. "Nina loved it." He chuckled. "But then complained it was too expensive."

It was an exceptional thing though. When Arleta was ten,

her father had surprised her mother with the large cast-iron stove, just like the ones used in the elven baking contest from the sign in town. He'd had a good year with his business and had the stove delivered straight to the cottage.

"It *was* too expensive," Arleta said with a whisper of nostalgia, quickly wiping away the hint of moisture in her eye, "but so worth it."

It had made her mother so incredibly happy.

She turned to the orc. "Thank you for walking me home. Now, I need to get to baking." She eyed the bag on his arm. "And you need to eat your cookies."

His eyes lit up at the word. "I do! I almost forgot." Ervash flashed a toothy grin, letting her know that he'd never really forgotten. "And you are most welcome to come by for dinner tonight. I'm making roasted chicken with potatoes and carrots."

Arleta nodded, but they both knew she rarely accepted dinner invitations. She'd be too wrapped up in making the bakes for the market the next day. The hours would pass, and she'd have to grab something simple from her icebox in the kitchen's floor. Then she'd drag her exhausted self to bed and start all over again tomorrow.

Ervash held up the bag and tipped his head toward it. "I'll enjoy these, and I'll see you tomorrow."

Arleta opened her mouth in protest that he didn't have to but thought better. "See you after the market."

He gave her a slight bow, turned, and strode out the door.

After the orc left, the weight of the day pressed heavily on Arleta, but the thought of digging her hands into flour, butter, and sugar brought a burst of energy to her limbs. She walked to the kitchen counter and grabbed the tablecloth to place it to the side.

Underneath it were not only the price signs, platters, and her coin box, but also a large jar of amber honey with the comb floating inside, and a crusty meat pie that Ervash had obviously purchased from a vendor at the market.

Just for her.

# 3

T wo weeks later, Arleta was feeling quite proud of her punctuality that particular morning. She pulled her father's watch from her skirt, checked the time, and returned it to her pocket for safekeeping.

The wagon was already packed and waiting out in front of her cottage, and that morning Arleta actually had a few minutes to spare to make it to the market with plenty of time to set up. She wouldn't even have to take the horrible bumpy way around town.

Apparently the stars had finally aligned.

With her extra time, she quickly ran around the back of her cottage to gather rosemary, basil, and thyme to garnish her table. She had some special items this time, like a tasty blackberry and basil jam that could be popular if she marketed it well. The preserve paired wonderfully with the assortment of buttery loaves she'd made while baking late into the night.

Arleta reached the garden and plucked several sprigs of the herbs. The edible pansies had also bloomed in the morning sun, and she couldn't resist their cute floral faces. Several bunches of those went into her apron pocket as well.

Satisfied, and still not late, she made her way to the front of her house where a gigantic, speckled horse stood in the way of her wagon.

"Oh, hello," she managed in surprise, stopping in her tracks.

The horse blew out his breath and shook his head, but said nothing, of course.

Horses didn't talk. Everyone knew that.

The steed did, though, turn his attention to an ecru-skinned woodland elf, fairer than Arleta's tawny beige. He was dressed in cotton pants and a flowy, belted tunic with golden threads stitched around the neck and sleeves. The elf was about to knock on Arleta's cottage door, holding a letter with fancy writing on the front and a wax seal.

"Can I help you?" Arleta asked, but she didn't want to help anyone at her door, since she was suddenly being forced to deal with the enormous horse blocking her way. The seconds were ticking, and she was quickly losing her advantage of being on time.

The elf spun on his heel to face her, ready to speak. Upon taking sight of Arleta, however, his lips snapped shut, and his blue eyes opened as wide as the hand-painted saucers she stored with their matching teapot and cups in the second cupboard to the right of her stove.

The elf was tall, which was not out of the ordinary, since all elves seemed to have ample height—at least the ones Arleta had occasionally seen in Adenashire. He stood frozen, still clutching the envelope as if his life depended on it, eyes lingering on

Arleta. A tendril of his spun-gold hair, picked up by the wind, was his only movement.

Something about him was familiar, but Arleta had no idea from where. She was certain they'd never met.

"Can I *help* you?" Arleta repeated, scanning over the horse blocking her wagon once again.

"Um," the elf finally said with a heavy breath. "Uh…"

Elves, particularly woodland elves, tended to be most self-assured, and they had many reasons to be. One of which being that they were, more often than not, quite good-looking.

Undoubtedly, with his finely squared jaw and high cheek-bones, he had that going for him.

*Very intelligent as well.*

Which, at this point, was questionable in Arleta's mind due to his lack of conversational skills and gaping mouth.

*And highly attuned to nature.*

They had flora and fauna magic, specifically, and because their magic was often visible, it was more respected.

This one was almost sweating little sparks of green and gold magic from his hands.

Arleta pulled out her watch again.

*Stars!*

This ridiculous elf had made her *late*! Quickly, she made her way around the hoof-stamping horse and grabbed her wagon's handle.

"Excuse me," she muttered, and the horse stepped back as if on cue, giving Arleta room to pull the wagon forward and out toward the road.

Whatever the elf wanted, he could close his wordless mouth and leave a note. Arleta had places to be and portly quokkans to haggle with.

"Wait!" the elf called just as Arleta stepped onto the dirt path.

"I have to leave." The young woman waved her hand in the air, but didn't turn back to him, continuing on her way along the road.

"Are you Arleta Starstone?" the elf called after her. "I have a message for you. It's *important!*"

"Oh stars," Arleta muttered and stopped. She turned back just in time to see both Ervash and Verdreth emerging from the front door of their cottage. Verdreth held a book in his hand, a tiny set of spectacles perched on the end of his nose. Ervash, as per often, had no shirt on. His green skin, hulking muscles, and tattooed chest and arms were on display in all their glory. Ervash was the muscle of the couple, Verdreth the brains—at least in appearances. In reality, they were fairly equally matched in both departments.

"Is there a problem?" Verdreth asked with a growly undertone, peering over his glasses at the elf still standing on the path to Arleta's front door.

The elf cleared his throat and held up the envelope. "I have an invitation for Arleta Starstone."

"And I *really* need to leave for the market," Arleta called to Verdreth. "Would you mind taking care of this for me?" She tipped her head to the overloaded wagon and started on her way again.

"I must deliver this *directly* to the recipient," the elf called, and his boots pounded on the dirt behind Arleta, not giving up on his mission. "It's the rule."

She flung herself around, patience evaporating. "You really want me to be late, don't you?"

The elf kept coming, holding the envelope in the air. Right

behind him were the two orcs. Ervash was whispering something into Verdreth's ear, whose brows raised at whatever he was hearing from his partner.

When the elf reached Arleta, he thrust out the envelope. Ervash and Verdreth simply stood a few steps behind him, doing nothing but displaying goofy grins on their green orc faces.

Tightness building in Arleta's chest, she grabbed the fancy envelope from the elf's hand and ripped open the seal.

"I'm Theodmon Brylar, and you, Arleta Starstone, are cordially invited to take part in the Langheim Baking Battle," he blurted out like a nervous child before Arleta had even read the invitation. Several more sparks of green and gold magic floated from his hands.

This time, it was Arleta's eyes that went as wide as those saucers in her cupboard, the ones with the delicately painted lavender sprigs on their edges. But her face quickly collapsed as her brows pulled together. "This is a joke, right?" Her attention moved from Theodmon to the orcs and then back to the elf. "Because I didn't submit an entry."

None of the men said a word while Arleta stared the three of them down. The tension thickened as much as the lemon curd filling in the strawberry bites in her wagon, still waiting to be sold at the market.

"*I* submitted it," Ervash finally admitted, biting his lip.

"You what?" Arleta gasped, not quite knowing what to do with this new information. Yes, taking part in the Baking Battle would be huge for her.

But her chances of them letting her in the door were likely slim to none.

*And* she'd be humiliated, and she couldn't risk that. It had been hard enough to get as far as she had.

Arleta had already lost too much. She had to protect her heart.

"You shouldn't have done that, Ervash." Arleta kept her tone soft since, despite what felt like dragon fire burning in her stomach, she really didn't want to be *mad* at him.

She couldn't lose the orcs too.

"I don't understand," Theodmon said, not letting loose of her gaze. "It's an *honor* to be invited to the Baking Battle—"

"Yes, of course. I'm not going though," Arleta interrupted, stuffing the invitation into her pocket next to her watch. "I'm hum—"

"Hungry," Verdreth interrupted, stepping forward and placing his hand on Arleta's shoulder. She tipped her head in question at his interrupting her, which was quite unlike him. "She has hungry patrons waiting to buy her stock at the market. Why don't I help you get there in time, and you can think about all this later." He grinned down at her.

But Arleta shook her head and gripped the wagon handle. "I'll be fine."

Theodmon wavered his attention around the group, then landed back on Arleta. "I… I'll help," the elf sputtered. "We… we need to discuss this issue of you not attending the Battle."

Before she could say no, Theodmon had already taken the wagon and was pulling it off down the road. Arleta puffed out her cheeks, blew out the breath, and glared at the orcs. "No more cookies for you two."

"I didn't do anything," Verdreth said, holding his hands innocently in the air.

Ervash shook his head, a look of horror screwing up his features. "You can't *do* that!"

"Oh, I can." Arleta, of course, didn't mean her words, but

she spun on her heel and chased after Theodmon. "What about your horse?" she asked when she caught up with the elf, who pulled the heavy wagon with ease.

"Oh, Nimbus? He's fine," Theodmon said. His demeanor seemed to have calmed slightly from whatever had been going on back at the cottage. "I told him we'd be back and to stay put."

Arleta folded her arms over her chest, working hard to keep up with Theodmon's rapid pace. "You didn't say that."

Theodmon pointed to the side of his head. "Mindspeak."

In the chaos of the morning, Arleta had forgotten that some elves had the magical gift to speak to animals. "Fine."

They made it to the end of the street and Theodmon stopped, looking back and forth and scanning over the morning's foot traffic.

"Do you know where you're going?" Arleta asked.

"No," Theodmon admitted. "I've never been to Adenashire. As far as I know, you're the first from here to receive an invitation to compete."

Arleta kept her mouth shut about the fact *that* was because Adenashire was a town where the population's majority was made of the magicless, and those without magic were *not* invited to the Baking Battle. They would not even dare. But delving into the politics of the Northern Lands wasn't really what she wanted to discuss with this elf she'd just met, and who was also getting her to the market on time. Verdreth cutting her off when he did had likely been a good thing.

"It's this way, Theodmon." She pointed to her right, and he was off again. This time Arleta was ready and followed his pace.

"Please, call me Theo," the elf said as he kept up his quick steps.

She didn't respond to his request though. *As soon as he gets me to the market, he'll be leaving and off to his next invitation delivery.*

*It's not as if we're friends.*

During their journey down the familiar streets, Arleta was all too aware of the eyes landing on her. It wasn't completely unusual, since she was either the poor girl alone in a cottage *or* the woman who was recklessly spilling baked goods out onto the streets, but that day a well-dressed elf was with her. A *handsome* one at that. That fact alone was something that would likely spark rumors around the village for the next few days.

The market soon came into view, and the two of them entered the square.

"Which booth is yours?" Theo asked, his chest rising and falling quickly from the hurry.

A sprinkle of shame settled over Arleta. "I don't have a regular space. We need to find the owner and see what he has left over."

A curious expression furrowed Theo's attractive face. "Why wouldn't you have a permanent booth?"

"Because I don't." Arleta spotted Tonix across the way and gestured to Theo to follow her. "Mr. Figlet!" she called, as she had done so many times before.

The quokkan's eyes locked on Arleta, then quickly shifted to Theo. He spread his hands and arms out wide and walked directly to the elf, who was still pulling Arleta's wagon.

"Your face is new around here." Tonix put on his best airs and lowered his tone. "What can I do for you, fine sir?"

Theo pulled his chin back in confusion and eyed Arleta. "*She* needs to buy a booth for the day."

Arleta rolled her eyes at the familiarity of the situation.

Tonix flicked his attention to the young woman, then back to the elf, showing off his teeth. "And you need a booth as well?"

"Yes," Arleta piped in before Theo could. "This *elf* needs a booth, Mr. Figlet." She knew well that he'd treat Theo much better than her, but she'd probably regret what would happen when Tonix realized Theo was only here for a visit and the booth was actually for her. At the moment, she didn't care.

Tonix cleared his throat and put out his hand toward a large, still empty booth near the front entrance. "We had a cancellation today. I can offer you this premium spot for the low price of only three silver."

Arleta nearly choked on her own tongue at the paltry amount. She'd often been paying five to six silver, depending on Tonix's mood that day, for the *worst* booths. "Sold," she managed.

The quokkan shot a deadly glare in her direction. However, he was likely still too enamored with the possibility of a *woodland elf* selling baked goods in his market, and so close to the Baking Battle, to recognize that Arleta and Theo were together.

Before anything else could be said, Theo had three silver held out to Tonix, and the quokkan's greedy paws quickly snatched it up. His eyes flickered to Arleta, but he didn't have the chance to speak or even turn away, since she was already bounding after Theo toward her prized booth.

"Wait!" Tonix shouted, but at least for today, she knew he wouldn't stop her for fear that he might make anyone from the woodland elves angry with him.

Arleta giggled with excitement, like a young child. "That was *amazing*," she said when she caught up with Theo at the booth.

He just shook his head. "What is wrong with that quokkan? Why was he looking at you like that?"

Instantly, the questions popped Arleta's bubbling mood. Not because she didn't wonder the same thing some days, but because it brought her back into reality.

"I thought elves were supposed to be smart." Arleta began the job of unloading her wagon onto the waiting table by spreading out her favorite cloth.

And like it was as natural as breathing, Theo took the other end and helped her. The action of him touching something so dear to her sent an unexpected thrill around Arleta's stomach. Not so much because he *was* helping her...but because she didn't tell him not to.

"I have no idea what you are talking about, Arleta Starstone"—there the feeling was again at the mention of her name, taking another loop in her stomach—"all I know is *that* quokkan is rude. So many of them are so jolly and kind," he finished.

"To *you*. And maybe you're judging by their button noses and propensity toward flattery." She smoothed out any wrinkles in the lace and reached for the platters and price signs at the back of the wagon. Behind them the market sounds picked up, the aroma of sizzling meats and woodsmoke filling Arleta's senses once again. A few patrons were already trickling in.

"But not to you?" he asked, his eyes lingering on Arleta. "Because that is unacceptable."

Arleta had several jars of jam in her hands and placed them gently at the front of the table. Part of her was starting to like Theo, but she knew she wasn't going to see him after today. Plus, it wasn't as if the slighting of humans wasn't common knowledge. They didn't have magic capabilities, so they were

J. PENNER

what they were. There was no benefit in hiding the fact from him any longer.

"Not to those without magic…like me. I'm human."

Theo glanced up at her from taking out a basket of strawberry lemon curd bites from the wagon. "Starstone is a *wizard's* surname."

Arleta chuckled. Everyone in Adenashire knew the Starstones had zero wizard blood, which was unfortunate for Arleta, since wizards were some of the most powerful people in the Northern Lands. Not one drop. She'd been reminded of that more times than she could count. "By adoption, and way back on my father's side. The name just stuck. No actual magical abilities came with it."

"Oh," he said, but zero emotions became apparent on his face.

Arleta was nearly certain Theo would soon take his leave, after asking for the invitation still tucked safely in her pocket to be handed right back to him, but he didn't. Instead, he continued to place out the breads and other offerings Arleta had prepared the night before.

"So now you understand why I can't take that spot in the competition." She bit at her bottom lip but pulled out the fresh herbs and pansies from her apron and spread them between the different bakes. "And with that knowledge, you should probably go." Arleta held out three coins to him. "For the booth."

Theo pulled out the chalk from the wagon, rounded the table, and started filling in the prices on the wooden signs. "Why?" he asked without even looking at her.

She knew she was probably going to have to lower the prices once she checked what he'd written. "Because I can't let you pay for my booth." Arleta thrust her hand in his direction again.

Theo straightened. "No, not the silver. I'm fine with you

repaying me." He took the coins from her and pocketed them as though to prove this to her. "Why can't you compete?"

She laughed, uncomfortable down to her boot-covered toes. "You heard what I said, right? I'm *human*. No magic."

The elf eyed her for a second and then plucked a strawberry lemon bite from its basket. "I'll pay for this." Before Arleta could say a word, he popped the pastry into his mouth, and Theo's blue eyes went bright. The two of them stood there while he chewed so slowly it was as if he never wanted to swallow the sweet treat. When he finally did, he said, "*That* is the best thing I have ever eaten. It's magic."

Arleta gulped hearing him talk about her—no, not *her*—her baked goods like that.

With the side of his palm, he erased whatever prices he'd marked on the signs and quickly wrote in something else.

Arleta scoffed, came to the front of the table, and froze at the prices Theo had marked on the signs. They were at least five times what she'd normally ask. "I can't charge that!"

"They're worth more." This time, he spoke *while* chewing.

"*No one* is going to pay that price," Arleta protested, pointing to the nearest sign.

A wide smile curled at the corners of Theo's lips, and he held out his hand just as a large crowd was moving into the market. "I'll make you a wager. By midmorning you'll be sold out and have little old ladies battling over who gets to pay you the most for the last of everything here."

Slowly, she took Theo's outstretched hand. Somehow it felt right in hers. "So what's the wager?"

"If I'm wrong, you can go back to your life with a decent take from the day's sales," he said. "All yours."

Arleta arched one brow. "And if you're right?"

Theo's steely gaze locked onto hers, his confidence completely locked in. "You will allow me to accompany you to the Baking Battle and make sure you get the opportunity to compete."

"Why?" Arleta asked. "Why would it matter to you if I compete? There will be so many other excellent bakers there. They definitely don't need *me*."

Theo gazed at her for a moment, as if carefully gathering the words he was about to say, making sure they were right and true. When he finally spoke, he said, "I take my job very seriously. Losing contestants is not an option if I can help it."

Something in the elf's tone told Arleta that he was holding information back, but his explanation made some amount of sense.

Theo had a job to do and was just trying to do it.

Despite her roiling gut, Arleta shook Theo's hand.

He pinched his lips together as if digging up an old thought. "They don't *really* toss their kin at enemies to escape, right?"

"Who?" Arleta asked, confused at the sudden topic change.

"The quokkan," Theo whispered and glanced around the market as if looking out for Mr. Figlet.

As much as she disliked Mr. Figlet, she said, "I think that's an unfair rumor." As she said it, a woman with hair elegantly and complicatedly coiled on top of her head and wearing a crushed velvet dress batted her eyelashes at the elf, shimmying up to the edge of the table.

Theo returned his attention to the table, turned on the elven charm, bowed his head slightly, and fanned his hand out over Arleta's display as if it were a treasure trove.

"What may we get you, m'lady?"

# 4

W hat just happened?" Arleta stared in disbelief at the empty table and picked up her heavily laden money box. Everything she had brought that day was gone. The jam, the bread, the lemon strawberry bites. People had even taken all the decorative herbs and flowers.

And it was barely midday.

"*You* happened. Your baking, I mean." Theo shrugged as he waved off two disappointed halflings from the booth. "We're sold out. Check back in a fortnight."

Regret fell over their tiny features, but they nodded and turned away.

When they were gone, Arleta scoffed as she packed up the wagon. "This was all *you*. Everyone saw your pointed ears and just *had* to make a purchase. Your elfin charm made the sales. It really didn't matter how wonderful everything was."

"But I was right." Theo sat back on her worn stool and

placed his intertwined fingers on top of his head. One side of his lips arched upward into a self-satisfied grin that made his sea-blue eyes sparkle.

And he said nothing else.

Arleta pursed her lips. Again, she wanted to let annoyance at him burn in her stomach, but instead tiny fairies fluttered around in the space as if she were a teenager with a crush.

Not that she was going to give any indication *that* was happening. It was likely damsels were falling at his feet all the time. She would not be so silly. And she was long past juvenile puppy love.

Who cared about waving, sun-caught blond hair falling across the side of an ethereally handsome face, the square jaw with the lightest sprinkling of stubble…piercing ocean eyes…

And elves who won bets with her?

Not Arleta. No elfin charm would overtake her.

He was just doing his job.

She cleared her throat and pulled the lace tablecloth from the table.

Theo hopped to his feet. "If we leave at first light, we'll make it to Langheim with plenty of time, a day early, in fact. The castle doesn't lock down around sundown."

"I'm not going to Langheim." Arleta didn't look at him and finished placing the tablecloth over the money box in the wagon. Her fingers didn't let go of the hem as she refused to meet Theo's gaze—except out of the corner of her eye, where she was pretty sure his expression had moved from smug to astonished at her stubbornness.

"What are you talking about?" Theo twisted his muscular arms across his chest. "There's no need to admit I was right because, most importantly, *you* sold out of everything. Or any need to worry about any money you will have needed to earn while you're away at the competition. But *I* won the wager. We shook on it." His voice became lower and huskier with each word he spoke.

Arleta grabbed the weather-worn wagon handle and rounded the front of the empty table. Her heart pounded stronger than a galloping horse. Without answering him, she made her way through the still-bustling market. Even in her distress, she took care while weaving through the villagers haggling over exotic spices, teas, plush or utilitarian fabrics, and lumpy gourds. None of them even noticed the tears running down her face, tracing paths down her hot cheeks.

What they *did* notice was the tall, lithe woodland elf chasing after her.

"Arleta!" Theo called in obvious distress, while quite a few heads twisted to see what was going on.

Then the whispers started, stirred up in the Adenashire breeze.

Instantly, Arleta regretted what she had allowed to happen that morning. Tonix would be furious with her little con about the booth rental. She was sure that horrible, back-of-the-market leftovers would now be double the cost, if he'd even rent to her at all.

Worse were the potential rumors that would surely spin around her name. Once Theo left, people would likely twist what had happened, that somehow she had *tricked* an elf into helping her sell her goods, that the whole invitation to the Baking Battle was something *she'd* made up.

Because elves just didn't hang out with the magicless of their own accord.

Once more, she'd just be the sad, overworked woman with the dreams that would never come true.

Fueled by blind determination to get to the safety of her cottage, Arleta made her way past the market entrance with Theo hot on her heels, but she didn't look back. She just wanted to get home and immerse her hands into a bowl of bread dough. Dough never said rude things or made her do anything she didn't want to. Sure it might not rise properly, but that wasn't its fault.

"*Arleta*," Theo called again, and she realized he was right next to her. He might or might not have said Arleta's name multiple times during her escape, but by then, they were well away from the market and already halfway to her cottage.

Gently, he placed his hand on her shoulder, and the touch made her stop.

Arleta's emotions were a storm of turmoil and fear, but there was something about the elf that Arleta didn't understand that made her turn to him. She'd spent years pushing people away, building walls so she didn't get hurt. So *they* didn't get hurt. The orcs were her only real friends, and it was only because they were both terribly stubborn when it came to her. But she didn't even really let *them* in.

An arm's length was all that was safe for her heart.

"Everyone will look, Theo," she whispered. "You don't want that."

There were, in fact, eyes on them.

"I. Don't. *Care*. About. Them," he said, each word hammered out like a blacksmith defining a stubborn sword. Theo's eyes nearly burned with blue fire. "This is about *you*."

The declaration hung in the air between them, and Arleta did not know how the words could be true.

"Why? You just met me." She gulped, a knot of disbelief winding itself tightly around her throat. "I thought this was a job."

"Um. Well, yes, of course. It's that too." He quickly tore his gaze from her and ran his hand through his hair, a small trail of magic following his action.

But she couldn't look away and couldn't make sense of the words that had just tumbled out of Theo's mouth. "You... you've known me for approximately five hours. So I'm not sure how you could care that much for my well-being."

But something in her believed what he had said concerning it being about *her*. A tiny seed of belief. It was buried deep, but it was undeniably there.

His stiff posture relaxed, and before Theo spoke, he eyed the cobblestone street, as if searching for the right words etched in their patterns. "Let's keep walking," he said at length.

With a small head bob, Arleta tightened her grip on the wagon's handle and pulled. The pair didn't say another word until after they'd pulled up to the cottage, where Nimbus, Theo's horse, was still waiting patiently directly in front of the roses.

A sigh, long and frustrated, slipped from Arleta's lips, and she knew full well that Theo was simply not going to leave without her.

She wasn't sure if she wanted him to.

But that was beside the point.

For the time being, he was going to need some kind of explanation. Then he could leave her in peace so she could figure out how to patch things over with Tonix. That, and come up with an excuse the orcs would believe for her decision to skip the Baking Battle.

Instead of bringing Theo inside the house, which was still in mild disarray from last night's baking spree, she maneuvered the wagon behind her cottage to the garden, where Arleta parked it in its usual spot. She slumped into one of the two weathered chairs that her father had made years ago so the family could sit back there and enjoy the plants.

Theo didn't sit. Instead, he strolled farther into the garden, all the while running his hands over the foliage. As his fingers brushed the leaves and blooms, a hit of green and yellow magic danced in the air, quickly dissipating like a summer firebug. He looked completely relaxed and in his element.

"They like you, you know," Theo said, his back still turned to her.

Arleta's brow furrowed in confusion. "Who likes me? The plants?"

Theo nodded as a leaf curled toward his palm.

Any frustration Arleta had felt moments ago melted from her. "Is that so?" It felt like his words were a bit of a joke, but she knew they weren't.

Apparently, as Theo could communicate with his horse, he must also have had the magical gift of reading plants.

"They say you're just like your parents." This time, the elf turned back to Arleta, concern etching deep lines on his features. "They…passed…didn't they?"

Her stomach dropped at his words. She hated thinking about the fact that, indeed, her parents were gone, even though she still liked to pretend they were not.

They'd been killed when she was sixteen, in a carriage accident. Even nine years later, every once in a while, the wounds of losing them still felt fresh.

But by the stars, she would prove to them she could succeed, and she would do it with no one's help. Not even the orcs, and certainly not an elf.

With a terse nod, Arleta shifted her attention to the ground, where she shuffled her boots through the dirt. Her heart thumped with a dull, nervous ache that had become a familiar friend over the years.

"I'm sorry," he murmured and retraced his steps to the other wooden chair, keeping his fingers over the plants the entire way as if to ground himself. The air swirled with the colored glimmers of his magic. "If I brought up painful memories."

Arleta shrugged. "It's been a long time."

After Theo lowered himself into the seat, he hunched forward and rested his elbows out onto his knees. "The sadness never quite goes away, does it? It lingers like a morning fog that never seems to lift completely."

"I miss them," Arleta admitted in a soft confession. Tears stung at the corners of her eyes, but she didn't allow them to fall...to show her weakness. "What else did the garden tell you?"

"That they, your parents, would want you to follow your dreams." Theo rubbed his thumbs together.

Arleta flitted her gaze to him and arched a brow, but the elf wasn't looking at her. Instead, his eyes traveled over the garden, as if he was still talking to it.

"How do you know that?" she asked, hesitant and curious.

"The plants." He chuckled nervously. "It sounds like a fable, I know, but there is so much love here. The generations of seeds and the older growth, they've borne witness, passed it from year to year. Your parents' legacy, your story, even the stories of the orcs next door are here." Theo twisted slightly to look at her, then inhaled a deep breath as if to drink her in. "Human or not, Arleta Starstone, your life is steeped in magic. You're surrounded by it. You just can't see it yet, but it's out there, waiting."

Arleta opened her mouth to speak. Likely to protest. To tell him he was full of sh—

But he spoke faster. "You *deserve* to go to the Baking Battle," Theo said, his tone firm. "*That* is why I'm determined to get you there."

Arleta crossed her arms over her chest in defense. "They'll probably just disqualify me."

"There are no rules against those who don't possess magic," Theo countered. "We already know you can bake without it."

"How will I *get* there?" She looked around at her lack of transportation. "I don't own a horse. I don't have enough silver to pay for the journey and the living expenses—even *with* my market windfall."

Theo beamed, as if sensing impending triumph. "I've already told you. I've delivered all the invitations. You were the last, and so I will take you with me back to Langheim."

A growl, low and grumbly, left Arleta's throat. "On *one* horse? There will be *talk*."

Arleta didn't really know if there *would* be talk of an elf with a human, but it felt like there might be, and she didn't want to risk it.

He shrugged, unperturbed. "I'll buy a cart. I've needed one anyway. Nimbus won't mind pulling it."

Before she had the chance to argue that Theo was probably lying about saying he needed a cart, heavy footsteps sounded just around the corner. Verdreth appeared, shoeless and in a smart blue button-up vest and linen pants, a half-eaten meat pie in one hand. He used the other to push his spectacles higher up onto his nose. "Oh, I didn't know anyone was back here." He shot Arleta a quizzical look. "You're home early."

"That's because we sold out of everything," Arleta said.

"And she made enough silver to last at least a moon," Theo added.

A grin curled onto Verdreth's green-tinged lips. "Does this mean you'll be traveling to the Baking Battle?" He crammed a massive bite of his meat pie into his mouth, reducing the remains to a lonely corner of pastry.

Arleta sighed and raked her hands through the loose top of her braided hair. After a few long moments, she muttered out, "I don't even know what to pack."

With a mischievous, *I thought you might say that* grin, Theo dug into his pocket, pulled out a folded parchment, and held it high into the air like a victory flag. "I have a list for all the participants of what is allowed and what isn't."

She rolled her eyes, a playfully exaggerated gesture, and let her gaze settle on the lush garden. "But these are my secret ingredients. How do I even know what herbs will be available at the Battle for me to use?"

"Oh, woman of many excuses." Theo unfurled the paper with a flourish, scanning it briefly before he plunked his finger directly on top of a section of text. "'Participants may bring a small bag of edible ingredients to incorporate into their competition dishes.'" He lowered the parchment and let his smile grow just a tad too much. "They'll be checked upon your arrival, of course, but there is no reason your special herbs should not be approved." Theo leaned into Arleta as if to unveil a secret. "Unless you try to smuggle the entire herb garden in."

Verdreth broke into a hearty laugh and slapped Theo on the back. "I like this elf."

Theo's eyes widened at the smack, but he quickly settled and let out a chuckle.

The orc ambled over to Arleta's side, his footsteps softer than one might expect for a being of his size. "You need to do this. If you don't, you'll regret it for the rest of your life. The Northern Lands are waiting to discover the culinary magic you create."

"What happens if we *don't* make it in time?" she asked.

Theo tipped his head at her, looking slightly frustrated at that point. "We'll leave early and make it in plenty of time. I'll make sure of it."

For a brief second, she clenched her teeth to stave off the roiling in her stomach. After a pause that felt like twelve moon cycles, she released a sigh of half relief, half resignation. "Yes. I'll go."

The orc gulped. "Oh, *good*. Because otherwise I would forever be on the receiving end of Ervash's laminations about missing out on tickets to the finale." He shot a glance at Theo. "You can help me with that, right?"

Theo bowed his head. "At your service."

# 5

At first light, puffy gray clouds filled the sky like meringue dusted in ash. Arleta tipped her chin to the sky. Her chest was tight with anticipation.

No. With anxiety.

The bad weather *had* to be an omen. If only the crows were there. That would solidify her suspicions. But the murder and their chorus were nowhere to be seen nor heard.

With a shiver edging its way down her spine, she pulled her cloak tighter around her shoulders to stave off the chill of the morning air.

"Do you have everything on the list?"

The deep rumble of Ervash's voice snuck up on her as he sidled up beside Arleta. She hadn't even heard him come out of his cottage. Right behind him was Verdreth, holding a delicate teacup in his ginormous hand. The hot tea inside sent trails of vapor into the air. Both orcs' tired demeanor told Arleta that they'd risen hours before normal just to see her off.

Arleta absently scratched at the back of her head. She only owned a few changes of clothes, but she'd included those and other odds and ends in an old leather satchel. Along with that were a dozen lavender vanilla shortbread cookies from a stress bake session after Theo had retreated to the Tricky Goat Inn for the night. The rest she'd left in a box on the orcs' porch to tide them over until their second round of breakfast.

"I think so. But do you think I could just...not go?" She gazed up again at the leaden clouds, seeming to echo her hesitation as they churned in the sky. "Look at the weather—"

"I know this is difficult." Ervash drew her into a tight, reassuring hug. "We love and support you."

Arleta squeezed him back. His muscular body was extra toasty since orcs ran hot compared to humans. She didn't exactly want to let go, for more reasons than one.

"Thank you," she managed when she finally convinced herself to loosen her grip.

Verdreth had already collected her satchel and a cotton bag holding an arsenal of her secret ingredients. Inside was a small tin of cardamom, basil, rosemary, and thyme bunches, a few containers of her favorite finely ground teas, whose blends always made an interesting and surprising addition to some sweets, and an assortment of other spices she'd surely regret leaving behind even if she didn't need them.

Seconds later, and just as she made it through her final mental checklist, the sound of clopping hooves was followed by Theo pulling up to the cottage on his newly purchased wooden cart. It was actually quite nice, and from the detailed craftsmanship, it looked like he'd paid a pile of silver for it, maybe even gold. Nimbus, however, hitched to the cart in all of his white-and-gray-speckled glory, looked supremely unimpressed. If horses could scowl, he was.

"Morning," Theo greeted them, in a tone that was a mite bit too chipper for the time of day as he brought the cart to a halt. Ervash tipped his head toward the elf. "Yes, it is."

Theo flashed him a quick, confused smile, climbed down from the wagon, then turned his attention to Arleta. "We'd better get going," he said with a lopsided grin.

Too nervous to care how attractive Theo looked that morning, Arleta gave him a curt nod and turned her attention to the orc with her bags.

Verdreth's chuckle rumbled through the crisp morning air. "For stars' sake, one would think you were being sent to the dungeons instead of the Langheim Baking Battle, Arleta."

Ignoring what he'd said, Arleta puffed her cheeks out wide while he loaded her things into the wagon. She finally spoke up when he got to the bag of her secret ingredients. "I'll take that." She held her hand out to him. "I want it up front with me."

The orc handed it to Arleta. Once the bag was safely in her possession, she hopped up onto the passenger side of the wagon all on her own, then placed the herbs safely at her feet.

Theo and the orcs exchanged glances, and the elf climbed back up to his spot. "I guess that's it then."

"Apparently," Verdreth chimed in, dipping his head to Arleta, who was staring directly ahead. "But, there is one last thing." Verdreth quickly glanced at Ervash and then back at Theo. "Now, Arleta is a *very* special neighbor to us."

Arleta swiveled further toward the orc, her thick eyebrows nearly knitting a sweater in anticipation of what else he was about to say.

"Yes," Ervash agreed quickly. "So, when you're steering that cart…be hasty, so you are not late, but do not go *too* fast."

Theo simply sat there, nodding, but Arleta's cheeks burned like the inside of her stove when she was baking a loaf of bread.

The look on Verdreth's face was deadly serious as he pushed his glasses up on his nose. "We only have one Arleta, and we can't replace her."

Ervash shot a meaty finger in the air. "Treat her with resp—"

"All right, all right," Arleta interrupted, her voice dripping with embarrassment. "I think he has the point. We're all adults here."

Ervash laid his massive hand on the edge of the carriage, holding it in place and waiting for a response from Theo. He edged in and lowered his already bass rumble of a voice. "We know where Langheim is too. This means we can *find* you."

Arleta wanted nothing more than to bury her head in her lap as the orc bared his teeth slightly at Theo.

Arleta shot an *Are you serious?* expression to her neighbor.

"I understand, sirs," Theo assured them, offering them both a respectful nod.

With that, Ervash removed his hand from the cart, his lips upturning in utter satisfaction while the two orcs stepped away from the carriage.

Theo leaned in close to Arleta, voice low as he asked, "Was he threatening me?"

She pinched at the bridge of her nose. "I think he was."

With a shake of his head, the elf took the reins into his hands and prompted Nimbus into a smooth trot.

And off they went.

"Don't forget the tickets to the finale!" Ervash called after them, his tone completely changed from moments before. "And Arleta, break a biscuit!"

Arleta couldn't help but let a sigh escape her lips as she gave a quick wave back to both of the orcs. She could never stay mad at them.

"It will be late when we arrive," Theo said once Adenashire had disappeared behind them. "But barring any unforeseen circumstances, the road between Langheim and here should be smooth traveling."

The words were barely out of Theo's mouth when lightning splayed across the sky. The bolt illuminated Mount Blackdon far off in the distance, where dragons lived.

"And you're supposed to be in tune with nature," Arleta said, reaching into the back of the wagon for her satchel. She flung open the top and grabbed the wooden box of cookies, popping open the lid. Picking out a sugary biscuit, she took a comforting bite. The tangy, floral flavors of the herb blended with the perfect amount of vanilla soothed her soul, and without a thought, she handed one to Theo. He gratefully took the biscuit and bit into it.

"This is incredible, Arleta," he said as he chewed.

Her stomach flitted with excitement at the sound of her name on his lips. "Could you not do that?" she blurted while her cheeks grew hot. Sitting so close to him, she suddenly became keenly aware of his intoxicating scent.

*Do all elves smell this way? Like cedarwood and sage?*

What was wrong with her?

Smelling delicious, Theo gently guided Nimbus onto the left fork in the road. "Do what?" The elf seemed genuinely confused.

Arleta gulped and moved over, putting another hand's length between herself and Theo. He had to know his effect on women. No one was *that* clueless. "Never mind," she deflected, pulling her gaze toward the road ahead. Mostly.

But Theo continued gazing at her as if something unsaid would not leave his lips. Instead, he cleared his throat and declared, "The cookie is deceptively simple, but the…layering of flavors. It's like something new hits my taste buds every second as I chew."

"That's the point." Sheepishly, she cast her eyes down to the edge of the wagon in front of them, tracing the patterns of the wood grain in her mind.

"Yes, I guess it is." Theo finished the last bite of shortbread and eyed the box.

"I suppose you want another?" Arleta teased.

"For the rest of my life." There was an uncomfortable pause before Theo let out a hearty chuckle. "I mean, yes, please."

Arleta handed him a second, and an hour later, between the both of them, the cookies were gone. However, the clouds were not. In fact, it had started to rain. Both Theo and Arleta had pulled the hoods of their cloaks over their heads to block the moisture, but it was growing heavier and heavier by the passing minute.

Darkness had blocked out the sun, making it difficult to stay on the path. Poor Nimbus, who didn't even have a cloak, looked soaked to the bone with his stringy, drenched mane and tail.

Heaviness settled onto Arleta's shoulders. Any shred of confidence that she thought she might have had to compete in the Baking Battle vanished like old magic into the air. The only upside was that the rain had drowned out Theo's enchanting scent. She was glad of that.

Theo abruptly yanked on the reins, *hard*. "Whoa, Nimbus."

The horse and wagon bucked up into the air and slammed back down on the muddy path, shaking its occupants. A stag with enormous horns raced across the road as if the wagon hadn't almost hit him.

Theo immediately twisted to Arleta, his face creased with concern. "Are you okay?"

Her heart had picked up with tremendous speed, but Arleta was fine. She managed to nod and slow her rapid breath but couldn't help the urge inside her that wanted to turn back to Adenashire. "Is Nimbus okay?" she asked instead, shifting her attention to the winded animal.

The horse twisted his neck to look back to Arleta and snorted, his breath clouding the chilly, wet air.

"He's well," Theo assured her. "And he says thank you for asking."

They sat in the road, not moving.

"We should get going," Arleta finally said to stop herself from insisting they turn around.

"Oh. Yes." Theo gripped the reins. "Can't be late."

But the rain did not let up. It only worsened as they traveled, pouring from the puffy gray clouds above, drenching both Arleta and Theodmon. She eyed him next to her on the wooden cart's seat as he steered Nimbus along the sloppy path, not complaining about the weather or the bumpy ride.

"You shouldn't have bought the cart," Arleta said under her shivering breath. "Taking Nimbus on his own would have been faster. We'd probably be there already."

Theo shook his head. "It would be wholly inappropriate for me to share my horse with a lady."

"You mean you'd hate to be seen with a magicless," Arleta muttered.

"What? *No.*" His tone was incredulous. "It would have been disrespectful of *you.*"

Arleta clenched her teeth and sighed. She didn't understand why he would say that, and an unexpected sting of tears came quickly, but the rain hid any that fell. She was grateful for this small mercy, since she barely wanted to cry in front of people she cared for, let alone this elf she'd just met.

"There's an inn not too far down the way," Theo said, breaking the heavy silence. "We can stay there for the night and leave for Langheim first thing in the morning."

As the words left his mouth, Arleta's heart leaped as multiple thoughts twined in her brain.

They were supposed to arrive in Langheim *today*, not tomorrow.

Plus, a single human woman staying at an inn with an elf may appear scandalous, even if they slept in separate rooms.

And they could be late for the competition deadline if anything else slowed them down.

The thoughts twisted and turned. She didn't really know why she'd let herself get talked into going to the Baking Battle. If Ervash and Verdreth…no…if Theo…no. It wasn't them.

*She'd* decided to go all on her own. All for vanity. All for dreams that did not belong to her.

She shook her head in a mostly failed attempt to rid herself of the jumbled thoughts just as the wagon pulled up in front of a small inn. Golden light flickered from the windows, and over the door was a sign reading THE DOUBLE UNICORN TAVERN AND INN. As expected, under the words were two unicorns standing on their hind legs facing each other, frozen in eternal battle.

"The innkeeper always has something tasty to eat and drink," Theo said as he leaped from the cart.

*Has he been here before?* she thought. "And two rooms, right?" Arleta called through the incessant rain. At least she'd made extra silver at the market and could pay her way. That was something.

Theo bowed his head. "Of course."

With a slight grunt, Arleta dismounted the wagon. Her boots squelched as they sank into the mud in front of the inn. Fumbling in the near darkness, she raked her fingers around where her feet had been for the sack of precious herbs and spices but found nothing.

"No, no, no!" Frantically, she ran her hands over the wooden floor of the wagon, but still, nothing. The bundle must have fallen out when they nearly hit that stag in the road about half-way from Adenashire to the Two Unicorns. Neither Arleta nor Theo had noticed.

She cursed under her breath, her voice as drenched in resignation and frustration as her cloak was in water. "Of *course*."

Nothing was ever simple for her.

Arleta pinched at the bridge of her nose and stomped through the muck all the way to the door, shaking off clumps of mud before daring to enter.

Once in and over the threshold, she was hit with the aroma of fresh biscuits, thick, savory stew, and burning logs, promising warmth and a full belly for the right price. She immediately shrugged off her wet cloak and hung it on a hook near the entrance. Water dripped and puddled onto the floor underneath it, mingling with what had fallen from Theo's cloak.

The room was crowded. Boisterous patrons sat in conversation at every table, and there wasn't exactly an abundance of space to start. Arleta spotted Theo's blond hair and quickly averted her eyes from the customers' gazes, but everyone had looked when she had entered. There was no denying they all had seen her and were watching her next move.

Maybe they *weren't*, but it felt that way to Arleta.

Bracing herself, Arleta combed her fingers through her rain-soaked hair and wrung out the wavy strands. She steeled herself, then marched directly to the elf, who was chatting with the inn-keeper, a dwarf with a fiery beard who stood behind the counter.

"My herbs are gone," Arleta whispered to Theo, and his eyes quickly darted to her in concern, then back to the dwarf.

Raucous laughter erupted from the dining area, where a rowdy group of patrons, fueled by too much ale, hollered at some shared joke. She knew better, but to Arleta, it felt like they were laughing at her.

Panic rose in Arleta's chest. It was all too much.

The innkeeper leaned his elbows on the mahogany counter and spoke over the roused patrons. "We're completely full tonight on account of the storm, I'm afraid." His voice was a rumbling drawl, and his eyes conveyed nothing but the facts.

Arleta's stomach plummeted, as if following the very pre-dictable trajectory of her sinking hopes. What were they going to do? Why had she agreed to this journey in the first place? She should have listened to the crows.

"Not *one* space?" Theo's voice was tinged with desperation as he raked his hand through his drenched hair. He darted his eyes around the room, briefly resting on Arleta, then he refo-cused on the innkeeper. "We have plenty of silver," he offered, his voice edged with hope, as if reality might somehow change for the right amount of coin.

The fiery dwarf raised his beefy hands in the air, his expres-sion the same as before. "Silver doesn't conjure up beds, lad." His tone held a bit of levity, despite the bad news. "I'm not in the habit of kicking paying guests out. Unless they create a ruckus, that is."

The moment the last words left his lips, a giantess, whose head nearly touched the ceiling, stomped out from a back room. Behind her she all but dragged a much smaller gnome with a wide-eyed stare on his flushed face. The man was clearly overwhelmed.

"I will not stay here one more *second*," the woman boomed, her filed-to-a-point teeth catching the flickering tavern light. "I knew this entire thing was a mistake." Her stare locked onto the dwarf, who seemed to remain unmoved. "We'd rather brave the rain than that room."

Simultaneously, Arleta and Theo stepped back to allow a generous amount of space for the furious giantess and her unlikely tiny partner, who she continued to tug alongside, to step up to the counter.

"I demand a refund!" The giantess's demand reverberated over a group of laughing revelers, but they seemed to pay her no mind. "The family accommodations are absolutely deplorable!"

The dwarf stepped up onto a wooden crate in a futile attempt to meet the angry woman at eye level. "Unfortunately, ma'am, we cannot offer refunds. Inn policy."

Her eyes shot wide, and her nostrils flared in anger.

However, before another word could be spat, Theo pulled out a handful of gleaming silver. "Consider this your refund," he said, somehow keeping his voice steady, and pressed the coins into the giantess's large hand. As soon as she didn't drop it, the elf plunked more silver coins onto the counter. "And there is the payment for their beds."

The giantess scoffed but pocketed the coin.

Before the gnome was dragged away, he eyed Theo from top to bottom. "Good luck in there. You're gonna need it."

# 6

With Nimbus safely tucked away in the inn's barn and their bags clutched in hand, Theo and Arleta trudged to the back of the inn's apparently infamous family quarters. Above them, the continuous patter of rain onto the tightly thatched roof beat out an ominous rhythm, tying knots in Arleta's spine.

"The family quarters can't be as bad as those two said?" Arleta asked, trying to get her mind off the fact that her herbs were, indeed, nowhere to be found in the cart. But one thing was lumping up on another, and her nerves were not cooperating. The last thing she wanted to do was fall apart.

"I hope not. After we get settled in, we can head back into the pub and get something to eat," Theo offered as he walked behind Arleta. "The stew smelled good."

"I have no intention of going back out there until we leave

tomorrow morning," Arleta insisted, a hint of stubbornness peppering her tone. "I'm tired."

*And hungry. And completely overwhelmed.*

But she didn't say those things to Theo.

Theo pursed his lips. "That's fine. It's been a long day. How about I'll head out before the kitchen closes and bring a meal to you?"

She tensed at his kind words. *Why is he doing this?* Theo really had no stake in getting her to Langheim. *What did it matter if I entered or not? Surely there are droves of other hopefuls. One contestant dropping out isn't his responsibility, even if he said it was...*

And yet, his kindness felt genuine.

"Fine," she conceded, but those silly tears stung at her eyes again. She wasn't a child and resented all the emotions this "adventure" was stirring up in her. This was exactly why she avoided getting close to people or opening up. All it brought was pain, and she didn't need that. Stability was her refuge.

Arleta let her shoulder meet the wall, exasperated, but too tired to argue. Or even move. "What am I going to do about my herbs?" Her words were an abrupt shift, but with everything that had happened that day, she'd nearly forgotten about them. The memory of the stag sent a surge of energy through Arleta. Her hands raked nervously through her damp hair while her breath suddenly came quickly. Exaggerated, hyperventilated.

Like even breathing was impossible.

"Hey, hey, hey." Theo's voice was soothing as he made his way over to Arleta and stood in front of her. "Look at me."

His words were incredibly gentle. As if they had known each other for years. As if he knew just what to do for her.

Her eyes, wide with dread, met his as the elf leaned one arm up against the wall next to her. He brought up his free hand, hovering it over her upper arm as if asking permission in her vulnerable state.

"May I touch you?" he asked, the warmth of his presence enveloping her.

Somehow, she bobbed her head that it was allowed. Even *wanted.*

Gingerly, his hand touched her damp sleeve and pressed slightly against her skin. "I'm going to count to five. I know it will be difficult, but try to hold your breath until I reach the count, and then breathe. Then we'll do it again until you want to stop."

The first time was a miserable failure, but a patient Theo tried again, coaxing her through the process once more. By the time they'd worked through eleven cycles of counting and holding breath, Arleta's breathing had calmed.

She gazed up into his eyes, then at his soft, tempting mouth. Theo was only inches from her, and the close heat of his body intensified the cedarwood fragrance he carried.

Coming back to her mind, she cleared her throat.

She still didn't know what she was going to do about the Baking Battle.

"I'm already at a disadvantage, Theo," she confessed, her voice a soft plea. "No one is going to want me there, and now I don't have my herbs. Everyone else will have their secret ingredients." Arleta rubbed at her temples, feeling a headache coming on.

The elf stayed close to her, regarding her hazel eyes with a soft intensity. "I want you there."

She froze for a second, then said, "And why is that? Why are you really going to all this trouble?" Her hands raised up in the air as she edged away from him. "Did you wager a bet on the underdog before you came to Adenashire?"

Theo's eyes crinkled at the corners as he stepped back and clasped his hands in front of him. "No. No bets were involved."

Arleta's patience, like her energy, waned. "Then why?" she demanded as the hall's lantern flickered orange, casting light and shadows all over the small space. But as she stared into Theo's eyes, waiting for his answer, she almost forgot about the rain pattering on the roof, and the worries of losing her bag almost fell away.

Almost.

There was something between them. She didn't know what it was, but it was *something*.

Perhaps he was this kind to everyone. Had all the women falling at his feet.

But she'd never felt this for anyone before.

Not that she'd have let anything happen. Too risky and foolish.

"Every pastry, cookie, bread I've tasted that you've made has been magic, Arleta." The sincere words fell off his lips like sugar. "You *are* what the Baking Battle aspires to. Why would I let someone as talented as you miss the chance to compete? And..."

Arleta's breath caught in her throat. "And what?"

Theo gulped and seemed to draw back his intended words. "To *win*. You have a real chance at winning with or without your herbs. I believe in you. I know talent when I see it. Now..." He paused for a second before he spoke again, a grin quirking at his lips. "Now, we have to brave whatever is in that room."

Ahead of them waited the door labeled FAMILY QUARTERS.

Together, they made their way to it. With a shaky hand, Arleta pushed the metal key into the keyhole and turned. Just as she pushed, something thudded against the door, forcing it shut again, but not before the scent of musk and wet fur accosted Arleta's nose.

"I'm gonna get you!" a muffled, youthful voice sounded through the door.

"Um." Arleta glanced back at Theo, who was biting his top lip.

A quick smile took over, hiding the flicker of uncertainty she'd seen. "It's either this or the barn."

Arleta blew out a quick breath and shoved the door as gently as she could to get it open but not hurt anyone who might be right behind it.

The momentary resistance was followed by a high-pitched squeal—not one of pain, but of excitement as someone scampered away from the entrance. When the door was open, the sight inside was quite one to behold, not to mention the even stronger smell.

An exhausted-looking mother castor, the size of a large dog and just as furry, sat on one bed, her chestnut head in her paws. Her large, paddle-like tail flopped over the bed behind her. She didn't look up or say a word to Theo and Arleta as they entered.

Castors often lived in marshes or wetlands, so Arleta was a bit surprised to see a family in the area.

"Kits!" another castor with a baritone voice said from their left, his short, rounded ears twitching on the top of his head. He was apparently trying to establish some sense of order. He slammed his wide, flat tail against the floor several times, nearly shaking the room, as two young castors bounced up and down on the bottom bunk behind him, explosive giggles leaving their mouths. On the other side of the room, a set of older youths occupied two single beds and stared blankly at the wooden puzzle games held in their paws.

"Pop!" one of the youth kits moaned, their furry brow creased. "Tell them to be quiet. I need to focus here!"

The other youth didn't even look up from their game.

"What do you think I'm doing?" the father said, exasperation ringing through his words, still not making any sign he'd noticed that others had entered the family quarters. "Look what you're doing to your ma!" He thrust out a paw to the other castor, her head still buried in her paws.

His mate groaned, the sound muffled by her paws. "Why did I agree to this holiday?" The sentiment went unanswered.

Meanwhile, from under a bed, a set of small, digited paws grappled in the air.

As the scene unfolded, Arleta stood frozen in place, fully understanding why the giantess and her mate had left. She'd heard of the spirited nature of castors but had never expected this.

Breaking through her thoughts, Theo let out a cough behind her. "Hello," he announced with surprising calm and cordiality. He shut the door behind him, sealing them into the furry chaos.

Arleta caught her breath as both the adult castors shot their attention toward the elf and human.

"I'm so sorry about—" the mother started, her expression a mix of surprise and worry, cut off when the two younger kits jumped to the floor and started dragging the third out from under the bed, kicking and screaming the whole way.

"No, no. We've all been there," Theo said over the racket, waving off the mother's half-spoken apology with an easy grin.

Arleta had no idea if Theo had actually "been there." She

undoubtedly had not, but somehow she appreciated his patient sentiment. And the whole thing had helped take her mind off her own troubles for the moment.

"I'm *hungry*," one kit complained.

Without missing a beat, Theo quickly took Arleta's wet bag and walked toward two unused—other than the blankets being pulled almost entirely off—beds on the right side of the room. Alongside them was a privacy screen for changing.

Arleta forced herself to follow him.

When their bags were stowed on the bedsides, Theo swung back around, a spark in his eyes. "How about I go back out there and get everyone something for dinner?"

This announcement instantly closed the mouths of the three young castors, and their eyes grew wide.

"Oh," the mother said hesitantly, "I have a few snacks in our bag."

"Please save those for later. Dinner is on me if you like." Theo swept his hand into the air, pausing for a moment as if waiting for the castor's reply.

She nodded with a grateful, yet exhausted expression.

"Then," he glanced at the three youngest, "I can't remember the last time I made blanket forts to sleep under."

The trio of young castors grinned, their buck teeth bright against their furry faces.

Before they could speak, Theo quickly added, "How about you start to plan the fort, and when I get back, I'll help you build it?"

The kits nodded in unison and scrambled for blankets and pillows.

Mother castor glanced up with a weary expression and mouthed, "Thank you."

Theo nodded and started to walk, but Arleta caught his arm. "Are you okay with this?" she whispered.

"Yes," he said with confidence. "Now get settled in." He tipped his head to the adult castors and left the room.

With Theo gone, Arleta quickly gathered the dry clothes at the bottom of her satchel and made her way behind the privacy screen while all the castors seemed occupied. When she stepped out, the parents had laid on their beds while the youths were still engrossed in their puzzle games and the kits sat on the floor with pieces of chalk in paw, sketching out their fort plans.

"What about a dam? Like at home," the first kit proposed.

"You said damn!" the third, who had been the one under the bed, squealed, his brown eyes shining in delight.

The father groaned, the sound resonating across the room. "*Kits!*"

The admonishment had little effect on their jovial mood, but the three went back to their drawing.

Arleta pulled back the bedcovers and climbed beneath their warmth. Somehow, for a moment, she felt safe and with a clear head, even with the noise.

It wasn't long before the door creaked open, and Theo was back with a large tray balanced in hand, bringing with it the savory tang of hearty stew. He distributed bowls of food to each of the castor family and then one to Arleta.

"I didn't even ask if lamb was your preference. I ordered vegetable for them," he admitted as he handed her the wooden bowl and spoon. "If you want something different, please let me know."

"It's perfect," Arleta assured him, taking the bowl. She took several quick bites of the savory meal, full of large chunks of potatoes, carrots, and tender lamb as she watched Theo leave his bowl behind and head straight for the kits, who were more than ready to start the build.

"Now remember," the elf said, sitting on the floor with them with a playful grin, "forts are for sleeping. You probably have a big day tomorrow, and you want to have lots of energy and not doze off in the middle of it."

Theo's voice trailed off as Arleta finished her stew, laid down, and turned over on her side.

Maybe things weren't so bad after all.

Her parents would want her to keep going. To not give up on her baking dreams. Face this challenge head-on.

Ervash and Verdreth would want the same. And not just for the tickets to the finale.

*She* wanted this. She'd always wanted this.

The thought curled her lips into a soft smile as her eyelids drooped.

# 7

As light crawled into their quarters, Arleta flopped over in bed and forced open her heavy eyelids. It took a moment for her to recognize the unfamiliar room, but she quickly remembered when she caught a whiff of castor musk. Across the room, the three young kits were snoozing in their fort. The blanket walls, supported by chair legs and bed frames, had somehow held up overnight.

The rest of the family was out as well, both the mother and father snoring like ogres. One youth was fast asleep with the wooden puzzle stuck on their face. They'd likely fallen asleep while still playing with it.

Arleta hadn't even noticed the small window at the back of the room the night before, but it let in a tiny amount of light. Theo had made it into the bed beside her at some point in the night but was upside down at the wrong end. His feet stuck out from under the blanket while his head was underneath, just a tuft of flaxen hair visible.

She reached for her satchel and rummaged through it. Her fingertips brushed against the familiar form of her metal pocket watch. She pulled it out to check the time, squinting at the small numbers as the watch's ticking vibrated against her hand. Despite the sleep in her eyes, the numbers became clear. Too clear.

It was midmorning, hours and hours past the time they'd intended to leave the inn.

Her heart clenched and icy dread surged as she quickly calculated the time it would still take them to reach Langheim. They would never make it before the gate would be closed and the registration completely locked down.

"Theo," she said, her voice quavering with disappointment, "we've slept in way too long."

"Huh?" His gravelly, tired voice came from under the blanket.

"We're *late*!"

"What?" Theo threw the blanket off, straining to get a glimpse of the clock face in her hand. "Damn it. I promised you I'd get you there in time." He sprang from the bed like a startled deer, pulling his clothes on in a flurry, all the while muttering to himself that *this will not do,* and *it is all my fault.*

Several of the castors stirred but didn't awaken.

Arleta also threw a fresh top and skirt over the shift she'd slept in. She quickly gathered anything that had fallen from the satchel and stuffed it haphazardly back inside, but she didn't know what the hurry was. On the cart, they would never make it in time. This was assured.

"I suppose you'll be taking me back to Adenashire," she

whispered, her voice peppered with the defeat she thought she'd rid herself of the night prior.

Theo froze, silent for a moment, then cursed.

"You said shit," an obviously groggy and probably still asleep castor kit mumbled from inside the blanket fort, then went silent again.

Any other time, it would have been laughable.

Arleta fell back to sit on the bed, her mind whirling and attempting to come up with some solution from the entire trip's shambles. "When does the gate close again?"

"Sundown," Theo answered, keeping his voice low.

She held her breath for a second and then let it out. "That gives us a little under seven hours."

He bobbed his head grimly. "At top speed, the wagon won't get us there in less than nine. Not with the muddy roads. And that's *if* there aren't any other hitches along the way."

Arleta rubbed her chin in thought. Her stomach roiled at what she was about to suggest. It was bold, and she still didn't have her herbs.

"What if we left the cart here, at the inn, and just took Nimbus?" The question nearly caught in her mouth, but she forced the words out.

For a second, the suggestion hung in the air between them, audacious and desperate.

"But you are a lady," Theo protested. "It would not be appr—"

Arleta scoffed, cutting him off by sweeping her hand through the air as if to showcase the room. "I don't *care*."

The rosy flush spreading across Theo's cheeks could be made out even under the dim light. It was nothing short of charming, but Arleta ignored it.

She tipped her head back and forth once, considering the options. "I'm sure for a fee that red-bearded dwarf downstairs would watch over the cart. I could pay for the storage with my extra earned coin." She dug around in her satchel to find what she'd brought of her recently earned silver. A few coins should take care of at least part of the storage fee. She held them out to Theo.

"That's not necessary—" Theo started.

"It *is* necessary," Arleta said firmly. "I wouldn't be letting you do all this if I didn't have a repayment plan."

Theo's shoulders relaxed. He took the coins from her hand and sent her a gentle nod. "I'm at your service, Arleta."

His genuine offering sparked a wild fluttering in her stomach. The back of her neck and chest grew hot. "Thank you," Arleta barely got out.

"We should get going," Theo said, practicality creeping back into his tone as he pocketed the coins.

Within minutes, they were outside with their luggage and cloaks, leaving the still-sleeping castors. Theo had struck a deal with the innkeeper. In two weeks' time or less, he would head back to the inn with Nimbus and retrieve the cart.

The storm had blown over completely, leaving the sky as clear and crystal blue as Theo's eyes. While they walked to the barn, Theo handed Arleta a biscuit slathered in fresh, salty butter and strawberry jam. "You need to eat."

"Thank you." She took and ate the sweet and savory morsel in only a few bites. By the time she was done, Nimbus's speckled form stood before them, and he was munching feed from a trough in his stall. The damp, earthy smells of the barn wrinkled Arleta's nose slightly, but it didn't diminish her enjoyment of the biscuit Theo had given her.

The elf ran his hand over the horse's flank, and the animal twisted to look at him with his shiny, intelligent brown eyes. Offering a carrot from his pocket, Theo seemed to engage him in a silent conversation while the horse ate.

Apparently satisfied with whatever was said, Nimbus snorted.

"Nimbus is fine with you riding him." Theo paused for a second and raised one blond brow. "He says that you were right when you mentioned we should have done that from the start."

Arleta let out a chuckle. "Animals don't seem to care much about the silly things we do."

In agreement, Nimbus tossed his head in the air, his gray mane catching the midmorning light streaming into the barn.

Theo patted his friend. "He suggests maybe we should listen to them more often."

"Perhaps," Arleta agreed.

Not long after, Theo had the bags cinched securely and a few plain biscuits stashed within easy reach. Nimbus was ready. The elf mounted on top of the horse and extended his hand to Arleta. She took it and hoisted herself in front of the elf. His arms reached around her, sending a thrill through her entire body, but she quickly dismissed it as the three of them left the Double Unicorn Tavern and Inn behind.

But not before Arleta had checked to ensure her Baking Battle invitation was still secure in her pocket.

She didn't want to lose that too.

As the powerful horse's hooves clopped down the road, Arleta didn't blame him for his sour look yesterday when he'd been hitched to the cart. Nimbus seemed to have a free soul. Her thoughts wandered to the hope that Theo had struck an agreement with him for a lot of extra sweet carrots and apples on the return to Langheim.

Hours passed, and as the sun moved across the blue sky, they only took minimal breaks. The journey seemed to stretch out in the damp air and soggy ground, both still heavy with yesterday's rain. It was as if the Northern Lands and Arleta were holding their breath with anticipation of the group reaching the Baking Battle in plenty of time.

However, as they traveled through the thick heart of the Stouling Forest, a particular sight made them slow their pace. Up ahead, a faun waved his hands in the air in the middle of the road. To his side was a topsy-turvy wagon that lay halfway in and out of a ditch, plus a bewildered-looking black-and-white cow that appeared uninjured, but still stuck. Two small fauns perched on the other side of the road playing some type of game where the winner one-upped the other with a series of curious hand gestures.

Theo gently tugged on Nimbus's reins. "I know we don't have time," he said to the horse, as if in response to something the beast must have spoken in his mind.

"Oh, thank the stars." The faun sighed, padding on his little goatlike legs toward them. "We've been stuck here for hours. No one has stopped." His voice carried a hint of nervousness.

Arleta bit her lip, knowing full well the weight of their deadline, but also that stopping was the right thing to do. Nimbus *was* right. They really did not have the time.

"Hello, friend." She wanted to put the faun at ease and turned to Theo as the sight before them tugged at her heart. "We can't just leave them," Arleta whispered.

After all, despite the traveling sun, there was always time for kindness.

His eyebrows furrowed just slightly, probably not because he didn't want to stop, but because he was well aware that their own time was running out. The elf let his lips arch into a slight, friendly smile. "Do you have ropes?"

The faun bobbed his head multiple times and trotted to the back of the wagon. From there, he pulled out a long bundle of tan rope and held it up to Theo just as he swung down from Nimbus.

After helping Arleta safely off the horse, he took the coil from the faun's hand. The elf glanced at Nimbus, and the horse nodded as if he were agreeing to lend a hoof as well.

"Thank you. *Thank you.* I'm Dreap, and these are my twins, Rhegea and Ronorae," the faun said, genuine gratitude shining in his eyes. "Thank you so much for stopping."

"It's our pleasure," Arleta said, and warm emotion stirred in her chest at the thought of wanting to take the time for this faun. "I'm Arleta, and this is Theo. We're on our way to the Langheim Baking Battle." She didn't know why she'd blurted that all out, but what was done was done.

"The Baking Battle?" the twins said in chorus, finally distracted from their game at the mention of cakes and confections.

A grin spread across Arleta's lips. "Yes. I'm entering."

The elder faun hooted as he and Theo began their mission to save the cow. "Well, good luck to ya."

Arleta indicated her thanks and sat next to the twins while Theo and Dreap secured the rope around the cow, and then to Nimbus. It wasn't long before the cow, named Violet, stood securely on the road. Next was the cart.

"Do you have any samples?" Ronorae asked Arleta, their eyes wide with possibility. "We didn't get lunch."

Arleta chuckled at their hopeful faces. "No, but we have a biscuit left from the inn this morning." She stood and fetched it from the satchel, then handed it to the twins to split.

Overhead, a flock of unfamiliar white birds flew past, Arleta's eyes tracing their graceful arc across the sky. Maybe they were a good omen. They had done the right thing.

Before they knew it, Arleta and Theo waved goodbye to the fauns and were back on the road, albeit a half an hour behind schedule.

"It's okay," Theo assured her. "Nimbus says he can make up the time."

❖

Hours later, and just after the forest had opened wide to reveal the Langheim realm's castle, Arleta's breath caught in her throat at the sight of the almost iridescent towers reaching into the sky over the trees, bathed in the last light of the day. Each stone seemed to be touched with starlight.

Unfortunately, even with the horse's determined pace the entire way, they could not outpace the sun. The giant metal gate was drawing closed, growling the entire way to the ground.

They were too late.

# 8

O h no, no, no!" Theo launched himself from Nimbus's back, leaving Arleta, and landed with a thud on the soft green grass.

He raced to the castle gate, arms flailing like a windmill, yelling toward the nearly closed gate. Arleta sat in stunned silence on the horse's back.

"Stop!" Theo called to the unseen gatekeeper. "Stop, the sun hasn't completely set!"

At his words, the gate groaned, then halted with a deep clank, leaving just enough room for an elf to squeeze through.

Arleta could just make out his figure behind the crisscrossed metal of the entry.

"I'm Theodmon Brylar, and I've brought one last contestant for the Baking Battle," he said from inside, clearly winded. The elf Theo spoke to, still in animated gestures, was silhouetted as well, but finally, the gate reversed its course and raised enough for Nimbus and Arleta to pass.

Theo stepped back outside the gate with a triumphant grin and waved the horse forward. Nimbus tossed his head multiple times as he walked while the elf came up beside Arleta.

"I reminded the gatekeeper of the rule stating that the gate is *not* supposed to close until the last light," Theo said, his gaze meeting Arleta's. Just then, the sun completely fell behind the Colmore Mountains flanking Langheim, but Arleta didn't see it for more than a moment since the trio had hurried to the other side of the gate.

Safely inside.

The gate guard was a tall, muscular woman with a dagger resting on her hip and linen clothes similar to Theo's. She eyed Arleta before returning to her job, lowering the gate behind them.

Theo led Nimbus from the gate area to an open courtyard, and the entire experience was a feast for Arleta's eyes. Lanterns affixed to the courtyard's columns burned with a lustrous blue flame. Whatever the fuel was, it was magical. Vines with open flowers twined up the same columns, and multiple trees, reaching up to the open sky above, were heavily laden with unfamiliar red, white, and purple fruits. The scent in the air was sweet and heady.

Arleta caught her breath at the sight. "How do you ever leave this place?" she whispered, mostly to herself.

Theo chuckled and allowed his hands to sink into his pockets. "It is beautiful, I'll admit. But now and then I need a break from all the perfection. It all can get a tad...stuffy. Plus, you never know who you're going to meet on the outside."

Taking in all the grandeur, Arleta said, "I'm good with a little stuffy for a while. Do you think I could get down?"

"Oh, stars, of course." Theo patted Nimbus gently on his neck, and the horse stopped walking. Offering Arleta a hand, the elf helped her down from the saddle, and she immediately jogged over to a tree bearing luscious purple fruit.

With her hand hovering over the base of the fruit, Arleta turned. "May I?"

The elf nodded.

Arleta grasped the smooth fruit and pulled it from the stem. The sphere sat just in her palm as she stared at it.

"It's an iweocot," Theo said, leaning against Nimbus as Arleta pulled the fruit into two halves, revealing the gnarly pit nestled inside. The flesh was an ombre of purple to pink, meeting at the pit.

"Can I eat it?" Arleta asked, her gaze filled with curiosity about the flavor.

The elf's eyes twinkled as if simply watching Arleta enjoying something so simple and new was a pleasure. "You can."

She raised the iweocot to her lips and took a small bite. Immediately, her face lit with joy. "It's so sweet." Arleta tipped her head in interest, regarding the flavors on her tongue. "Spicy...with a mildly tart finish. I wonder if we'll be baking with these?"

"Possibly," Theo said, pulling Arleta back to the task at hand. "But we need to get going. Registration awaits."

Arleta nodded, savored the last bite of her iweocot, and pocketed the pit to take back to Adenashire while Theo retrieved their things and sent Nimbus on to the stables.

"I'll be there later tonight to take you home," Theo promised Nimbus.

The horse nickered and trotted his way down a corridor.

"You don't live in here?" Arleta asked, trailing after Theo.

"The castle is more like our city square. Big events and such happen here." Theo directed her through an intricately carved door full of elven symbols. "I live away from all the hustle and bustle—speaking of which, get ready for some."

Arleta barely had time to even think what Theo meant by that when a distinguished-looking elf barreled toward them. "Theodmon," he said, out of breath and clearly frustrated, "you were expected yesterday. Everyone has been looking for you."

Theo raised a brow in question. "Everyone?"

The elf, who appeared middle-aged—whatever that *was* for an elf—and had shoulder-length, slightly graying hair at his temples, lowered his shoulders. His clothes were luxuriously gilded in intricate patterns on the chest. "Well, you know who. You must find her." He eyed Arleta, giving no hint what he made of her presence.

"Devdan, you're her assistant. You can handle these things," Theo said, "I have one last contestant to get to registration—"

"Find her *immediately*." Devdan's lips puckered in concern, and after a beat he leaned in, adding, "She's causing quite the stir."

Arleta stood rooted in place, suddenly feeling the once delicious iweocot turning over in her stomach at the tension crackling between the two elves.

And who was *she*?

Theo sighed and turned to Arleta, dragging her from her thoughts. "If I send Devdan as an escort, will you be okay with finding the registration?"

Devdan spluttered in surprise. "Sir?"

Theo silenced him with a single glance.

Arleta, rallying her courage, offered him a determined nod. "I think so." She wasn't really sure at all, but Theo had already done enough, and she needed to take over. "Yes. I'll be fine."

With Arleta's assurance, Theo's attention moved back to the other elf. "Please escort Arleta *Starstone* to registration. She has her official invitation with her."

Devdan bowed his head slightly and began walking away.

Arleta didn't move for a moment, quickly eyeing Theo. "Thank you for everything."

His lips curved into a kindly arch, and he handed Arleta her bag. "I'll ask where your room is and find you later to ensure you've settled in."

With that, Arleta scurried after the rapidly disappearing elf. She was led through a labyrinth of ashlar stone corridors, illuminated by the ethereal glow of magic lanterns like those in the courtyard. As they traveled, they passed more elves and people from all over the Northern Lands. There were dwarves, fairies, fauns, even an ogre, who all must have been there for the competition. Excitement grew in Arleta's chest with each passing minute, and she wished she could take it all in, but she needed to keep up with Devdan's power-walking pace.

Finally, they arrived at the registration area, a large, open room where an elf with a medium-brown appearance tidied her workstation for the day.

"One more, Viessa," Devdan announced curtly to the elf, who looked up in surprise.

She held the participant list in her hand, then up in the air. "Right at the last second."

"Yes," Arleta said, blushing, but stepped up to the table and pulled the invitation from her pocket. After she gave Devdan a cursory head bow, the posh elf was off to something else without so much as a goodbye.

Viessa took the invitation and compared the name to that on the list. "You must be very excited about this opportunity."

"This is my first time here," Arleta admitted, the words tumbling out in a flurry of nerves. She gulped, half expecting Viessa to say something about her being magicless and show her the door.

Unfazed, the elf scanned down the list before plunking her slender finger on Arleta's name. "Ooh, I see you entered a thyme raspberry tart in the qualifying round. How delightful."

Arleta hadn't entered anything. That was all Verdreth's doing, but she found herself nodding along. "It is."

"Must be." Viessa smiled and looked up. "Clearly the entry was a hit with the judges since it earned you a spot." She produced a contract and a pen for Arleta to sign it with, placing them on the table in front of her. "Now read through that carefully. One of the key points is that you only have three opportunities to enter the Baking Battle, and they can only be nonconsecutive years. However, there are plenty of other details to keep in mind."

Arleta's heart picked up as she quickly skimmed her way down the document, looking for the mention of the word "human" or "without magic" and any rules against them, even though she'd been reminded several times there was no such rule.

"Oh," Viessa said, as though just remembering, "do you have any special ingredients to turn over for approval?"

Arleta's shoulders tensed, but she kept her eyes on the document, still trying to absorb every word. "Unfortunately they were lost on the journey."

"That's too bad." The elf fumbled with her stacks of paperwork on the table.

Arleta was barely halfway through the text when a voice echoed through the large room.

"Viessa," someone called out impatiently, "we need to wrap things up."

"I'm sorry," Viessa said as she winced and turned back to Arleta, "but I must close. If you could sign that, I can finish checking you in, get you the key to your room and a schedule."

A nervous thrill twisted Arleta's stomach. Hesitating only for a moment, she flipped to the last page and scrawled her name on the line with an X next to it. Once it was done, she passed the document back to Viessa, her heart pounding like a blacksmith's hammer.

The elf quickly handed over a key and several neatly folded papers, along with the invitation. "Everything you need is in there. The competition will start bright and early tomorrow morning."

Arleta gazed down at the precious papers in her hands, her full name spelled out on the front of them: *Arleta Starstone*, written in the same fancy elvish script that had been on the invitation. Below her name was *Room 206, Elyilon Wing*.

A surge of excitement trilled in her chest. She was *really* at the Baking Battle.

"Where is the Elyi—" Arleta started as she held the silver key in the air, but Viessa's backside was already around the corner.

Arleta puffed out her cheeks like a fish and blew out the air in a gust. "Stars in heaven," she muttered, steeling herself while flipping through the pamphlet. Maybe there would be a map inside. That would be incredibly helpful.

She looked up and spun around, intending to get a sense of the space she was in, but instead plowed directly into a feminine elf, causing her papers to fly up into the air and float gently back to the floor.

"I'm so sorry," Arleta barely got out as the scowling, auburn-haired elf took a step back in disgust.

"Get *out* of my way!" she snapped, her sharp voice echoing in the large space.

Arleta stood there, stunned, feeling as if she'd been caught naked in the wrong place. "I…I…"

"Ugh." The green-eyed elf stood several inches taller than Arleta and threw her hands in the air as she huffed off. "I just have to make it through this damn week without people getting in my way," she muttered, and then was around the corner and out of sight.

Shaking, Arleta bent to retrieve her papers.

"You look a little lost," a friendly voice chirped, causing Arleta to look up. Her gaze caught on just about the sweetest-looking dwarf she'd ever seen in her entire life, the opposite of the person she'd just encountered, a ray of sunshine instead of a starless night.

The dwarf was a vision in a corseted, buttery yellow dress. The bright, warm hue complemented her rich complexion and lush head of sable curls. Each hair coil seemed to dance with the same radiant joy shown by her twinkling brown eyes and pearly smile. Holstered on her ample hip, where one might expect a weapon, was instead a teacup and saucer, held together by leather straps.

The second Arleta saw the dwarf, all her worries were forgotten. Then, as reality edged back in, she found her voice again. "Um, yes. I need to find my room."

"May I?" The dwarf stretched out her hand, and Arleta gladly turned over the shuffled paperwork.

"I'm Dolgrila Butterbuckle," she said while reading. "But everyone calls me Doli." Her eyes lit up as she found the pertinent information. "Oh, what do you know? You're directly across the hall from me. I can take you right there."

Arleta didn't even have the chance to get in a word before Doli was pulling her into the nearest corridor.

"This is going to be so *fun*," Doli chirped, her wide nose crinkling, voice ringing with excitement and hope.

# 9

I'm Arleta Starstone, by the way," Arleta managed to squeeze in among Doli's nonstop chatter on their journey to the top of the stairs. The whole experience was still pleasant because of how Doli's voice danced as she spoke. She could probably make just about anyone feel at ease. It almost made Arleta forget all about the horrible elf she'd encountered and would hopefully never see again.

The dwarf bobbed her head multiple times. "Yes, that's what it said on your paperwork." She threw out her hand with a friendly flourish. "It's very nice to meet you."

Arleta shook Doli's hand. Her grip was firm and ever so faintly calloused.

She had already learned on the way to her room that Doli was from Dundes Heights, and that most of the dwarves there, as one would expect, were miners. But Doli had never taken a liking to the job and had devoted her life to baking the best cupcakes, as well as other baked goods, in the Northern Lands. It was her first year at the Baking Battle as well, but she had arrived two days earlier to get the lay of the land.

"My room is right over there," Doli chimed in, tipping her head to the room across the hallway, neatly labeled with a sign reading 207 before her attention turned to 206.

Arleta inserted the key given to her and turned until a satisfying click echoed through the hall and the door fell slightly ajar. She held her breath and pushed it open wide.

With a giggle, Doli gave Arleta just the slightest nudge, and the two stepped inside.

The room was the nicest place Arleta had ever seen in her life, and her mouth hung open to prove the point. A fluffy bed with a soft blue covering waited just to the left, and to the side of it was a carved chest of drawers with an elegant water pitcher on top. A large window was positioned in the center of the wall, but since it was dark outside, she couldn't appreciate the view.

"Looks like mine," Doli said, as if she'd been curious.

"Ugh, can you keep it *down*?" a low voice, nearly a growl, said from their right.

Arleta spun on her heel and dropped her paperwork to the floor for a second time. The sheets floated and scattered across the room. "Oh," she gasped, her voice caught in her throat.

Sitting crisscross on the room's second bed was a person with short-cropped snowy hair framing a pair of tall, pointed, furry ears. A bushy white-and-sand-colored tail twitched and thrashed beside her in irritation. Her skin tone matched the light warm brown of her tail, and a smattering of copper freckles lay over her nose.

She glanced up from the notebook perched in her lap, her

long, clawlike fingers clutching a charcoal pencil. "You can shut your open mouth," she growled, her voice low and throaty, before her eyes returned to the scribbling of her notes. "Haven't you ever seen a fennex before?"

"Oh, no," Arleta pleaded, as if she'd somehow offended the fox-like woman. "It's not anything like that. I mean, no, I *haven't* seen one of your kind, but mostly I didn't know I'd have a roommate."

"We all do." Doli shrugged nonchalantly as she walked straight up to the fennex with her hand extended. "I'm Doli, from Dundes Heights."

The fennex looked up briefly, raising a single white brow, and again returned to her work, ignoring Doli's outstretched hand. "I'm not here to make friends," she said, her light brown eyes narrowing. "With humans or anyone else."

Doli spun around to face Arleta and tipped her head in question. "You're human?"

Arleta's heart sank and she took an involuntary step backward, fixating on the scattered papers on the floor. The weight of her bag, slung over her shoulder, suddenly felt as heavy as a load of bricks.

"But you have a wizard's name," Doli said, almost in question.

The fennex chuckled and scrawled something in the notebook again. "No wizard blood in this one, that's for sure. I could smell her one hundred percent human blood mixed with castor musk the moment you two waltzed in here." She gestured dismissively toward the window while she wrinkled her small, sharp nose. "Perhaps you could open that and let some of the stench *out*."

Arleta wanted to sink into the floor. Sharing the family

quarters with the castors felt like it had happened a hundred years ago. Wavering between embarrassment and fear, she wanted to lie and say she wasn't human. But the fennex knew and there was no getting around it. "I...I didn't try to trick anyone," she said, raising her shaky hands in the air. "Starstone is my family name. A few generations back there was an adoption by a wizard, and the name just stuck."

Doli planted her hands on her hips, her grin widening. "Well, I'm glad to finally see a magicless in the Battle! Everyone has a different story to tell."

Letting out her held breath, Arleta gently placed her bag on her bed, the weight of the situation easing on her shoulders, if only a tad. "You won't tell?"

"Honestly, I don't care either." The fennex let out a huff. "I'm here to win, and if someone here has no magic in their blood, just means they're easier to beat."

Arleta released a long breath and forced from her mind any repercussions—no matter how bad—of her being found out by the judges. She'd come all this way and needed to stay on track. But that of course reminded her of the lost herbs and a flicker of disappointment crossed her face. Not that they were *real* magic, but they had been something.

"Hmph." Doli scowled for the first time since Arleta had met her, screwing up her sweet dwarven features. "That's not a very nice thing to say. What's your name again?"

The fennex slowly raised her chin and sighed, obviously over her new acquaintances. "Jez."

Anxiety gnawed at Arleta's chest as the tension between the two escalated. To offset the feeling, she gulped and absent-mindedly rummaged through her bag. Though she desperately wanted to find something useful, she couldn't shake the sinking feeling that she might need a new roommate soon. Just in case, Arleta didn't take anything out in case she needed to leave in a hurry.

"Jez *what*?" Doli scolded and stamped her foot when she said the fennex's name, her hands held out in question.

"Just Jez."

Doli's lips twisted. "Well, *Just Jez*, that's not a nice thing to say. We're here to bake, not conquer someone's realm."

Jez raised her rounded face to meet Doli's gaze. "I'm not very nice." She shrugged and went back to her work.

"At least you're honest," Arleta said, mustering a weak smile, still nervously digging through her bag for nothing in particular just to keep her hands busy.

The fennex chuckled, revealing her fangs. "Yes, yes, I am," she chortled, then deadpanned, "now keep it down and leave me alone."

Doli let out an exasperated groan, waving her hand in Jez's direction before bringing her attention back to Arleta. "Let me help you with that," she offered.

Arleta stepped to the side and allowed Doli to rummage around inside the bag. First she pulled out the cloak and, on tiptoe, hung it on a hook to the side of the bed. Arleta placed the small stack of shirts and skirts into one of the chest's drawers.

Doli peered into the empty satchel and back up to Arleta, disappointment pulling at her features. "You don't have anything for the ball?"

"Ball?" Arleta pushed the drawer shut. "What ball?"

Doli quickly retrieved the fallen papers off the limestone floor, including getting on her hands and knees and slipping her hand under the bed. When she finally sprang back up, her curls bounced with energy, and she triumphantly held the paper aloft. "Found it!"

The dwarf hopped up on the bed and patted the spot beside her for Arleta to sit and join her. With one hand, Doli released the teacup and saucer on her hip, then handed Arleta the paper. With her other hand she waved her fingers over the top of the cup and sparkling magic bubbled into the air. When the dwarf was done, the cup was filled with hot tea, clouded with creamy milk.

The magic was unusual for a dwarf since most were tied to soil, rocks, and precious gems, definitely not tea.

"I need a spot to settle my nerves," Doli said, taking a sip before she settled the cup back on the saucer.

Arleta glanced down to the page, which laid out the itinerary of six days' worth of events, starting with, *Welcome to the Langheim Baking Battle.* Then the welcome was followed by words like quatre épices, resplendent, Macaron Masquerade, and epicurean.

At that, the mess of flowery elven language sent Arleta's brain into overload, and it all quickly became one big jumble, but Doli scanned easily down the page.

"See, on day four we have the Macaron Masquerade," she said, pointing to the event. "You're definitely going to need something more fabulous than what you brought to wear. And don't forget a mask."

Doubt suddenly seeped into Arleta's stomach. She felt entirely out of place with the grandeur of the event. She was used to baking simply in her small kitchen, all alone in plain clothes.

Jez blanched. "She looks fine. Could she use a bath? Yes. But *I* don't have anything fancy for the party," she stated matter-of-factly, glancing down at her sleeveless leather shirt and simple black cotton pants. "I'm sticking with comfort…if I don't just nap."

"Well." Doli sighed, her initial insistence giving way to understanding. She swung her attention back to Arleta. "I suppose it's not the end of the world." She took another sip of tea. "Maybe we can make you a mask on one of the off days."

Arleta's shoulders relaxed and she flopped back on the bed. Just as she'd settled into the soft mattress, her stomach let out a growl that could have rivaled the fiercest ogre. "Oh stars, sorry. I haven't eaten much since yesterday when Theo and I started the journey."

"Theo?" Doli questioned, curiosity tugging at her voice. "Who's Theo? Do you have a traveling companion?"

Staying flat on her back, Arleta said with little thought, "An elf. We just traveled to Langheim together."

"Elves are entirely too stuck up," Jez said out of nowhere, pursing her petite lips. She didn't even look up from her notebook. "I honestly don't know what I was thinking coming to a realm full of them."

Arleta propped herself up on her elbows, ready to question the fennex about her choice to even come to an elf-run baking competition if that was how she felt about them. However, the doorframe creaked, and a figure appeared in it, his arms draped languidly over his chest.

"She's not entirely wrong," Theo chimed in, his voice laced with amusement, wearing a fresh change of clothes. "Anyone up for dinner before the welcome speech?"

Arleta's heart jumped at the sight of him, glad to see a familiar face.

# 10

Dinner had been both a feast for the eyes and the stomach. There had been a buffet with six choices of main courses, a staggering array of sides, five types of bread—including Arleta's favorite, sourdough—fifteen dessert options, ale, wine, and sparkling water from a Langheim spring. Not to mention the three giant statues—one a stag, the next a phoenix, and the third a dragon—expertly assembled by elven chefs using more types of carved fruits than Arleta could even identify.

She was stuffed, and more than completely overwhelmed.

*Everything* in Langheim was a feast for the eyes and mind when you were used to living in the sleepy village of Adenashire. Nothing of importance ever really happened there, and it was probably why rumors and gossip were such an important currency to its residents.

*If one isn't living an adventure, then make it up*, Arleta thought as she stood entranced with the elven musicians just outside the dining hall. Doli's voice yanked her back to reality.

"Arleta," the dwarf said, her tone as chipper as ever, "the welcome speech is about to begin."

Blinking twice, Arleta shook her head and caught sight of Jez leaned up against the wall, waiting for them. She'd sat at their table for dinner but had made it a point to keep several chairs between Theo, Arleta, and Doli, apparently so she didn't have to talk to them. Doli had tried to get the fennex involved with the conversation and had only received a few grunts for her trouble.

Theo was already waiting for them inside the auditorium lined with rows of wooden benches. His hands were stuffed deep into his pockets, and he nervously glanced around the room, as if he was looking for someone.

"You okay?" Arleta asked when she arrived next to the elf.

He gulped but managed a grin. "The Battle kickoff always makes me feel nervous."

It was an obvious lie, but it was his right to keep to himself, so she shrugged it off, allowing him space.

"Look." He leaned closer to Arleta, his voice lowered, and pointed ahead of them. "There are seats up there. Why don't you take them? I have something I really need to take care of."

Arleta's brow furrowed and she glanced at Doli, who stood just a few steps away, gazing up at the ceiling filled with twinkling, painted stars. Jez, on the other hand, seemed to have vanished into thin air.

"Should we save you a spot?" she asked as she surveyed the room, searching for any sign of Jez's whereabouts, although she didn't really know why.

"Um, yes." Theo smiled genuinely. "Thank you. If I'm back

before it starts, I'll join you." With that, he was off, swallowed in a sea of contestants and specially invited spectators for the event.

Arleta turned back to the open spots, following Doli's lead as they found their places. Just as they settled in, out of wherever she'd been hiding, Jez slinked past them and took the seat just to Arleta's right. The fennex immediately wasted no time in taking out her journal, scribbling on a page. Arleta peered over at the pages and her eyes widened. On them were the most beautiful pencil drawings of cakes, pastries, and cookies, all with meticulous notes in the margins.

Jez let out a growl and slammed the journal shut with an air of frustration, but she didn't move to a new seat.

"Sorry," Arleta muttered and averted her eyes. Doli quickly looped her arm through the crook of Arleta's and pulled her close.

"Theo is very attractive," she crooned. "For an elf, of course."

Arleta wondered who exactly Doli found attractive herself, but it was a question for another time.

"He was very generous on our trip here," Arleta whispered as her cheeks heated slightly. "And a perfect gentleman, but we're only friends." She stopped and worked out the timing in her mind for a moment. "We've only known each other for less than three days, really."

Doli let out a giggle, her eyes sparkling with delight. "Well, look at us. We've only known each other for a few hours, and we're already best friends. Did you know some elves are fated?"

"What does *that* mean?" Arleta asked, intrigued by Doli's quick change of subject.

Doli's eyes lit with pleasure. "I visited the library here—it's massive by the way—and read through a few books on elven culture. You know, to figure things out. I love libraries and books." She leaned in closer. "Some of them—not all—get night visions of their soul partner. They can experience these for years, starting when they are very young."

Arleta tipped her head in great interest. "Do they always find these soul partners?"

"No," Doli said with a hint of wistfulness. "If they don't, they will never settle for anyone else. They could never fully commit to another."

"That's sad." Arleta winced as the large ogre she'd seen before took his seat directly in front of her, completely blocking the stage.

"Or romantic," Doli sighed.

The two friends looked at each other, then the ogre, and giggled, since all the other seats had filled in and there was no place they could move to. Resigned to their own current fate, they returned to their conversation.

"And this soul partner is only between elves, right?" Arleta asked.

She couldn't shake off the fact that she was incredibly drawn to Theo. But then again, probably most of the people in the room were. Elves were attractive; it was just a fact. In no world that she lived in would Theo be interested in her as a partner, let alone would they be fated. If Theo *had* a Fated, Arleta would simply get in the way if she admitted anything concerning her feelings. She would probably even be laughed at.

Doli shrugged. "Probably, but I didn't have time to finish the book before lunch," she admitted with a sheepish grin.

"Welcome!" a feminine voice boomed from the stage, stealing their attention. "Welcome to the one hundredth Langheim Baking Battle! My name is Naexi Miraven, and I will be your host for the event."

Both Doli and Arleta split wide apart to peer around the ogre at the speaker. She was a lithe elf with raven hair and nearly the same complexion as Doli. Gold cuffs adorned her pointed ears, each studded with glistening rubies. Her red gown draped to the stage floor, sparkling like a lively flame. Everything about her looked as if she were floating.

Arleta glanced down at her own simple clothing, a twinge tightening her chest, but she quickly forced her mind from herself and back to listening to the speaker.

"I assume everyone has had a chance to partake of the wonderful meal provided by the excellent elven chefs of Langheim," Naexi continued, her voice carrying a touch of pride. "Their skill and magic with food is the best in the Northern Lands." She then held aloft the same papers Arleta had received earlier at registration. "Make sure every one of you reads through your Baking Battle introduction packet thoroughly. In it you will find your daily schedule, mealtimes, even events and entertainment. Don't miss out on everything we have to offer in Langheim." The elf held out her hand in presentation. "And next I have for you our two-time reigning Baking Battle champion, Taenya Carralei."

Most of the audience broke into loud applause as an alabaster-skinned, auburn-haired elf strolled out onto the stage.

Arleta gulped, and her heart nearly stopped as the cranky elf she'd bumped into at registration came into view. Arleta had only seen her name before but didn't know what she looked like from the posters that had been put up in Adenashire.

Taenya's emerald eyes were bright and beaming. Gone was the scowl, and she held her arms high into the air as if to invite more applause, a completely different demeanor than Arleta had seen her with only a short time before.

Doli clapped. Arleta was pretty sure she hadn't actually witnessed the exchange, so Arleta simply joined in with the applause for this master baker who was obviously quite full of herself when in public.

"Thank you, thank you," Taenya shouted at the crowd, who'd finally quieted down. "This year is quite special at the Baking Battle. Not only is it the event's one hundredth year anniversary, but this year marks my third and final opportunity to compete. By the stars, I *will* be crowned as one of the few contestants in Battle history to win three times."

This time people clapped, but a few other competitors raised their brows.

Doli leaned over. "Elves really are pretty full of themselves."

Arleta glanced at Jez, who was rolling her eyes. Not that the expression was unexpected from the fennex.

Taenya went on about herself for a good while longer, but Arleta heard little of it since she was instead wringing her hands in her lap and feeling like a fish who'd jumped into the wrong lake again. Taenya's confident words rolled around in her mind. Arleta knew without a doubt that her own skills and pastries were good—amazing, maybe—but did she have the kind of certainty to go up against elves like Taenya to prove it?

What would everyone think if she beat someone like that?

Suddenly her breath caught short in her chest.

The orcs had been wrong about her.

She couldn't do this.

"I need to step outside," she whispered in between gasps to Doli and rose just slightly.

Doli's thick brows furrowed in concern. "Do you want me to come with you?"

Arleta waved her hand in the air, still struggling to get a

full breath. "No. I'll be back in a few minutes." With that, she bolted from her seat, swiftly passing by Doli in a blur.

"Where's she going?" Jez's voice trailed behind Arleta, but she was quickly too far away to hear Doli's answer.

A few heads turned, but mostly no one noticed she'd even left. Arleta found herself in the empty space just off the auditorium. Her legs took her only as far as the wall next to a grand staircase, which probably led to yet another unimaginably beautiful space in the castle. She thumped her shoulder against the cold stone wall and brought her hands to her face, completely covering her mouth, nose, and eyes.

Doubt whispered in her ear in a repeated loop in her mind. *I'm not allowed to beat an elf or anyone else around here.* Even if there was no official rule, the only reason she'd even passed through the preliminary round was because she was assumed to be a wizard. If the judges had known the truth, they would have tossed out that raspberry tart Ervash had entered, never even considering her entry.

"What's wrong?" Theo's voice came from beside her, jolting Arleta from her thoughts. "Are you feeling unwell?"

Embarrassed, Arleta quickly uncovered her face, but something about the elf's presence at least calmed her erratic breath.

"I just shouldn't be here," she said, her voice laced in early defeat.

Theo licked his lips, thinking for a moment before he spoke. "This place can be completely overwhelming. Even I find it too much sometimes, and I grew up here."

Arleta just stared at him, not knowing at all what to say. She had expected him to do one of two things: either tell her she was right and she *didn't* belong here, or try to give her some kind of pep talk. But he did neither.

"What would you like to do, then?" Theo finally asked, genuine concern in his tone.

Arleta released a heavy breath. "Go back inside," she finally decided.

With the slightest head bow, he offered her his elbow. "We'll have to stay against the back, I think."

Arleta laced her hand into the crook of his arm, and he walked her into the back of the auditorium, where they leaned against the wall next to the door.

Naexi was back in the center of the stage. "And here are our esteemed judges," she announced as a posh, middle-aged elf with long silver hair, a flamboyant and rotund dwarf donning a fuchsia shirt and yellow pants, and a griffiner, their wings neatly tucked behind their body, dressed in a leather shirt and pants, made their appearance. Naexi continued, first pointing to the dwarf, then the griffiner, "Not that they need introduction, but here are Thiggul Honorton, Gaia Thornage, and our head judge for the one hundredth year of the Langheim Baking Battle, Shalina Brylar."

The richly dressed elf stepped forward, her presence commanding the attention of the entire auditorium. "Cake a diem, bakers! Cake a diem!" She held her chin up in the air as if she was better than everyone else, which was not an uncommon thought among most in the Northern Lands concerning elves.

The crowd went wild, but Arleta's attention shifted back to Theo. "Brylar," she echoed over the applause. "That's your family name. Are you related?"

Theo's lips stretch thin for a second. "Oh, *we're* related," he said with a tinge of fatalism. "That incredibly tiresome woman preening onstage is my mother."

# 11

By the next morning, Arleta hadn't slept a wink. Not only did Jez snore like a dragon with a head cold, but Arleta also couldn't get it out of her brain that Shalina Brylar, *the* head judge of the Baking Battle, was Theo's *mother*. The realization had kept her thoughts spinning like a whirlwind.

*Why didn't he tell me sooner?* she thought as she sat on her bed, absently braiding her hair before heading down to the start of the competition.

*Does it matter?*

She wasn't sure if it did, but it seemed like it might. Arriving with an elf made her stand out, and that wasn't something she really wanted to do, but arriving with the head judge's *son* really hadn't exactly made her unnoticeable to interested eyes. Standing out based on the merit of her bakes was fine but doing it as a magicless would not be.

The fact that she'd never had all the information she'd needed to make a good decision ate at her stomach.

*Tap, tap.*

The gentle sound came from the door, interrupting her thoughts.

"Are you coming?" Doli's muffled voice wafted through the wooden barrier like she had her lips pressed against the crack in the doorframe.

Arleta's stomach somersaulted, and she quickly tied off the end of her braid. "Um, yes," she called back, her voice doing a terrible job of hiding her nerves. Still, Arleta stood and forced her feet to the exit just as Doli swung open the unlocked door.

The dwarf wore a bright blue dress with tiny purple flowers speckling the fabric, and her curls were pulled tightly up onto the top of her head in a puff. "You've already missed breakfast. We need to get down to the start of the competition, otherwise we'll be disqualified." A hint of worry creased her brow.

Arleta shook her head but didn't say a word as the two of them left the room behind. All the way through the halls and down the stairs, while Doli chattered away, Arleta's stomach did uncomfortable little flips. Over and over her brain told her to hightail it back to her room and hide under the covers of her bed, as if *that* would magically solve anything and not make the situation worse.

The meeting room, filled with bakers, was already in sight when Theo unexpectedly strutted out from Arleta's right as if he'd been waiting. Of course she saw him, but her eyes immediately darted to the limestone floor.

"Arleta?" he called, keeping his voice down.

Everything in her wanted to keep going with Doli, but her feet stopped her. "What?" she replied in a guarded tone.

Doli glanced back, raising her brow.

"Save me a seat," Arleta said, waving her hand toward the meeting room.

The dwarf bobbed her head in understanding and went on her way.

Theo closed the gap between them, concern pulling at his features. "Are you angry with me?"

Immediately after he had told Arleta that Shalina Brylar was his mother, she'd excused herself to go back to her room with a headache and had avoided him ever since.

Frustration seeped through her huffy exhale. Arleta didn't look at him. "Why didn't you tell me who you were before last night?"

Theo kept his voice low. "You know who I am."

Finally, exasperation winning out, Arleta raised her eyes to him. "You know what I mean."

"You mean my moth—"

"*Yes*, Theo. Your mother." Instinctively, Arleta crossed her arms tightly over her chest, protecting herself, as she always had. "I don't think you can quite understand how difficult being here is for me." She leaned in closer to him. "Being without magic. If most of these people knew."

"I apologize for not telling you about my mother." Theo's brow furrowed with remorse. "That was wrong of me, selfish, even. I thought if you knew too soon that you'd insist we turn back to Adenashire."

"I would have." She tightened her arms around herself, but at the same time appreciated his apology. "Everything here is perfect, Theo. You live in a realm of perfection. I don't. Every day, and not just here, I'm reminded of the fact that no magic runs in my blood. That I am *less*. That's not something you have to deal with."

Confusion knit between Theo's brows at her words, and he released a long, steady breath. "Before you go in, I wanted to let you know I did a little research at the library."

"For what?" Arleta asked, slightly frustrated with his change of subject.

"If a contestant arrives without their allowed baking ingredients, they will be permitted a replacement," the elf relayed, his lips quirking up at the corners.

Arleta's arms relaxed, falling to her sides. "Oh? But where will I get them?"

"I'll take you," Theo offered. "Our forests have many edible ingredients that could be of interest. Tonight we'll go on a tour. It won't help you for the competition's first round, but there are three more."

Arleta's stomach tightened into a jumble of nerves and hope. To stand out, she was really going to need her specific "little dash of magic," so she nodded. "Fine."

Theo chuckled and his eyes darted to the meeting room. "Looks like it's about to start. I'll see you later?"

Arleta rolled her eyes and turned. "If I don't get eliminated first."

"You're not less than," Theo said in a gentle voice when Arleta had gotten no more than three steps away.

Her heart skipped a beat at his words, but she resisted the urge to turn back. Doli was inside and waving for Arleta to come and join her. She picked up the pace and slid into her seat just before the large double doors closed. Just to her side, Jez, with her journal clutched in her clawed hand, sat in the same row with no one between them. Arleta couldn't help but wonder if it was actually Jez who'd saved the seats by growling at anyone who'd dared to try to sit in them, anyone other than Doli.

Arleta gulped and quickly glanced around the room. From the looks of it, there were twenty-five baking contestants of all different shapes and sizes, ranging from the large ogre to a petite halfling. But mostly, there were elves. And, of course, Taenya Carralei was seated in the front row. Her auburn hair was pulled back into a tight bun, making all of her features, including her very pale pointed ears, appear even more severe. She wore a simple cotton shirt and pants. The elf was ready to win.

The judges were nowhere to be seen.

"Behind those doors"—Naexi Miraven held out her hand and gestured to two more double doors Arleta had not noticed the prior day, with intricate wooden spoons and various baking ingredients carved into the wood—"is the fabled kitchen of Langheim. I'm sure you're all anxiously waiting to get inside. Some of you have been here before, and some not, but either way listen carefully, as the instruction may differ from in years past."

Arleta wrung her hands as the elf described how each baker would have their own station equipped with the necessary bowls, utensils, cold box, and oven. All basic ingredients would be waiting and ready for them at each station, as well as their preapproved brought ingredients.

Arleta winced, pressure building in both her heart and mind.

At the start of their time they would have two minutes to choose any additional ingredients from a specific pantry area, but once they chose, they must use at least a portion of them in their final bake.

"So choose wisely," Naexi warned as she grinned, then paused, likely to increase the drama, before continuing. "As outlined in your schedule, day one will be your signature bake. It's your time to shine and show off the bake that has made you who you are. This is the pastry your family adores, the cookie your friends beg you to make again and again. It might even be the reason you are *here* today."

This was another problem that had kept Arleta up all night. Her signature bake was simple: lemon bars with a delicate shortbread cookie crust. But she had always added something unique to make the bake hers, and cardamom was her favorite choice to elevate the flavors. Now, if they provided her with some, she'd be fine. But if not, since few other bakers used herbs and ingredients considered savory in their bakes? Then they'd just be lemon bars, which were delicious, but would they stand out?

Her heart raced as she missed most of the remaining bits of Naexi's speech, except the parts where the winner would have immunity in round two, and that of the twenty-five contestants, ten would be eliminated today.

The large double doors creaked as they opened, snapping Arleta from her thoughts. The contestants were all rising and heading to the baking arena, and it wasn't long before Arleta realized that Doli was pulling her by the sleeve to stand.

"You're going to do this," Doli ordered in the sternest voice she could muster.

"Yes, ma'am," Arleta managed and followed at the back of the group toward the already bustling kitchen.

The second she got into the kitchen, her heart nearly stopped. The massive place smelled *heavenly*, like spices and sugar. Around the baking stations, up on risers, waited row upon row of seating, most likely for the finale. Ice fairies that couldn't have been any bigger than a small rabbit buzzed their wings around the room, leaving trails of magic in their wake, apparently there to provide their magic to help cool any creations for decorating and serving. Arleta's eyes darted around the room as she found her station, labeled with her name in fancy elvish scrawl, somehow remembering that Naexi had told them they would have five minutes to adjust themselves to their baking station.

The oven, while an upgrade, was very similar to the one she had at home, the one her father had gifted her mother years before. On her workstation were, as promised, an array of wooden bowls, metal baking trays, utensils, and the standard baking items of sugar, milk, flour, water, salt, and several other necessities. What was missing from hers, though at everyone else's station, was a wooden box of "secret ingredients." But she pushed down her apprehension into her shoes and straightened up.

Arleta was ready.

Sort of.

She glanced over to Doli, who was just across the way from her, and smiled.

The dwarf nodded and returned the expression. Jez's station was on the other side of the room, and it just so happened that Taenya was immediately to her left.

The elf carefully scanned over each of her station's pantry ingredients and went as far as tasting each one. Arleta raised up on her toes, trying to manage a glimpse at what was inside Taenya's special ingredients box.

"Keep your eyes to yourself, wizard," the elf growled. "Don't make enemies."

Arleta's cheeks heated. "Sorry."

But she didn't have the chance to say anything else, even if she'd wanted to, before the fairy bell rang for the contestants to gather the rest of their ingredients.

"One last thing." Naexi's voice somehow floated magically through the air. "The ingredients are limited, so hurry to gather what you need."

And the race was on. For a split second, Arleta was confused, but she quickly realized she needed to grab a basket from a stack outside the baking arena and head immediately to the overflowing cold and dry pantry areas.

If she intended to make lemon bars, she for sure needed lemons. Weaving around the other contestants in a dance of chaos, she immediately raced to the section of fresh fruits and gathered enough lemons, plus a few extras, for a single recipe. If they would have been gone, she'd have been back at square one.

To her side, two contestants fought over the last of something already, and Arleta made a mad dash to the dry goods section to see what was still available. While bakers scrambled, grabbing jars of spices off the shelves, Arleta's eye homed in on the last jar of cardamom pods. A stroke of luck. She thrust out her hand for the prize just as a clawlike hand did the same. Only they got there first. Arleta twisted to see Jez, the jar of cardamom wrapped in her fennex fingers.

Time slowed as the two stared at each other, neither moving.

"Take it," Arleta conceded and whipped away from the fennex, not waiting for any type of response. Quickly, she scanned over what was left, but anything she had experimented with for this recipe was gone, and she didn't want to take anything she might regret. Other herbs worked, but she didn't like them with lemon as much as without. The judges might not either.

Play it safe.

Plain lemon bars it was.

Before the two-minute fairy bell rang again, Arleta was already back at her station with her oven preheating, measuring out her flour.

"Bakers!" Naexi called. "Bake!"

A commotion of baking ensued as the small fairies continued buzzing overhead. Arleta did her best to block everything out as she moved into an automatic mode. This was her saving grace any time she had a stress bake session. It was almost as if the baking happened all on its own, guided by instinct.

Lemons.

Sugar.

Flour.

Butter.

Vanilla, salt, eggs.

Arleta lost herself in all the basics of lemon bars.

And as if no time had passed at all, she suddenly had the neatly cut bars on a platter in front of her, each piece garnished with a tiny sliver of candied lemon peel and dusted with a powdering of sugar.

She knew they were good. She'd sampled a tiny corner of a small test pan she'd prepared alongside the primary bake. The lemon curd was creamy and rich, tempered with the tartness of the lemon and sweetness of the sugar.

But they were basic.

And when she glanced over to Taenya's perfect pink, white, green, and red four-layer cake, decorated with a virtual fairyland with a large, meticulously created marzipan toadstool, complete with a green toad perched on top, she knew she was out of her league.

Taenya hovered her hand over the cake, a sparkle of magic vibrating over her fingertips.

Maybe she should have fought harder for the cardamom or at least made a meringue topping for her bars.

The final bell rang.

Round one was complete.

# 12

The round one judging was blind, so the bakers hadn't seen the judges, and the judges were not allowed to see the bakers. Apparently they were not even informed whose bakes were whose once the creations had been taken away.

To make sure it all stayed that way, no one could leave until the judging was complete and the winners were announced.

Which meant that the twenty-five contestants, many of which complained they'd been too nervous to eat breakfast before the start of the round, were all stuck in a room together.

For *hours.*

Doli, Arleta, and Jez sat leaning their backs against the ashlar stone wall of the holding room. Other contestants paced or wrung their hands, including several of the many elf bakers. The only one who appeared any bit calm was Taenya, but that was probably because she'd begun meditating only a few moments after the group had been led into the area, allowing her to ignore everyone else.

"When are they going to tell us the damn results and let us go back to our rooms?" Jez grumbled, rubbing her clawed hand on the back of her neck. She seemed even grumpier than normal.

"It *would* be nice if they brought us lunch." Doli reached out to pat Jez on the shoulder, but the fennex instinctively shrugged the dwarf off without even looking at her.

Arleta sucked her teeth, already resigning herself to the fact she would go home today.

*How will I get back to town?*

That was entirely another problem. Plus, once she got back to Adenashire, she'd have to tell Ervash and Verdreth there would be no final-round tickets for them, since first-round eliminations didn't receive them.

*And* she wouldn't get to go on her evening herb hunt with Theo.

Her stomach sunk as she remembered his invitation. None of that would happen. She probably would never even see Theo again once she returned home.

Or Doli. Or even Jez.

Arleta flicked her gaze up to the two. *Why are they friends with me?* If what Jez was doing could be considered friendship.

"What?" Jez growled.

Arleta shook her head. "Never mind. What did you use the cardamom for?" She realized neither of them had even told each other what they had made, and the creations had been whisked off so quickly to the judges the only one Arleta had seen was Taenya's annoyingly massive cake.

Jez sighed, sounding tired and annoyed. "A blood orange

cardamom loaf with pink citrus icing and candied orange slices."

Both Arleta and Doli leaned out onto their knees to listen to the fennex.

"The sweet, spicy, and tart combination is the ideal blend," Jez continued. "It's the first recipe I ever perfected." She opened her mouth to go on, but when she noticed the others staring at her and hanging on her every word, the fennex snapped her lips shut and averted her gaze.

"Go on," Doli encouraged with a glimmer in her eyes. "We're famished here. If we can't eat actual food, at least we can hear all about it."

"No," Jez growled, curling her legs closer to her chest. "I don't know why I was sharing it with you in the first place." Her voice was tinged with irritation, but the fact that she'd not moved away from them spoke louder than words.

Doli and Arleta eyed each other and grinned.

"Mine was a dozen butterscotch cupcakes," Doli mused and floated her hands in front of her at least four inches apart. "The frosting and cake was *this* tall. To. Die. For." Her eyes lit up as she turned to Arleta. "What about you?"

For some reason, Arleta hadn't really thought that far in advance, that she would also likely have to share what *she'd* made. She gulped, embarrassment heating her chest. "Um… lemon bars."

Instead of the underwhelmed reaction she expected, Doli clasped her hand to her chest and gasped dramatically. Maybe *too* dramatically, since the gesture caught several eyes. "Those are my absolute favorite!"

"They weren't special," Arleta protested. "They didn't have all the ingredients I needed."

"I'd trade a mountain of gold for a single lemon bar right now," Doli crooned.

Jez scoffed as she returned her attention back to Doli. "That's a bit over-the-top don't you think, dwarf?"

Doli chuckled and raised her brows. "Look who needs a lemon bar now."

The fennex threw open the journal wedged on her lap and buried her face in it, ears twitching on the top of her head.

Suddenly, Arleta remembered her sample bake. After the entries had been taken away, the small tray of lemon bars remained behind, so she had wrapped the extra bars in parchment and stuck the package in her pocket.

"I actually have some," Arleta admitted, sliding her hand into her pocket to retrieve the package.

Both Jez and Doli perked up in unison, their gazes trained on Arleta.

"You had food this entire time and you didn't *tell* us?" Doli leaned in close and whispered in semi-mock offense.

"I completely forgot." Arleta presented the small pack to the others. "I think I just took it automatically. I try to never waste food."

Jez hungrily snatched the bars and turned to the wall so no one else in the room could see what they had. Inside the parchment there were four pieces, one with a corner missing where Arleta had taken a taste. Powdered sugar still dusted their tops, and by the giant smile on Doli's face, the sight of the bright lemon filling gave her an instant mood lift.

Jez took one and passed the rest to Doli, who quickly chose her own. The two took a bite, their teeth sinking into the tangy goodness. Meanwhile, Arleta's stomach flopped over several times, waiting for their judgment.

"*Wow*," Doli breathed, still munching on her bite. "These are heavenly."

Jez nodded. "Yeah. Really good," she mumbled in approval, reaching for the third bar still in Doli's hand. She had it in her mouth before anyone could stop her.

Before the fennex could, Arleta grabbed the last bar and took a small bite. The lemon burst in her mouth and was quickly tempered by the rich shortcake. "They're good, but—"

"No buts, Arleta," Jez groaned. "Those are better than I wanted them to be."

Doli twisted her lips and rolled her eyes at the fennex. "What a *delightful* compliment."

"It's as good as you're gonna get," Jez muttered, returning to her journal.

Arleta quickly glanced around the room to see if anyone had noticed they had just been eating. No one had. "You two are just being nice."

"I'm never nice," Jez quickly added, apparently needing to keep up her reputation.

Doli shrugged, laughter playing at the corners of her lips. "I *was* being nice, *and* those are some damn good lemon bars."

Arleta was just about to ask if Doli thought they were good enough to keep her in the competition when the door to the holding room flew open, revealing Naexi holding a long parchment high in the air.

"I have the results!" the elf declared.

# 13

Are you *sure* you didn't have anything to do with my moving on in the competition?" Arleta asked Theo as they strolled out of the castle. Her chest still tingled from the announcement that she, Doli, and Jez had made it through to the next round. Although Doli's roommate, a halfling, who Arleta had not even met, would be going home.

Theo feigned a scoff. "What do you take me for?"

The sun was just setting, and an array of sparkling stars appeared in the newly darkening sky.

Arleta stopped in her tracks and threw her hand on her hip. "What *should* I take you for?"

"An honest elf," he said.

"You didn't tell me about your mother," Arleta reminded him and didn't move from her spot on the path.

Theo bowed his head slightly. "You're right. But it's not like I'm able to interfere with any Baking Battle judging. Even if I could, I would never, because when you win... You will do that all on your own."

Arleta's heart fluttered at his words. Not only because they were coming out of Theo's mouth, but because maybe she *did* have what it took to win. Taenya had taken first place and had earned immunity in the next round, but no one knew the scores of the other contestants that had made it through. Arleta could have been closer to the top than she even imagined, and she knew her bars were not even the best she could do.

"But for tonight," Theo said and signaled to the path in front of them, "let's get your secret ingredients."

Arleta's lips tugged up into a smile, and she put any hesitation behind her—at least for the evening. "My little dash of magic."

Theo's eyes crinkled. "Yes."

Along the way she found some wild thyme and a sprawling rosemary bush, all from which she cut multiple sprigs and tucked them into a sack she'd brought along.

Farther into the trees, she spotted what appeared to be a small outdoor amphitheater. At the entrance was a large archway covered in beautiful leaves.

"*Bay laurel?*" Arleta exclaimed, and before Theo could stop her, she'd raced toward the lush arch.

Theo trailed behind her. "You really have a gift, don't you? I can't imagine how you even noticed the variety in the dark without magic."

Arleta glanced up at the sky. "There's enough light with the stars." She hiked up her skirt and climbed the leafy arch. "My father taught me all about finding edible plants and herbs."

"There are lower branches filled with the same leaves," Theo said, a hint of laughter in his tone.

"I like the ones at the top better." Arleta reached for a bunch, plucked several leaves, and stuffed them into her bag. "Adenashire doesn't have any laurel, but when I have some, I give it to my neighbor for tea when he has a bit of...stomach upset." Arleta didn't want to go into all the details of what happened when Ervash had eaten too many of her pastries, which was often. She dropped to the ground with several leaves stuck in her hair.

Stepping backward, Theo studied her and let out a long breath.

"What?" Arleta asked, brushing herself off and shaking the laurel from her hair.

"It's nothing," the elf replied, but there was hesitation in his voice.

"Oh, come on. It's definitely something." Her chest tingled with curiosity. "Are we running out of time or something?"

The moonlight spilled over Arleta's face. Theo opened his mouth as if to speak but didn't.

"Out with it, elf," Arleta playfully demanded.

The corners of his lips curled into a shy grin, and he glanced down at the earth. "This is where I first met...my Fated." He bent down and picked up a loose bay leaf. As his fingertips brushed the leaf, his hand sparkled with magic.

"Your Fated?" Arleta's lips curled up at the edges, but inside her stomach dropped. She knew well that anything she felt when she was with Theo was simple infatuation, but hearing him talk about his Fated stung a little. To offset her illogical disappointment, she pulled a few more bay leaves from the vines and stuffed them into her sack. "Doli told me all about how some elves have a soul partner or something. Sounds fascinating." Arleta cleared her throat. "Where is this person?"

Theo slipped his hand into his pocket. "I know them from my dreams only."

"So you haven't found them yet? Here in Langheim?"

Theo brought his hand to his neck. "No. She doesn't live in Langheim. Believe me, I've searched. Delivering the Baking Battle invitations all over the Northern Lands for the last few years has given me the opportunity to look elsewhere though."

Nervousness played in Arleta's chest, and suddenly she didn't really want to talk about Theo's Fated anymore. Still, she asked, "Do you think you'll find her?" Arleta spotted a kossleaf plant a few feet away, which was a good substitute, maybe even better, for basil. Just five times the cost, so she never purchased it at the market.

"I hope so," Theo said. "If she'll have me. I've been waiting for her under that bay arch for a long time."

Arleta chuckled nervously and plucked as many bunches of kossleaf as she could find, still fighting what very well could have been jealousy in her roiling stomach from their current conversation. Even if the elf *was* interested in her—which he obviously wasn't, since he hadn't named her as the person he'd met under the arch—they could never be together.

He was an elf. She was a human with no magic. To be with her, he'd have to lose the respect he was accustomed to. Not to mention he had a Fated waiting somewhere in the Northern Lands for him.

They would be friends, and that was that.

"I have a garden back at my cottage if you'd like to see what you can find there," Theo offered.

She stuffed the last of the sprigs into her bag, happy Theo had changed the subject. "That would be allowed?"

"I don't know why not," he said. "It's not far either."

"Do you have any bergamot tea?" she asked.

Theo nodded. "I do. Would you like a cup?"

Arleta grinned. "No, but I'd love a small amount of loose leaves."

True to his word, the residence was not more than a few minutes' walk away, the forest path opening to a lovely, simple cottage not that much different from the one Arleta lived in. The door, painted a soft green, was lit by a lantern sparking with a flame of white magic.

It was like something out of a tapestry, lovingly woven together with the finest threads.

The pathway to the door had perfectly placed stones embedded in the ground leading the way. Even in the moonlight, she could see the rows of plants running along the front of the cottage, nearly beckoning them into the cozy space.

"*This* is your home?" Arleta asked, slowing to admire it.

Theo tipped his head to the entrance. "Did you expect a castle?"

"Kind of?" Arleta's nerves settled slightly. "But this is better."

Theo clasped his hands behind his back and headed for the door along the stone path. "Before we go out to the garden, there's someone you should meet."

Arleta caught up to the elf just as he opened the door and called, "Faylin? Are you here?"

"Who's Faylin?" Arleta barely got the question out before a large brown and white cat stretched and sauntered out into the small foyer.

Faylin sat on all fours, had tall ears tipped with small tufts of fur, and had two tiny, curved horns coming from his forehead. The cat yawned and eyed Arleta with a typical mix of feline curiosity and aloofness. "Is this human what's been keeping you, Theodmon?"

Theo walked directly up to Faylin, whose head came up to his thigh, and stroked his chin several times. The cat let out a deep, most contented purr.

"You'll like her," Theo said as he made his way the short distance into the kitchen and poured two glasses of water from a pitcher on the counter, then filled a bowl on the floor for Faylin. He then took out a tin of bergamot tea and spooned at least half of his stash into a small cotton bag.

"I'm Arleta," she said to the cat while continuing to stand in the foyer.

"Arleta the human." Faylin was direct, as most cats are.

Arleta nodded, a dash of amusement in her eyes. "And you are a…?"

"A majestic forest lynx, of course." He stretched his shoulders up tall.

As Arleta's eyes adjusted even more, she could see that Faylin's ears were dark, nearly black, as was his striped tail, while his back was a slightly lighter mix of brown spots and stripes, leaving his underside and legs mostly white.

"Of course," Arleta agreed, although she'd never seen or heard of a forest lynx before in her life.

The cat turned and padded to the kitchen, beelining for his water.

Arleta followed. "So you have a cat?" she asked Theo.

Faylin paused mid-drink and turned his head to Arleta. "*I* have an elf."

"He does." Theo chuckled and held out a cup of water to Arleta. "Faylin is my family, and I wanted you to know."

He also handed her the tea, and she tucked it into her sack.

Arleta raised her cup and took a sip of the water as the cat rubbed his face affectionately against Theo's hand. Then Faylin sauntered over to her and did the same, his right horn gliding along her thumb. Finally, he pressed his muzzle into the palm of her free hand and softly kneaded his paws on the floor. The cat's fur was the softest that Arleta had ever felt.

When the feline was done, he sat, his steely blue-eyed gaze shifting between Arleta and Theo. "You are right. I do like her."

❖

Leaving Faylin draped over a chair, for what Theo said was likely his tenth nap of the day, the elf and Arleta stepped out the back door and, in an instant, found themselves in the garden where light magic glittered and danced over the plants like fireflies.

"This is huge!" Arleta exclaimed. And the garden *was* enormous. There were rows upon rows of fruits, vegetables, gourds, and then there were the herb plants, almost exploding with their aromatic leaves. Beyond them, lit by the moon and stars, lay an orchard of fruit trees alongside a fenced pasture and the silhouette of a barn.

"I've been working on it for…quite a while," Theo admitted.

Arleta jogged up to several towering tomato plants and plucked a tiny, juicy fruit. She popped it into her mouth and the skin burst with flavor. "For quite a while? This is a garden of a lifetime."

"It helps when you can talk to the plants," the elf said, gazing in Arleta's direction while she enjoyed a second tomato, but he quickly looked away and blew out a long breath. He steeled himself and made his way into the rows of herbs. "Think there's anything else here you might like to take back to the competition?"

But the second the words left his lips, what had been a light twinkle of magic only a moment before exploded into a radiant display. The garden lit up as if it were nearly daylight.

"Uh...um," he stammered.

Arleta's brows raised and her chest quivered with what felt like the same magic. "That makes it even easier to see the selection." She quickly bent to gather some lavender, since it had a floral flavor that could work in some sweet recipes. When done, she swept her hand out toward the pasture and barn. "Is that where Nimbus lives?"

"Yes," Theo said, keeping his hand tucked squarely in his pockets, but the over-the-top display of magic remained unchanged. "He's probably settled inside for the night."

Arleta nodded, desperately trying to think of what else to say. "And how long have you known Faylin?"

"Oh, since he was a cub," Theo said, the memory seeming to ground him for a moment. "I found him injured and abandoned in the forest and took him in." He chuckled. "I didn't know quite how much I liked cats before Faylin. It's nice to have someone in your life who'll always tell you the truth. Felines don't mince words."

"I've heard that," Arleta said, finding her way to a worn wooden bench placed just outside the garden's perimeter. She nestled her bag at her side and leaned back on her palms to gaze at the stars. "My father and I used to do this all the time. After my bedtime, he'd come get me on extra bright nights, and he'd teach me the names of the constellations."

Theo ambled over and lowered himself on the other side of the bench. He followed Arleta's gaze and pointed to one of the brightest in the sky. "What's that one?"

Arleta shook her head. "You really don't know?"

"I'm sure I learned at some point," Theo said, giving her a sheepish shrug. "But I've forgotten."

Arleta chuckled lightly, wondering if he was being completely honest. "That's Eliana, or more commonly, the Little Mouse." She traced her finger in an invisible line to point out the trail of three stars forming the tail. "My favorite."

"And I picked it first?" Theo kept his gaze lifted, continuing to study the constellation as he spoke.

Arleta bit at her lip. "Apparently so."

"Your father must have been really wonderful," he said.

She paused for a moment, remembering the conversation she'd had with Theo back in her own garden about her family. "They died traveling out of Adenashire, my parents." She didn't really know why she was talking to Theo about the topic. She tried to mention her mother and father as little as possible. Somehow, here, the moment felt different. Somehow it seemed like he cared.

Theo immediately dropped his gaze back to her, as if to give his full attention to the story.

"I was sixteen, and Father wanted to take Mother on a little adventure," she said. "He'd saved up enough for a few days away. On the way back, they were ambushed. They...didn't make it."

The elf sat next to her with space enough for two others between them, but he leaned closer. "That's horrible," Theo said in a whisper.

"Yes," Arleta nodded, "it is. At that point, the orcs next door took over anytime I needed parents."

"Honestly," Theo said, "those two seemed pretty great. Despite threatening me a little bit before we left."

The memory of the orcs' kind and sometimes gruff nature

brought a smile to Arleta's lips. "They really are wonderful. Like parents."

This was something she had known for a long time but had never said out loud to another person.

"On receiving the news that my parents had died, they immediately took me into their home. I was only sixteen, and I had no idea what to do. While I hid in my room, Ervash and Verdreth sorted out everything. They made sure my house's ownership was transferred to me and took care of the funeral." Tears stung at her eyes, but they didn't fall.

"So have you ever been out of Adenashire since?" he asked after a few moments.

"First time," Arleta admitted. "Just the thought of leaving was pretty frightening to me."

"Undoubtedly." The elf shifted slightly away from her, as if to give her space.

A question sat on the end of Arleta's tongue for a moment. She hesitated, unsure if she should ask it. "And who did you lose?"

Theo twisted his neck to face her, not speaking. A ghost of sorrow pulled between his brows in the starlight.

"Back in Adenashire, you said something to me about grief." She thought for a moment. "You compared it to morning fog that never lifts completely."

"You remembered that?" Theo's tone was surprised.

"I could barely forget." Arleta's breath shortened, waiting for the elf's next words.

His palms edged out onto his knees. "It was my younger brother. When I was quite young…a child…he was always unhealthy. I took it on myself to be his protector, but when he became really sick, I couldn't save him from the disease by building blanket forts for us to hide away in."

Arleta's heart clenched for Theo, remembering the blanket forts he'd built with the castor youths at the Double Unicorn Inn so she could get some sleep.

Theo shook his head. "We were never the same after his death. My father packed his bags and went south, and my mother?" His lips stretched into a thin line. "Well, she threw herself into work. You've seen her."

"Your father is still alive?" she asked.

Theo shifted and trained his focus in the distance, looking toward Nimbus's barn. "As far as I know. I haven't seen him in years."

Arleta smiled, but in her jumbled thoughts all she wanted was to comfort Theo, to help ease his grief, and him to ease hers, even though it was entirely impossible, and maybe even selfish.

Fear crept its way back into her heart. She's said too much. Theo had said too much.

She'd gotten too comfortable with him.

Arleta gulped down her nerves and managed, "Why did you bring me here?"

"Um, you needed the herbs," he admitted plainly, but there was an edge to his tone, the tension obvious. Theo quickly broke from her questioning gaze.

"That's not why." Arleta's breath picked up as she anxiously waited for the truth. "Why did you care if I met Faylin?"

"It bothered you that I didn't tell you about my mother as a judge," he admitted. "You and I... We're friends, and I didn't want to keep things from you. Faylin is part of my life. He always will be."

Arleta draped her arms over her chest as her gaze remained transfixed on the frustrating elf in front of her. "But *why* did it matter? We barely know each other, and after the Baking Battle is done, we probably won't see each other again."

As the words slipped from Arleta's mouth, her heart clenched. She barely even knew why she was asking. She wanted it to be a lie so much that it pained her.

The elf gulped, and the light in his eyes reflecting the magic dimmed. "Do you have what you need?"

"Why, Theo?" Arleta demanded. "Why did you bring me here?"

"I told you," he said. "You're my friend. I enjoy your company, and you needed to get your herbs. I had them, so it worked out for both of us."

Arleta stared at him for several seconds, waiting for him to say more, but he didn't. The fact was that he'd told her he had a Fated, and if Arleta was having feelings for Theo, she could *not* keep spending time alone with him. Why couldn't he see this? Not only would it end up hurting her when she left Langheim, she also wouldn't be able to focus on the Baking Battle if half her mind was taken up with this off-limits elf.

She tucked her hands behind her back. "Thank you for helping me tonight, and for everything you've done." She bowed her head. "But I think it's best for us not to see much of each other at least until the competition is over."

# 14

The sun rose over the mountains, its rays spreading over the sky like melted butter. Somehow, the sunrises and sunsets were even more spectacular in Langheim than in Adenashire, but none of the beauty lifted Arleta's mood.

After the incident in Theo's garden the night before, he'd agreed to take her back to the castle and not see her again. Normally, she would have made the journey on her own, but she hadn't known the way and didn't want to end up lost in the forest.

Frustrating.

They barely spoke on the return, and Theo left when he saw she was safely inside the castle. She could tell there were things he had to say, as if he really cared about her, but he held them back.

All the more frustrating.

Of course Theo had to have acted like a perfect gentleman

and didn't even *try* to convince her to stay back at his cottage since she had said she felt uncomfortable.

The only good thing about the night was that she had been able to find Viessa, the elf who had registered her for the Baking Battle on her arrival, and give her the herbs she had gathered. Viessa had said if everything checked out, Arleta would find them waiting at her station in the next round.

And that was that.

Arleta wrapped her arms around her legs and tightened her cloak around her neck and head as she remained tucked into the small castle inlet. With a sigh, she settled further onto the granite bench as dozens of tiny, sapphire-bellied finchlettes chirped an annoyingly cheerful tune in a nearby crabapple tree.

*If Theo is at the castle, I'll just ignore him from here on out,* she thought. *He has a Fated elf mate, he told me so, just like Doli read about in the book at the library. And he would never choose me, a magicless, anyway.* The thoughts pinged their way around her head.

If she wanted any chance at winning, or even progressing in, the Baking Battle, *that* was what she needed to do. She needed to stay focused, keep her head down, and mind her own business. It was the only path forward.

Getting involved with elves was ridiculous. She shook her head and internally scolded herself for getting swept up into something that was not there.

But in reality, waking or sleeping, Theodmon Brylar would not leave her mind. It was as if he'd set up a home complete with a raging fireplace and bearskin rug there...silver free in her mind.

"*Ugh,*" she scoffed, scolding herself at the childishness of the entire situation. The finchlettes chittered on above as if they were laughing at her.

"What else do you want from me?" a voice drifted from farther out in the castle's garden. The words dripped with frustration, not too different from the irritation Arleta felt. Two figures emerged into view, forcing the birds to scatter, silencing the air.

The muscles in the back of Arleta's neck twitched when she saw the tall, auburn-haired elf, one of the last people she wanted to see or overhear arguing with someone.

Arleta did her best to shrink away from view by ducking behind a bush flanking the inlet to avoid being seen by Taenya or the elf with her. As she leaned back, she noticed the purplish-blue berries on the bush. They were almost like blueberries, but the color was slightly lighter, the fruit smaller. Someone with an untrained eye would think they were the same, but Arleta recognized them as yageberries. They weren't poisonous but had a strange ability to make sweet foods taste sour when mixed with sugar.

She looked back at the figures, and other than the scowl on his face, the other elf was just as perfect looking. He had a chiseled jaw with high cheekbones and perfectly arched eyebrows, though all elves seemed to appear as if magic preferred their faces over everyone else.

Which, of course, made her think of Theo. There was that fire and bearskin rug again, with him on it. Waiting. For her.

"Ugh," she scoffed again lightly, hating her ridiculous brain and the stars that must have cursed her at that moment.

"I want you to do better," said the elf, his long dark hair pulled back into a low ponytail. "I saw the judging numbers, and while, yes, you prevailed, there were first-year bakers who were too close to your score. You're losing your touch."

First-year bakers? Arleta's mouth became dry at the words. *What if that was her?*

She immediately shook the thought aside. There was no way her simple lemon bar recipe even came close to Taenya's cake.

*But what if hers had tasted better?*

Sometimes bakes that present beautifully aren't always the tastiest. Or maybe the other elf meant Doli, or maybe Jez. She hadn't sampled anything from them yet, but they had made it to the next round too.

The masculine elf stepped in close to Taenya, and this made Arleta lean out on the bench to better hear what was being said. "There are *too* many bakers coming from different realms in the Northern Lands this year. This is an *elf* contest, and a great many of us were eliminated in the first round." He lifted his slender hand and touched his middle and index fingers to Taenya's chin. "Do not let this be you."

The baker elf scowled but didn't pull away. Although, by her stiff shoulders, it was apparent that was exactly what she had wanted to do. "Yes, Vesstan."

"You *will* win this for the third time, Taenya," the raven-haired elf insisted. "I'm your brother. I know things." He turned on his heel and left Taenya standing alone next to an orange tree.

The feminine elf let out a long sigh and ran her hands through her loose hair, then quickly threw them down, like she was trying to shake out the anxiety running through her blood. When she turned, Arleta could see the far-off look in her eyes, as if the person behind them was slowly being stripped away.

Arleta teetered on the edge of the bench, doing her best to keep her balance, all while simultaneously regretting not minding her own business when she'd only *just* decided to do that.

Making her best attempt to steady herself, she quietly reached out to the wall beside her.

Instead, Arleta's behind slipped from the bench and she landed directly on the ground with a thud.

A curse slipped from her mouth.

"Who's there?" Taenya demanded, her eyes narrowing with suspicion. She made a beeline for Arleta's hiding spot. With a flick of her hand, a light green magic shot from her fingers and parted the bush hiding Arleta precisely in half. Dozens of yageberries flew off the plant, several of which smacked directly into Arleta, one square in the middle of her forehead.

Arleta, still on her sore backside, looked up at the frowning elf.

"*You*," Taenya growled. "Why are you always around? Are you spying on me?"

Arleta wiped the dripping berry juice off her forehead, staining her fingers blue. "What?" she protested. "No! I was out here trying to get some peace and quiet."

Taenya narrowed her green eyes at Arleta as if she were trying to read her mind. "I don't trust you."

Arleta gulped, wanting to say something that would get this elf to back off. If Arleta had wanted to keep to herself, she'd obviously gotten the wrong attention. "Um, I don't know what to say to that, since we don't know each other, but congratulations on your win yesterday. That cake was something."

The elf took a small step backward and lowered her shoulders slightly. "Yes," she replied curtly, every ounce of her guard obviously still up.

"Arleta?" an annoyed voice called. "Is that you?" Jez came trudging up the path behind Taenya, making the elf take several more steps backward.

Taenya rounded toward Jez, gave her a once-over, then

twisted to scoff at Arleta. "Just stay away from me," she spat before she stormed off.

"I'm trying to," Arleta mumbled, pushing herself from the ground. By the time she was upright, Jez stood a few paces from her.

"What was that?" the fennex asked, quick eyes scanning over all the strewn berries, the mangled plant, and then Arleta as she wiped the soil from her skirt. "You're a mess."

"Thanks for pointing out the obvious." Arleta shook her head. "How'd you even know I was out here?"

Jez immediately pointed to her nose with a clawed finger. "I could have scented the trouble between that elf and you if I were a day's ride away."

"And you cared why?" Arleta tucked her hand into her pocket.

Jez's brows furrowed. "Well, let's just say there are certain bakers I'd rather see advance in the competition." She pinched her lips, as if there was more to say.

"And?" Arleta prodded.

Jez sucked her teeth, allowing just the tiniest amount of guilt into the twitch of her nose. "And Doli would never let me hear the end of it if something happened to you," she said. "I came down here promising to look for you just to get that dwarf off my back."

Arleta chuckled at the fennex's eventual honesty—and possibly deeply buried underlying concern. "And where's she?"

"Searching the castle." Jez rubbed at the spot just below her large, pointed ears as if she might have a headache coming on. "When you weren't around this morning, she got worried. And I…accidentally told her you smelled stressed last night when you came in."

"You were asleep. *Snoring* even. How did you smell me?" Arleta asked, rubbing at the spot on her forehead where she knew there must still be yageberry juice.

"Mhm," the fennex grunted. "My kind's senses are sharp. Sometimes *too* sharp. And you people want to talk about everything all too much."

Arleta crossed her arms. "I didn't want to talk to *you* about anything either."

Part of that statement was true. Arleta never wanted to talk about her issues to anyone. But since she'd met Doli, and maybe even Jez, for reasons unknown to her, that had started to shift. At least a little.

"Good," Jez said. "So. What was happening between you and Taenya?"

Arleta eyed the fennex, who was suddenly in a talking mood.

"This is different," Jez said.

Arleta cast her gaze to the ground. "Nothing. It was all a misunderstanding."

The fennex squinted slightly, her tail flicking from side to side, but then she waved at Arleta to come along. "Let's find Doli, then. I'm sure she's running around the castle like a perky chicken with their head cut off."

Arleta winced. "Eww."

But she followed the fennex.

The castle was so large, with all its stairs and winding corridors, it took them over thirty minutes to find the dwarf. But once Jez caught her scent, it didn't take long at all.

"Oh, I'm so glad to see you!" Doli threw her arms around Arleta's waist and squeezed her so tight she could barely breathe.

"I'm fine, Doli," Arleta conceded, managing a smile. "I just needed some time to myself to clear my head."

The dwarf released her hold, stepped back, surveyed both Jez and Arleta, and then opened her mouth to speak.

But Jez cut her off by turning to leave. "I'm going back to bed."

Doli reached out and grabbed Jez's wrist. "No more escaping! We just all need some breakfast." She flung her other hand into the air and stuck up her finger as if she had an idea. "We'll have a ladies' morning—"

"Then you don't need me, since I'm not exactly what one might call very ladylike," Jez interrupted, pulling away.

Doli's eyes grew large, and she grasped Jez's shirtsleeve before she could get far. "I apologize. *Friends'* morning. And it's not an excuse to get out of our bonding session. I'll get tea and bring it up to the room." She eyed Arleta. "We have to figure out what you're going to wear for the ball."

*The ball.* Arleta's heart clenched just at the thought of it. "That sounds lovely, Doli."

The dwarf waved Jez off. "You go back for a power nap. Arleta and I will be up soon—with tea!"

The fennex grunted. "I'm going to need something stronger than tea."

*That makes two of us.* The thought rolled through Arleta's brain, but she only smiled at Doli, who was already pulling her down the corridor.

"Oh," Doli said to Arleta, pointing to her own forehead, "you've got a little blueberry right there."

Arleta didn't have the energy to correct her.

# 15

Doli apparently had multiple hidden pockets in her skirt, since that was where Arleta had watched her stuff multiple pastries from the breakfast buffet for their *friends'* morning. In her hands she balanced a tray of filled teacups and utensils. The dwarf was nimbler up the stairs than Arleta ever would have expected from anybody carrying so much. She didn't spill a drop the entire way.

In her own hands, Arleta carried several apples, oranges, and a handful of iweocot she'd spotted on the buffet table.

"Can you reach your key?" Doli's mouth was stuffed with a cheese pastry, yet she somehow still got the question out clearly as the two arrived at room 206. She really had many talents.

"I think so." Slowly, Arleta edged her hand into her skirt pocket. She had just touched the metal key with the tips of her fingers when the door flew open, sending fruit flying in all directions.

Jez's face appeared in the doorway. "What are you two lurking around out here for?"

"Maybe you can help," Arleta grumbled as she bent to retrieve the bruised iweocots from the floor.

Jez simply opened the door up wider for Doli and Arleta. "Looks like you got it all by yourself."

The dwarf hurried inside after Arleta had all the fruits back in hand. "There was a lot more, but this was all we could carry." She plunked the tray of tea down on Arleta's bed and unloaded the pastry from her pockets. By the time she was done, there was a stack big enough to feed at least four others, as long as they were not orcs.

Jez retreated to her bed and Arleta closed the door behind her with her hip. Looking at the mountain of pastries, her stomach rumbled.

"I'm starving." Arleta let the fruit roll from her hands and arms onto the bed, grabbed a jam-filled donut, and took a massive bite. The sweet fruit coated her tongue while the flaky donut's slight saltiness balanced everything out. "Tea please." She held out her hand, surprising herself at her newfound comfort level.

Doli chuckled and placed a cup and saucer into her friend's open palm.

"I have something stronger if you want it." Jez held a flask in the air, waving the silver receptacle suggestively.

"How'd you even get that in here?" Doli said, picking up her own teacup from the tray. She didn't have her special holster on her hip that morning.

Jez shrugged. "I have my ways." The fennex swung her long legs over the side of the bed and stood to retrieve her cup. Despite the steaming tea inside, she shot the entire cup down and poured in some of whatever was in her flask, then held the silver receptacle out to Arleta.

Arleta put up her palm in refusal, although something in the back of her mind said yes. But she fought the urge because she wanted to keep control of what could come out of her mouth otherwise.

"More for me." Jez topped off her cup, grabbed two pastries from the stack, spun on her heel, and crawled back into her bed.

Doli sipped her tea and placed it back on the tray. "How about we start thinking about a mask for the ball?"

Arleta's stomach pinched. "You really don't have to do that." She hated others doing anything for her.

Doli's smile lit up her face. "I *want* to. Can I borrow some of your paper and a pen?" she said to Jez, who was already ignoring the others and staring intently at her notebook.

When the fennex didn't reply, Doli cleared her throat.

"What?" Jez snapped and finally looked up.

"Arleta needs a mask," the dwarf said. "I thought maybe I could sketch something. But I don't have any paper."

Jez scoffed, but flipped to the back of her notebook, tore out a slip of parchment, and held it out to the dwarf. "Don't ask for more."

Doli walked over and gently took the paper. She raised her brow and her lips turned up at the corners. "Do you have a pen you could spare?" Her tone was sticky and sweet.

The fennex scoffed again and dug into her pocket. When she finally found a pen, she flung it out to the dwarf.

"Thank you," Doli said and skipped back to Arleta.

Arleta sat sipping her tea, slightly amused at the situation between the dwarf and fennex, almost forgetting herself. She took another bite of her pastry, savoring the sweetness.

Doli hopped up onto the bed next to Arleta and gazed up at her face, staring for just long enough to bring her back into the present. "You have lovely eyes." She quickly sketched something on the loose page with a light stroke.

Arleta turned her gaze down. She wasn't embarrassed; she just knew that she had shared her father's hazel eyes. Kind, gentle, and not there anymore. "Thanks," she muttered.

Doli's expression grew concerned, and she stopped drawing for just a second and then furiously sketched something else on the page. "I apologize if I made you feel uncomfortable."

"It's not that," Arleta said.

"It is that," Jez interrupted and took a drink of her spiked "tea." She didn't look up at them.

Both Doli and Arleta flipped their attention to the fennex but didn't say a word.

"Hey, I get privacy and all," Jez said, "but sometimes you should just say what's on your mind. That's what I do." She eyed Arleta. "For whatever reason, Doli's compliment made you feel scared."

"That sniffer of yours is something else, huh?" Doli said.

"Yeah," Jez agreed. "Scent magic is a blessing and a curse for all fennex." She swung her legs to the ground and brought her attention back to Arleta. "You don't need to tell people all your business if you don't want to, but you can tell them to back off. Stand up for yourself."

Arleta sighed, then pursed her lips. "Um…thanks?"

"If you don't want to do this right now," Doli said, taking a break from drawing, "I'm okay with that."

"No," Arleta admitted. "This is actually nice. Your compliment just reminded me of my parents. They died when I was sixteen."

Doli placed the paper down and laid her hand on her ample chest. "I'm so sorry to hear that. I assume you were close?"

Arleta placed her tea and unfinished pastry back onto the tray. "Very. I miss them a lot."

Strangely, Arleta's initial discomfort from Doli's compliment dissipated as the dwarf went back to her work. "If I win the Battle, I want to buy a bakery in Adenashire to make them proud." Saying the words out loud felt a bit like a relief. Arleta actually felt like she had a chance to win, at least a small one.

Doli lightly touched Arleta's shoulder. "Sounds like you really loved each other."

Tears stung at Arleta's eyes and brought her back to reality. She'd said too much about herself. "How about you? Why are you all here?"

Jez didn't seem like she was paying attention, but Arleta included her anyway.

Doli picked up the paper again and resumed her work. "Because I don't care about the family gemstone business." She laughed. "They all want me to take it over, and I want to do my own thing."

"Like what?" Arleta asked.

Doli tipped her head back and forth several times. "Other than baking, clothes and how they make people feel have always interested me, so maybe something about that. I haven't thought that far in advance. But I do know my life path will *not* involve mining." As if on automatic, Doli placed her hand over her empty teacup. When she lifted it, the cup was full and steaming. "Even my magic capabilities are completely different from theirs."

"Making tea?" Arleta asked.

"Making tea," Doli echoed. "Dwarf magic involves precious

stones. *Always.* Believe me, my family tried. When my magic was different, I leaned into it. They still don't see why I didn't try harder to be 'normal.'" She made air quotes with her fingers. "Who wants to be *normal* when you can be spectacular?"

Jez chortled and downed her "tea."

"And what about you?" Arleta asked.

Jez let out a little cough. "Me?"

"I mean, you're listening to our conversation and all," Arleta chided, though she was half joking.

Jez raised a furry brow. "It's not as if I can opt out." She glanced around the room. "Where am I going to go?"

Arleta shrugged. Although if Jez truly wanted to leave, she had an entire realm to explore outside the room. "I'm here for the silver and to make my parents proud. Doli is here to be spectacular." She winked at the dwarf.

"Exactly." Doli nodded and penciled in a few more details on her paper.

"So, do you want to share what brought *you* to the Baking Battle?" Arleta asked, glad to keep any more attention off herself.

Jez gave an awkward half grin and got out her flask again. This time, she simply unscrewed it and raised it to her mouth, taking a big drink. "I don't know why I'd even consider telling you all this."

"You don't have to if you don't want to," Arleta echoed Jez's sentiment from earlier, but inside she was eager to hear the answer.

Jez narrowed her eyes at Arleta. "I'll do or not do what I want, thank you very much." She paused for a moment, as if in thought, and then took another swig. "I'm here for *me*."

Both Doli and Arleta gave Jez puzzled looks. The answer

was a surprise. From what Arleta could tell, Jez didn't seem to enjoy herself much at the Battle, and Arleta had assumed that someone else probably wanted her to compete.

"What do you mean?" Doli asked, sincerity in her tone.

Jez bit her lip, as if what she was about to admit was difficult for her. "When I was a pup, I was small. I actually still am." Her tail swished back and forth nervously.

Her comment about being small was also a surprise to Arleta. Jez was more than a head taller than she was already. But Jez was also the first fennex she'd ever met, so she had no idea how tall most of them were.

"A lot of things weren't right," Jez continued. "I got tired quickly, overwhelmed." She eyed Doli. "And my family? Let's just say they're more you than me. I just wanted to be alone."

Arleta had to fight back the urge to say to Jez that her family probably loved her, even if she was different. The thought may have been true, but Arleta didn't know if it was with absolute certainty, so saying it would have been trite.

"Needless to say, I saw too many wizards trying to come up with some potion to fix my problem," Jez said, exhaustion creeping into her tone.

"And?" Arleta asked. "Did anything help?"

Jez shrugged. "Not everything is magic's damn business to solve." She paused for a second before she narrowed her eyes at Doli and Arleta. The fennex blew out an audible breath. "Damned alcohol overshare."

Doli chuckled and continued working on her drawing.

"Now that we've *bonded*, you two be quiet. I'm taking a nap. I have to beat you both tomorrow in round two."

With that, Jez laid down, rolled over, and snored. It was likely fake, but it made her point.

Arleta and Doli gave each other looks.

"I think Jez likes us," Doli said.

"I do not," Jez insisted without moving.

Doli picked up the piece of paper she was working on and showed it to Arleta.

Her eyes widened when she saw not only an illustration of a mask but also a figure resembling herself in a lovely dress.

"It's a quick drawing," Doli said. "But I brought several dresses. I think I can alter one a little bit and add to the length so it will fit you. The color will bring out your eyes."

"No—" Arleta started to say, but really, she was touched.

"Don't say no," Doli insisted. "Really. I *want* to. I have trouble sleeping, and my roommate is gone after round one. I need something to do other than talk your ear off all night."

"Yes," Jez mumbled from across the room. "Let her."

A wide smile stretched over Arleta's lips, and she reached over to hug Doli. "I'd like that."

# 16

The second round was about to begin, and the arena bustled with activity. However, Arleta's heart thundered in her chest so loudly she was positive everyone present could hear it. Although the fact was that most of the other fifteen contestants appeared to be fully focused on their own baking stations and their closed and locked basket of mystery ingredients.

Not Arleta.

She was watching the three judges pacing the room. Devdan, who Arleta remembered from her first encounter at the castle, trailed behind them dutifully. As the head judge's personal assistant, he clutched an imposing pile of notebooks in his arms, displaying impressive balance. Every so often the judges would swivel toward him, a question hanging between the members of the group. With uncanny precision, Devdan would whip out the correct tome from the stack, flipping to a relevant page while the remaining books teetered precariously in his grip. The judges would nod, seemingly satisfied for a few moments, and then the entire process would begin again like some strange dance. Behind the spectacle was a viewing gallery, and inside it was what appeared, by their luxurious clothing, to be rich sponsors who'd been given the opportunity to watch the competition. Some of them looked interested and chatted with those around them, but others yawned and stretched, likely due to the early hour.

Somehow, Arleta had been placed smack in the center of the room with Jez on her left and Doli on her right. Neither of them had said a word to her since they'd all arrived in the arena, even Doli.

Arleta finally glanced around at her station, first at the mystery basket that contained the base ingredients for the day's bake, and then at the box labeled "secret ingredients"—her herbs and tea that she'd gotten with Theo.

*Theo.*

Just the thought of the elf stung at her mind. She'd nearly forgotten about him the day before, when she'd been hanging out with Doli and Jez.

Not seeing him was the right thing to do.

*Isn't it? Ugh.*

Something inside her tugged at the thought of Theo, but it was only a silly crush, something for children.

But Theo was handsome, he smelled delicious, and the thought of being with him sort of sounded amazing. A shiver ran up her spine at the memory of how he'd taken care of her when she'd panicked at the inn. No judgment, he'd just taken care of her needs.

She shook aside the thoughts. The idea of keeping away from him was to ensure she could focus on the Battle, but instead there he was, distracting her when he'd done nothing but what she'd asked him to do. To her knowledge, he hadn't even come to the castle yesterday.

She bit the inside of her cheek until it pinched just slightly and shook her head back to the present.

Taenya was across the way, next to a high elf from the south. Something about Taenya looked frazzled too, though not really in appearance. That, like always, was immaculate. Her long, reddish-brown hair was pulled back into a tight ponytail, and her pale face maintained the all-business attitude. But something in her eyes gave her mental state away. It was the same bothered look Arleta had seen in the garden.

Arleta knew she shouldn't care. Taenya was her competitor and not a friend like Jez or Doli. The elf wasn't even *nice*, for that matter. Still, something close to concern stirred in her at the elf's distress.

To get her mind off Taenya, Arleta reached into the box of her secret ingredients and inspected them. From the temperature of the box, the herbs and tea had been kept cold, so they still appeared fresh, but they also may have had some type of simple magic applied to them to help deter any degradation over the course of the competition.

Relief at holding the herbs calmed her nerves. Having her "little dash of magic" available to use in her recipe, whatever it was going to be that day, would give her a leg up—plus some internal confidence she'd been lacking in the first round. The fresh aroma of the leaves mingled and made its way to her nose, the scent transporting her back to her garden at home, reminding her how much she loved this.

"Contestants, contestants," Naexi said with a flourish of her gown. "May I have your attention?"

Arleta caught the movement out of the corner of her eye and quickly set her herbs back into the box. Anticipation tingled in her veins.

"Good luck," Doli whispered nervously, drawing Arleta's attention to the dwarf, whose station had a small platform running the length of it so she could reach the counter comfortably.

Arleta nodded.

The judges had taken three seats at a long table in front of the viewing box where everyone else seemed to settle in for the "show."

Arleta wrung her hands together as Naexi cleared her throat.

The umber-skinned elf held a piece of parchment aloft and declared, "Today is a technical challenge. Sometimes even the simplest-sounding delights can be the most difficult to perfect, but today, the judges are in the mood for *scones* with their afternoon tea."

Arleta's heart fluttered. She *loved* scones. She adored filling them with fruits, sometimes nuts, or maybe chocolate. Even plain with cream and jam were delicious. But plain would not do for that day when she knew she had gotten the bergamot tea, and it was inside of her box, ready to use. Scones with a hint of lovely tea flavor were always a delightful surprise to the person enjoying them.

Suddenly, Naexi rang a fairy bell and jolted Arleta from her thoughts. The other contestants were already off and running toward the pantry, including Jez and Doli since they must have been paying attention instead of daydreaming.

*Ugh.* She didn't even know what she had in her base ingredient basket.

Quickly she flipped it open, as the lock had released with magic, and peered inside. Flour, sugar, solid, cold butter, a rising agent, salt, eggs, fresh, creamy milk.

Her heart settled just slightly, knowing she wouldn't have to fight for any of the basics. All she needed was a fruit that would pair with the ground tea. Blackberry, raspberry, even cherry, and hopefully those were still available.

She bounded toward the fresh pantry, where contestants grabbed ingredients from the left and right. Arleta scanned over what remained, and her eyes focused on a basket of dried cherries. Quickly, she picked up her pace and dove for the basket just as the high elf's hand reached for them, but Arleta was quicker that time, albeit clumsier. Her palm hit the basket and the cherries shot off the table, tumbling onto the floor.

The high elf scoffed and turned to gather a basket of cranberries, still unscathed, waiting in front of her.

Arleta didn't care that the cherries were on the floor. They were what she needed and could easily be washed. She kneeled down, picked up the basket, and swept all the errant fruit back inside, then scurried to her feet to race back to her station with her prize.

Jez and Doli had already returned with their ingredients, but Arleta didn't have time to see what had been chosen. Instead, she blew out a quick, audible breath, did her best to block out what was going on around her, and got to work.

First, she gathered her bowls, utensils, measuring cups and spoons, and a baking sheet. She heated her oven and focused on her available ingredients as her favorite scone recipe flitted its way around in her head.

As if she'd done it a thousand times before, her hands

grabbed for the necessary ingredients, adding and mixing them in just the right order.

When the dry ingredients were prepared and set aside, she found a mortar and pestle and measured out the perfect ratio of tea, but not before she removed a small handful of pretty tea leaves to garnish the top of the scones. When the tea was ground to her satisfaction, she added it to the dry mix.

Next was the butter. Fortunately, it had been kept extremely cold, almost frozen, so she took the opportunity to grate it before adding it to the dry ingredients since doing so improved the incorporation, resulting in a tender pastry.

After, she mixed in the eggs and cream.

The dough quickly came together with a nice marbling after she washed, rinsed, and patted dry her cherries, gently folding them into the mixture. So as to not handle the mixture too much, instead of individual scones, Arleta formed a ball with the entire thing and hand pressed the form down into a large circle on her parchment-covered baking sheet.

Finally, she cut her circle into eight generous slices and popped the entire thing into her waiting oven.

Quite satisfied with herself, she crossed her arms over her chest and turned her attention to making the glaze to top her scones.

But before she got far, an "Oh dear!" came from her side. It was Doli. Beside her on the stovetop looked like strawberry jam, completely boiling over in a saucepan. But her hands were elbow deep in her bowl with her scone mixture.

"Let me get that," Arleta said without much thinking.

As she left her station, an audible gasp came from the viewing box. Arleta's eyes trained toward it. She couldn't tell who'd made the sound, but many eyes were on her, including Shalina's from the judges' table. She didn't look pleased.

But Doli's sticky jam was about to go everywhere, so Arleta grabbed a cotton potholder and pushed the pan off the heat. Immediately, the fruity mixture deflated.

"Thanks, honey," Doli said, giving Arleta a weak smile. "I'm really nervous today for some reason."

"No problem," Arleta said and quickly returned to her work.

Jez was busy working on her scones, and they looked ready to put into the oven.

"I didn't break a rule, did I?" Arleta kept her voice hushed as she reached for a container of cream next to a glass jar of powdered sugar for her glaze.

Jez quickly eyed her. "Not that I know of."

Arleta sighed in relief, not wanting to get herself or anyone else in trouble, but as she straightened, her sleeve caught the sugar jar, which flew off the counter and sailed into the air.

"Oh shit," Jez said, throwing out her hand and catching it before it could shatter on the floor.

This time laughter came from the viewing box, and several of the viewers seemed to enjoy the antics of what they were seeing.

Arleta's eyes widened, and she quickly took the sugar from Jez, who then immediately got back to work.

She looked back at the judges' table, where everyone but Shalina Brylar seemed slightly amused.

"Sorry," Arleta mouthed as she held up her hand with the sugar, but the apology didn't seem to appease Theo's mother, since her scowl held.

Arleta dropped her head and made her way back into the center of her station, where she focused her mind on her glaze.

When she was done, and the consistency was just right, her scones were done too. She took them out of the oven to see they'd raised beautifully and were just a touch golden on the tops. When she'd placed the baking tray down, a light bronzed fairy with ebony hair swooped in and fluttered above Arleta with their sparkly wings.

"Ready to cool?" they asked in a small treble voice.

Arleta touched the top of the scones to feel for doneness and nodded with assurance.

The fairy smiled, raised their hands, and cool magic radiated over the scones, effectively bringing the temperature down to the range in which they could be glazed.

"Thank you," Arleta said.

"My pleasure," the fairy replied before flitting off to another station to do the same, sprinkling a bit of ice magic in their wake.

Wasting no time, Arleta brought the eight scones over to the counter to complete the presentation. After glazing, she chose a pretty platter from below her station and sprinkled the tea leaves she'd set aside onto the tops of the scones.

Jez and Doli were just behind her in time but had their offerings ready not long after hers. All three of the bakers were done and pushed their presented scones to the front of their stations for judging.

Before she knew it, Viessa, the same elf who'd checked her in at registration and handled her secret ingredients, gathered up her platter of bergamot tea cherry scones.

Viessa winked as she picked them up. "Beautiful."

With that, she was gone, placing the entry on the judging table.

Arleta's head felt light just as Doli came to her side.

"How do you think you did?" the dwarf whispered.

"Great." Arleta leaned down. "But what *they* think is what matters."

Jez came up to the other side of them and leaned her hip against the counter, crossing her arms over her chest.

The next thirty minutes were tense as each of the scones were tasted. Doli's strawberry cheesecake scones, Jez's double chocolate variety, Taenya's iweocot and date scones, and of course Arleta's and the rest of the competitors'.

Arleta had hoped for direct feedback this round. It was a big elimination round, paring them down from fifteen to six.

But instead, Shalina looked as if she were going to blow the entire time the public deliberations went on. When the judges finished, she finally threw up her hands and pushed the finalized choices to Gaia Thornage.

The griffiner, with Thiggul Honorton at their side, made the announcement, and with the last word, Shalina left the arena in a huff.

That said, Jez, Doli, Arleta, and, of course, Taenya, along with two other bakers, were on the list.

They would all be going to the third round.

# 17

The celebration was short-lived.

The second Jez, Doli, and Arleta walked out of the nearly empty Baking Battle arena, they were met by the three judges.

"Oh *shit*," Jez muttered under her breath, and Doli shot her a scolding look.

"We need to speak with you three," Shalina demanded, her facial features tense with anger.

Thiggul and Gaia, to be honest, looked more confused than the head judge, as if they were about to explode with questions.

The side of Arleta's neck pulsed and her palms went sweaty, but she did her best to brace herself for whatever was about to happen.

"In my office." Shalina waved the group forward. She took them up several flights of stairs to an ornate door not unlike the one leading into the baking arena. But instead of cooking and baking themed carvings, it was covered in flowers and plants from the realm. The elf grasped the handle and flung the door open, practically stomping inside.

The trio of bakers followed, with the other judges trailing behind. Gaia's black wings rustled slightly behind their back as they closed the door.

The room wasn't massive, but had a large window overlooking the Colmore Mountains, and behind a large oak desk hundreds of books lined a wall of shelves. One titled *A Compendium of Berry Varieties in the Northern Lands* lay on the desk and immediately caught Arleta's eye.

Shalina perched on the edge of her desk with her arms crossed tightly over her chest. Finally, she tipped her head to a scarlet brocade couch on the right-hand side of the office, silently gesturing for Doli, Arleta, and Jez to sit. Like school children, they did so without question.

Thiggul, dressed in a brightly colored pair of baggy pants and a silk shirt with yellow jewels sewn onto the collar, spoke first, keeping his attention on Shalina. "I believe we should have had a longer conversation concerning this matter."

Shalina whipped her head toward the dwarf. Her narrowed eyes glittered, ready for battle. "We *did* have this conversation," she retorted sharply.

The dwarf snapped his rosy lips shut. Gaia Thornage, a typically regal griffiner, brought their birdlike gaze to the intricately designed rug sprawled on the office floor.

For what seemed like an infinitely long time, a tense silence hung in the air.

The baking trio sat with their shoulders sandwiched together on the couch—almost, since Doli's frame was so much lower than the others. Doli and Arleta had their hands neatly folded on their laps while Jez had hers crossed over her chest in the same defensive manner as Shalina.

The elf finally uncrossed her arms and broke the silence, her voice thick with dissatisfaction. "What you three pulled off today is completely unacceptable. This is *not* what the Langheim Baking Battle stands for."

"Cooperation?" Jez groaned.

"This is the centennial anniversary of the Battle, not a child's party," Shalina spat. "Your antics are making a mockery of it."

Doli tried to sit up straighter, her voice gentle. "We meant no harm, ma'am. There are no rules about *not* working together to finish the bakes, are there? It all just kind of…happened."

Shalina's gaze iced over. "And what about professionalism? Have you simply thrown that concept away?"

Arleta bit her tongue, holding back a lot of words she knew better than to say. The last thing she wanted to do was bring more attention to herself.

"Shalina," Gaia said before Doli could reply, if she even wanted to, "we are actually hearing different things from the sponsors."

"And those are?" the elf hissed, her eyes flashing.

"This continued conversation should have been in private, but as you are the one who called these three in already"—the griffiner inclined their birdlike head just slightly, but at the same time puffed up their body and flexed out their wings— "the Baking Battle has lost some of its allure in the Northern Lands in recent years."

"I must agree," Thiggul said, with slightly more hesitation than the griffiner.

Caught off guard by the shift in direction, Arleta shot puzzled looks at Jez and Doli.

"This is all gossip," Shalina shot back, her tone brimming with denial and sheer outrage that such a topic would even be uttered.

"It's not gossip. Thiggul and I spoke with them directly after you left the arena." Gaia bowed their head once more and continued in a calm tone. "There was a lot of excitement and energy today in that baking arena. The sponsors loved it." They brought their attention toward the trio. "What these three did today was unorthodox, I will admit that. But perhaps it's just the spark of novelty this competition needs to regain its former glory."

Shalina puffed up with indignation and opened her mouth to speak, but Thiggul lifted his hand, halting her words. "Once more, I must agree with the griffiner. The Northern Lands are changing. In Dundes Heights, many dwarves tire of clinging to the old ways as well." His eyes slid to Doli while the corners of his mouth twitched upward. "We yearn for fresh opportunities. In fact, this is why I'm even here as a judge this year… and hope to be for many more years to come. Mining is a noble profession, but there are many other paths a dwarf can choose as their life's work. Seeing these competitors cooperate gives me hope that the people of the Northern Lands are open to a little more than dogged adherence to tradition."

"We have the opportunity to all come together and put on an event like we've never seen before," Gaia said.

Silently, Shalina edged her way around the back of the oak desk as if to use it as a shield between her and everyone else in the room. Her porcelain skin flushed red. She placed both hands down on the top, barely resting her fingers on the wood, then looked up. "And you two would have this competition descend into chaos? Permit the contestants to dictate the rules?"

In unison, Jez, Doli, and Arleta shrank back a fraction on the couch.

"This is not what we're suggesting at all," Gaia reassured her, holding their clawed hand toward the elf in a gesture of peace. "I propose, for the time being, since teamwork during a contest is an uncharted territory, we should clarify to the remaining six contestants that it will not be tolerated in the following rounds."

Shalina straightened her body as if in victory.

"*This* year," Gaia continued. "But possibly next year, once we've had the chance to discuss the matter, we may entertain the idea in some form. To make things more interesting."

A small growl came from the elf's throat.

"Just *us* being here, as a newly diverse set of judges, has attracted several more sponsors this year," Thiggul added. "The Baking Battle is no longer simply an elf-run competition. You don't want to lose all the new interest you've gained if we were to suddenly...resign."

Arleta's eyes widened at his threat.

Gaia clicked their tongue, a hint of amusement in their eyes. "Imagine the scandal it would cause." They shrugged their shoulders while their wings fluffed slightly behind them. "The dwarf and I can make our own opportunities."

"And what will we do with these three?" Shalina flung her arm out toward Jez, Doli, and Arleta as if presenting them as evidence of some sort of heinous crime.

The griffiner swiveled their head toward the couch. "Ah. I nearly forgot you all were here. I suggest you make your exit while we judges continue our discussion about the future of the Baking Battle."

"And we're still in the competition, right?" Arleta blurted out, nearly in shock.

Thiggul shrugged. "You earned your spots based on the merit of your bakes. Now go and speak nothing of this."

The friends bolted off the couch and dashed out the door without a backward glance, but as the door clicked shut, Shalina's voice could be heard through the woodwork. She didn't sound happy.

Jez rounded on her friends at the top of the staircase. "What just happened?"

Doli spun around and grasped for Arleta. "I have no idea. But we're all still in this game, and that's all that matters. Let's not ruin everything by asking too many questions." She held up her finger as if she'd remembered something. "And it gives me time to finish your dress for the ball."

# 18

With a slightly awkward—because of the height difference—but grand twirl, Doli spun Arleta around to face the mirror in her room. "See how pretty you are?"

Arleta was hard pressed not to admit it was true. She looked good. The yellow dress, borrowed from Doli's wardrobe and quickly altered, was originally too short. But Doli had added a ruffle from another skirt she'd brought with her that put it almost right at Arleta's typical length.

It was the first time in a long time that she'd seen herself looking that way. Pretty. *Happy.* Her skin was clear of the flour that too often dusted her cheeks, and her hazel eyes sparkled. Her chestnut braids were pulled back into a low bun with the ends neatly tucked away, while her suntanned complexion was radiant against the golden fabric.

Doli leaned her head against Arleta's arm. "I hope you like

it. I knew that color would be perfect." She wore a pink dress herself, a perfect contrast to her rich, dark-umber skin tone. The dress had small, clear crystals sewn onto the amble bodice that Arleta was pretty sure were gems from her family's mine, but she hadn't asked, thinking it might be rude. Her impressive coiled hair was loose, dotted with several fresh miniature peonies at the front. Laid over her eyes was a pink mask, the same little crystals lining the edges.

"I do." Arleta's eyes welled up, and she turned to hug her sweet, generous friend. "How in the stars did you get this done in time?"

Doli squeezed Arleta back. "Oh, I just stayed up all night."

Arleta pushed Doli back slightly, concern tensing her features. "You can't stay up all night for me. You need rest for tomorrow."

The dwarf dismissed the worry with a bat of her eyelashes and waved her hand in the air. "I'll be fine. Now, let's go show Jez."

Arleta chuckled and slid on the simple mask Doli had sewn out of extra fabric she'd brought. "I'm sure she'll be thrilled." Sarcasm peppered her tone.

The two of them scampered out of Doli's room and over to 206 with Arleta half expecting that Jez might be asleep with the covers over her head just to avoid the ball. They burst through the door, and what greeted them instead was Jez decked out in a pretty fantastic outfit of her own. She wore a luxuriously tailored pair of cobalt blue pants along with a matching shirt that was gilded with golden thread on the edges. A matching gold mask, nearly as regal as a crown, was fixed on her round face. The tones were a perfect complement to her sandy complexion.

Doli and Arleta stood stunned.

"Ok, maybe I brought something." Jez cast her gaze down at

her polished leather boots. "I didn't know if I'd feel up to going to the ball, so I didn't want to get anyone's hopes up."

Doli let out an excited squeal, darting over to Jez with her arms thrown wide open. Before the dwarf had the chance to tackle the fennex into an embrace, Jez, with her quick, fox-like reflexes, caught Doli by the forehead, effectively keeping her at arm's length and stopping her in her tracks.

"Let's not be ridiculous here," Jez said. "It's *just* some cloth and thread."

Doli pulled back and crossed her arms over her chest in a quick pout. "Fine. But you are absolutely stunning, and I'm so glad you're coming."

"It's not *just* cloth and thread," Arleta added. "And I'm really glad you're coming too."

At that, Jez flashed a half grin, fangs and all, and tipped her head to the door. "Since we all look so good, let's go get this over with."

With Doli and Arleta holding hands—Jez had, of course, refused—the trio made their way downstairs and out to a large courtyard nestled on the east side of the castle. The grounds buzzed with excitement, as guests were already eating and drinking from what was another massive buffet. This time it was a secret forest theme, great animals meticulously created from brightly colored macarons towering over the heavily laden dessert table. A stag, not unlike the one Theo and Arleta had almost hit on their journey to Langheim—other than it being colored lime green—stood among them.

Arleta's stomach twisted at the thought of Theo. It could have been longing, but Arleta didn't want to admit that. She hadn't seen him since the garden…except in her dreams, where he kept appearing in the shadows.

She pushed the thoughts away as the music from a full array of musicians swelled.

"This is *incredible*." Doli pointed up to the twinkling fairy lights hung between the trees in the courtyard. Each illumination was a tiny spark of magic.

The guests, comprised of both the remaining and eliminated contestants, the elven elite, the sponsors, and other possibly important people from around the realm, were already dancing and enjoying the buffet and fine elven drinks. Arleta glanced around for the judges, particularly Shalina, since she expected that the head judge was still not happy with her. Soon enough, she spotted the elf at a table with the other two judges and some faces she didn't recognize.

Shalina looked as stunning as ever, with her silver hair worn loose and flowing around her bare shoulders. The full-length dress she wore was made of plush emerald velvet with a cascade of falling leaves delicately embroidered and tumbling along one side of the gown.

Arleta made a mental note to stay out of Shalina's vicinity. She didn't need to draw attention to herself for any reason.

"I'm going to get something to eat," Jez said and made a beeline for the mountain of dinner options, leaving Doli and Arleta behind.

"I'm pretty hungry too," Doli chirped. "You want to join us?"

Arleta forced up the corners of her lips. "I think I'm going to wander around for a bit. I haven't really gotten the chance to get a good look at the castle yet."

Doli patted her on the shoulder and winked. "Don't forget about us."

This made Arleta chuckle out loud. "Oh, I don't think that's possible."

Safely distancing herself from the judges, she made her way to the other side of the room. There, she absentmindedly picked up a plate from the dessert table and placed a few treats onto it: a miniature chocolate cherry tart, a tiny square slice of lime vanilla cake, and a coconut cream square with strands of toasted coconut on its top. It was beautiful, almost too beautiful to eat. From there, Arleta passed under an elaborate plant arch that led her completely outside into the serenity of the main garden. Alone in the still air, she tipped her chin up to the twinkling stars overhead and took a bite of the coconut cream square. Coconut came from the southeast shore of the Northern Lands, and it didn't make it to Adenashire much. When it did, it was often too expensive to purchase.

The creamy flavor melted on her tongue, and she instantly wanted to congratulate its baker for a job well done. It was a taste so rare she was transported back to childhood in her mind.

When she was a young girl—eight, if she remembered right—her mother had splurged and made her a coconut cake for her birthday. The memory was still as sweet as if it were yesterday. Even the orcs had come over to celebrate, and they didn't eat too much cake. A gentle laugh escaped her lips at the thought. Her father had also made a flower wreath for her head out of lavender, and they danced and laughed all night until her feet ached.

A pang of sadness tightened her chest. Not only did she miss those days she'd spent with her parents, but she missed Ervash and Verdreth too. The orcs had never left her. Not for one day since her parents had died. They had been there for her, offering a hearty meal, a hug, or a helping hand.

And she had never fully admitted to herself how much they

meant to her until that minute, out under the stars in the castle's calm garden. They'd refused to let her shut them out, no matter how many times she'd tried. No matter how high she had built her walls, they were always tall enough to see over them.

They not only acted like fathers to her, they *were* her fathers. And something solidified that fact in her heart.

At that moment, she vowed to make sure to tell Verdreth and Ervash how important they were to her. Life was unpredictable, and one never really knew when someone they love might not be around anymore.

"This isn't even what I *want*."

A hushed but urgent voice broke Arleta from her thoughts. It was Taenya. *Again.* She was dressed in a long gown that fit tight on the sleeves and bodice. And another elf was with her, the same one as before; Vesstan, her brother.

Caught off guard, Arleta quickly wiped the tears running down her cheeks and frantically looked around for an escape, but they were in short supply. If she were to try dashing across the garden back to the open courtyard, they would spot her. Instead, she ducked down behind a bush and hoped for better cover than the last time Taenya had caught her "spying" when she most certainly was not.

"I don't want to wear this ridiculous dress," Taenya snarled, gathering up the hem and then throwing it to the ground again. "I don't *want* to talk to any of the people at this party."

Vesstan clicked his tongue, his disapproval echoing throughout the garden. "You have responsibilities to this family, Taenya. We had an agreement."

Realizing she still had a plate in her hand, Arleta carefully set it down with the last two desserts still on it.

Under the moon and starlight, Taenya narrowed her eyes. "No, *you* had an agreement that I wanted nothing to do with. I never wanted to enter this damned Baking Battle in the first place. I have dreams, you know. I want to do…things. Experience life outside of Langheim."

Arleta's chest ached with empathy at the elf's words. She could hear the desperation in Taenya's tone, pleading for control in a life she apparently had not chosen.

Arleta could relate.

Vesstan leaned in close. "You will *not* dishonor us by losing your winning title, sister." The last word came out like a curse. "Now get in there and make a good impression." He strode off back to the party, leaving his sister behind in the moonlight and shadows.

A slight breeze picked up and Arleta took the opportunity to hunker down even further, pressing her hands into the soil beneath her.

Just a moment later, and after a shake of her head, Taenya followed Vesstan into the courtyard and out of Arleta's sight. Arleta made sure to keep ducked down for a few extra seconds to guarantee she'd not been seen.

Leaving her plate behind, she stood and began dusting off the yellow dress, careful to make sure she hadn't gotten any plant or dirt stains on it since it didn't belong to her. Just as she finished and took a step forward, Arleta ran smack into someone's chest.

"I'm so sor—"

Her words trailed off as she craned her neck upward, meeting Theo's unexpected gaze.

The elf was dressed in an upgraded version of his typical wear; slightly more fitted pants and a gauzy shirt underneath

a jacket made in the latest elvish fashion. And he smelled…
intoxicating. First of delicious cedarwood and sage, then like
her garden in full bloom, like freshly baked bread slathered in
butter and raspberry jam on a rare lazy morning.

His eyes skimmed over Arleta as if he were parched and
drinking her in. "You're radiant."

Arleta pushed all that deliciousness and his compliment
aside. "What are you doing here?" The words nearly caught in
her throat.

"I didn't know you were out in the garden," Theo said, his
eyes crinkling at the corners. "I was required to come, but
planned to keep my distance, as you asked." He looked up
into the sky. "The fireworks are starting soon, and I wanted to
get a good view. I saw Doli and Jez across the courtyard, but
you weren't with them. I thought maybe you'd decided not to
attend."

Arleta whipped her attention around the garden and spotted
a nearby stretch of wall with enough privacy for the moment.
"Come," she commanded and pulled him by his jacket toward
their destination.

Theo did not resist her order. Not one ounce.

When they arrived, she impulsively pushed him against the
wall, and he put his hands up in the air at his sides as if in mock
surrender. Moonlight painted a glow on his elvish features and,
for a brief second, Arleta struggled to get her words out. They
were tangled up somewhere between her heart and her throat.

"What is this all about?" she demanded, finally discovering
her voice again. Her words sliced through the charged silence
between them. What she really wanted to say was how much
she desired him and didn't know why.

"This?" Theo echoed the question. "What is *this*?"

"You being out here, taking me to your garden, encouraging me to come to the Baking Battle." She narrowed her gaze at him through her mask. "Calling me radiant."

Theo leaned his back into the stone wall and slid his hands into his pockets. "Would you rather I lie to you?" The words dripped from his lips like tempting honey.

But the tempting honey part may only have been Arleta's hazy interpretation.

"You have a Fated, Theo." Arleta flung her hands into the night air and stepped toward him. "You told me in your garden, so stop flirting with me."

He winced and magic trickled from his hands, still in his pockets. "I really didn't know you were out here."

Anger burned at Arleta's chest, and she took two more steps toward him until the space between them was no more than a few inches. The anger wasn't even at Theo, but herself for even toying with the idea of wanting him. Even so, she refused to back down even as her heart threatened to escape her chest. It pounded so hard.

She wanted little more in the world than his lips on hers, his hands on her waist, pulling her close to his chest, offering forever.

But there he was. So close and so off-limits all at the same time.

The sudden crack of a twig sounded behind them, and Arleta jumped back from Theo just as Devdan stepped around the corner.

"Sir," he said to Theo, his voice formal, "the fireworks are about to begin. You are needed out there."

Arleta took another nervous step backward, allowing Theo plenty of room to leave.

The elf pushed himself from the wall and followed his mother's assistant, but not before he turned his neck and sent Arleta a lingering glance.

And she did her best to stomp out any of her own fireworks trying to ignite. They were too dangerous, and she knew it. If she was going to win the Baking Battle, she needed to keep Theodmon Brylar *out* of her mind.

⬦

"Bakers!" Naexi Miraven's voice rang out across the baking arena, and all eyes seemed to move to her. "Today is the third round of the centennial Langheim Baking Battle. Those of you that are still here are part of an elite group of bakers. It's an exciting day for those remaining, for all but two of you will go home."

There were only six of them left—a high elf named Esta, a halfling named Pepin, Arleta, her two closest friends, and Taenya—and the air was thick with anticipation.

Arleta tensed as the host's words hung in the air, and she couldn't help but feel a twinge of guilt. That day she, or at least one of her friends, would be out of the competition. If she were to move on it would mean Jez or Doli would likely not. She didn't even know how to process that. And there was the fact that, as far as she knew, she was the only being without magic that had ever been in the Battle.

*What if she were to win?*

Everyone would find out.

How they hadn't already, she had no idea.

"Today our theme is cookies!" Naexi announced with infectious enthusiasm, her voice carrying the excitement of the crowd. "And I can't wait to try your offerings." She played to the packed viewing box, including many of the eliminated bakers, as well as sponsors. They gave out a few whoops.

The first recipe that popped into Arleta's mind were the blueberry cookies she'd made for the first time shortly before the Baking Battle. The orcs had loved them, although they loved most everything she made, and they had been a big hit at the market. She had lavender in her secret ingredient box, and if she wanted to up her game, she knew a hint of the herb would be a great, unique pairing to the basic version she'd made back home.

Paying no attention to the halfling or high elf, Arleta glanced at Doli and Jez, who'd been moved across the arena far from her. The other stations waited empty. Jez stood stoic, with her hands behind her back, and Doli's smile was ear to ear. She must have already had her cookie in mind too.

"*But*," Naexi quipped with an air of mischief in her voice, and Arleta's attention shot back to her, "today we have also thrown in an extra challenge. One ingredient available at the fresh or dry pantry is one you will not want to choose, lest it ruin your bake." She held up her finger. "I cannot give you any more details, and because of this, while you may smell them, none of you may *taste* your creations, or the components in them, at any point. But if you know your ingredients well enough, you should be able to steer clear of any danger." She continued with her cryptic words. "We will also not be announcing your recipe choice today before the tasting, to keep the mystery going."

Arleta's heart picked up. This meant that any one of them could be eliminated simply because they'd been tricked. It seemed unfair. But when she glanced up at the overflowing viewing box, filled with eager spectators, she was pretty sure she knew what was going on. Several viewers leaned forward as if on the edge of their seats from the extra drama of seeing one of them possibly lose theatrically. Shalina had forbidden them from using each other, but the judges had to keep the excitement up somehow, and this was how they were doing it, making hazards the contestants might fall into and ruin their bakes.

If they only knew Arleta, a non-magic human, had infiltrated the Baking Battle. Now *that* irony would create some drama.

At that point, the judges came onto the scene and preened a bit in front of the viewing box. Shalina waved while the other two gave several bows, as if they were who everyone was there for. They were given a standing ovation before they sat at their table below with a view of each of the six bakers.

Naexi continued with her instructions for a few more moments, reintroducing the bakers and reminding them of the rules of the game. This time she made sure to emphasize that there was to be *no helping* between the bakers.

"Yes, yes, yes," Arleta muttered under her breath, steeling herself for the upcoming task.

A few seconds later, the bell rang, signaling the start of the third challenge. Unlike the last round, Arleta wasted no time running to the overflowing fresh pantry to find her blueberries. With only six of them left, there would likely be no fighting today over ingredients, but it was a critical moment, and no matter what happened, she needed to keep her wits about her.

The pantry was stocked full of all sorts of fresh and colorful fruits. They were beautiful, and any one of them could be the ingredient that needed to be avoided.

All the other bakers had visited the dry pantry first.

She scanned over the huge stock, and her eyes landed on a

basket of juicy blueberries nestled among the abundance. But when she stepped forward to grasp them, her heart stopped.

They were not blueberries. They were yageberries. The same berries that had ended up all over her when Taenya had caught her hiding in the bush outside the castle. The same blueberry clone that would completely ruin any dish made to be sweet because when the fruit was mixed with sugar, it turned the entire flavor sour.

That was the trap ingredient.

She stepped back and away from the pantry. Quickly, she looked up and found both Doli and Jez engrossed in choosing their dry options. Everything in her wanted to warn them, but she knew she couldn't. The rules were clear: *no* helping allowed. They were also picking out dry ingredients, so they might not have even been using fruit in their recipes. Either way, they would have to navigate the challenge on their own.

With Arleta lost in her thoughts, she barely registered when Taenya swept by her.

"Better get moving," the elf muttered under her breath, and Arleta had no idea if she was talking to her or not.

But the advice was good. Arleta needed to pivot from her original recipe idea.

Another orc favorite and, a market bestseller, were her sea salt, browned butter, chocolate chunk cookies. No herbs, but it was a solid contender that melted in the mouth in a sweet and savory dream.

At least those were the words Verdreth had used the first time he'd tried them.

The salt added a unique ingredient in the way it was used on the top of the cookies, and unique was often the goal of creating her bakes.

With a renewed sense of purpose, she spun on her heel to the dry station to see if some type of chocolate was left—dark, semisweet, milk—any would work, although she preferred the semisweet.

As she made her way to the dry ingredients, Taenya was already back to her baking station, and Jez had turned to go back to hers.

But Doli was on her way to the fruit.

She quickly eyed the judges. Shalina's attention was on her. Had she seen Arleta reach for and leave the yageberries in their spot? Was the judge testing her? To see if she'd warn Doli?

Arleta put her head down and whispered into the air, "Don't take it," half hoping that the stars would carry the message, and Doli would hear it and understand.

The odds were low that Doli would take them anyway. There were so many other gorgeous options.

Arleta blew out her breath and kept walking.

Seconds later, she stood in front of the unlabeled chocolate options and did not look back at Doli.

The fragrance of the chocolate hit her nose, teasing her taste buds as she studied the lighter to darker color options. She reached out and plucked up the dish of what looked to be semisweet chocolate since it was lighter than the dark chocolate and darker than the milk. Arleta brought it to her nose and took in the vanilla and caramel notes of the choice. It was the right one.

Quickly, she grabbed a bottle of flaky salt from a shelf above, and that was all she needed, since the other ingredients for the cookies were already at her station.

On the way back to her bench, she scanned over the remaining two bakers, but her view was blocked. She couldn't see their ingredient choices, so she continued to her station and began her bake.

She had to focus, but Doli kept entering her thoughts. Again, she looked up and made her best attempt to see what Doli had taken, but it was useless since her view was obscured. She was pretty sure that the judges had placed them at the exact stations where they could not see the other bakers clearly.

Forcing herself to focus, the recipe for her cookies filled Arleta's mind, and she dove in.

Brown the butter.

Mix the dry ingredients.

Add the butter, vanilla, and eggs.

Fold in the chocolate chunks.

Portion.

Bake.

Sprinkle on the flaky salt.

Have the fairy cool her cookies to just the right temperature.

Present her offering.

Serve to the judges.

Arleta took in a deep breath as she eyed her platter of cookies. She'd made them jumbo sized, and honestly? They were truly a masterpiece. Some of her best work that she'd be proud to serve to anyone. Each cookie had been individually tested for perfection using the tips of her fingers to ensure the ideal texture and doneness.

The tantalizing scent of home enveloped her, sweet and creamy caramelized brown butter, vanilla, and roasted cocoa. The gentle sprinkle of salt on the top would heighten the entire eating affair. From experience and the recipe she'd chosen, the texture was crisp while the insides remained slightly chewy.

The fairy bell rang, jolting Arleta from the reverie of her cookies.

"Bakers, please present your bakes to the judges," Naexi announced.

Arleta's eyes widened. This was new, but possibly it was because there were only six of them left.

Hastily, she grabbed her platter, clutching it tight. She joined the bakers' procession toward the judging table. As they approached, she stole a glance at the other cookie platters, her eyes finally settling on Doli's creation.

She was relieved to see that the cookies were entirely golden brown, with a drizzle of white glaze over the top of each. Not a yageberry in sight.

Arleta found a spot in between what she guessed were Jez's cinnamon roll swirl cookies and Taenya's peanut butter chocolate cookies. On the table lay Doli's and what appeared to be a mint chocolate variety from the halfling and a jam-stuffed gingerbread from the high elf. They all looked lovely and delicious.

The six bakers stood back while the judges eyed the offerings.

Gaia, the griffiner judge, finally spoke. "I commend you all on your accomplishments of getting this far with your bakes. You all have scored highly, and each of you deserve your spots in the top six."

"That said," Thiggul piped in, "one of you has unfortunately earned an automatic elimination for today's competition."

The audience gasped.

Arleta's stomach dropped. Quickly, her eyes ran over the cookies again to confirm that Doli had not used the yageberries.

"Dolgrila Butterbuckle," Shalina announced, keeping her head up high. "Please step forward."

*No, no, no!* The words spun in Arleta's mind.

Doli's always cheerful expression drooped, but she followed the instructions.

Shalina picked up one of the dwarf's cookies and broke it open. The inside was stuffed with a purple-blue filling.

The yageberries.

A buzzing sounded in Arleta's ears while the head judge's mouth moved, likely explaining to the audience the mock blueberry, and what it did to the entire bake, essentially ruining it.

Her cheeks flushed, and all Arleta wanted to do was sink into the floor. She should have warned Doli. She hadn't to save her own hide, afraid of the consequences. Her breath picked up, growing panicked, short, as Doli stepped back and away from the rest of the bakers. Tears glistened on her full cheeks.

Guilt tightened its grip around Arleta, and she watched a hazy scene of the judges evaluating the rest of the cookies, but Arleta heard none of it until a fairy tapped her on the shoulder.

She quickly saw that Jez, the halfling, and the high elf were also standing to the side. She had been left standing in front of the judges with Taenya eyeing her at her side.

"Congratulations, Taenya Carralei and Arleta Starstone," Gaia said. "Your elf and wizard baking skills have served you well to get you this far."

But Arleta's mental state teetered on the edge of collapse. Her friend had lost because of *her*. If she had not entered the competition and shook things up, they never would have instituted the yageberry problem, trying to create more drama for the viewers' sake.

In a moment of overwhelming frustration and shame, and no one there to talk her down, Arleta's emotions bubbled over. Without a second thought, she flung her hands into the air.

"I'm not a wizard!" she blurted, her voice carrying both desperation and indignation. "I'm human, magicless, and I shouldn't even be here."

The arena went as silent as it had ever been.

# 19

Immediately following Arleta's declaration, the third round came to a halt. Everyone was asked to leave the arena. Doli and Jez had tried to console her, but it was useless. Doli had tried to tell Arleta the mishap with the berries was not her fault and that she had won on her own merit, but *was* it a mishap? Arleta couldn't shake the unsettling thought that if she wasn't at the Baking Battle in the first place, none of this would have happened.

Everything was stuck in an indeterminate state. Yes, Arleta had placed in the top two, but no one would confirm she was staying, even with the final round looming. She spent the next day hiding in her room, not letting Doli in and not speaking to Jez. She knew it was completely illogical and she should have been focusing on Doli, but she couldn't seem to bring herself out of her own stupor.

Just after sunrise the next morning, Arleta found herself wandering into the small courtyard behind the castle gate, the first place she had explored after she and Theo had arrived.

Guests for the finale were being funneled through a separate entrance at the back side of the castle, leaving the courtyard empty. She walked to the iweocot tree, plucked some fruit, and took a bite, but the sweet flesh only turned her stomach. She tossed the partially eaten fruit under the tree.

"Are you okay?"

Theo's voice echoed softly in the courtyard, breaking Arleta's train of thought.

Arleta spun around to face him, finding herself looking at his *incredibly* concerned gaze on his *incredibly* attractive face. "I don't know."

"I know you don't want to see me," he said. "But Jez and Doli are so worried about you, they were willing to try anything."

A tiny piece of her wanted to tell Theo to leave her alone, but the rest of her desperately wanted him to stay.

"They're letting you stay," Theo said, his tone steady and reassuring.

She eyed him. "Are you sure? Shalina doesn't want me here."

"She was overruled." Theo took several steps closer to her, his footsteps light against the cobblestones. "You and Taenya have the overall highest scores by far. All the judges agree."

"But Doli still could have won the round instead of me if the berries would have been correct," Arleta said.

"I saw her previous scores versus yours. She would not have won," Theo assured her.

Arleta blew out a long, deliberate breath. "But magic—"

"Your bakes don't need magic to be amazing," he said. "The talent is all you. That fact is going to make people upset, jealous even, but they can't deny the facts when so many people know the truth."

Arleta breathed out a sigh of relief while a warm smile crept over Theo's lips, seeming to remember something.

"Oh, and I checked, your orc friends from Adenashire received their invitations, so I'd guess they'll be arriving soon."

Just the thought of Verdreth and Ervash being at the Baking Battle shot up Arleta's heart rate in anticipation and nerves. But honestly, she couldn't wait to see them.

"Thank you for taking care of that." Arleta looked the elf in the eyes and quickly cast her gaze down, because all she could think about was kissing him.

Theo bowed his head and started to turn.

"Theo?" Arleta whispered, and her shoulders tensed at what she was about to ask. "Why did you do all this for me?"

The elf rounded back to her. "You are probably the strongest baker this competition has ever seen. I've already told you."

"No." Arleta shook her head firmly. "You have not."

Theo stood frozen, then waved his hand dismissively in the air, but concern clouded his eyes. "This is not the time."

She glanced around the courtyard and threw her hands into the air. "You're right, it's not. But win or lose, I'm leaving tomorrow, and I can't *do* this anymore, Theo. *Tell* me." Her tone was pleading, and she was not going to let him go without admitting whatever he had to say.

Theo pinched at the bridge of his nose, obviously fighting what was about to come out of his mouth. "Please, just let me go."

He turned to walk away, but Arleta grabbed his arm, and the second she touched him, the words spilled from his mouth.

"I...I *need* to be near you." He pounded his fist to his heart. "It hurts when we are apart."

As if a thread connecting the two of them tightened into a knot, Arleta dropped her grasp, but took a step forward. She gulped. "I don't understand. You have a Fated, so this should not be happening."

"You don't understand that being fated is something you must choose with your whole heart. Nothing can be held back," Theo admitted. "My telling you will only complicate your thoughts if you have not already accepted it. Doing so will affect you in ways I can't stop."

Arleta's eyes widened and she threw her hands back into the air in exasperation. "Can't you see I'm already affected by you, Theo? Whatever we have here, it's complicated."

For too long of a moment, the elf and human stood in the courtyard, staring at each other. Yearning. Not saying a word.

And yet saying everything.

Theo finally broke the silence, keeping his voice low, his breath ragged. "I told you I met my Fated under the bay arbor."

"Yes." Arleta's heart pounded against her rib cage. She both wanted to hear what he was about to say and run away at the same time.

"I met *you* under the arbor. I've met you there so many times."

As the words left his mouth, Arleta knitted her brows in confusion, then her stomach dropped like a brick. Somehow, she knew his declarations were true, but they *couldn't* be. "I...I'd never been to the arbor before that night," she stammered. "And that's not where you met me. We met in Adenashire."

"In my dreams I did. The night world is different. Surreal. But I couldn't just tell you. Not here, not now. The Baking Battle was enough, and I wanted to put *you* first, not my feelings. How could you concentrate otherwise? I barely can, and I've been waiting for you for years. It's not simply information a person dumps on another when they've never even heard of a Fated." He raked his hand through his hair while nervous magic poured from him, then disappeared into the air.

Arleta wrapped her arms around her chest and squeezed.

"I had zero doubt from the moment I met you on the path outside your cottage that you were my Fated, Arleta Starstone. And my garden?" Theo held both hands out. "It's so large because every time I plant something new, it is for you."

"But you don't really know me," Arleta protested.

Theo's chest heaved for breath. "I have known and loved you for a hundred lifetimes."

Heat rose on Arleta's cheeks. She was suddenly overwhelmed with embarrassment at not seeing what had been so obvious, with guilt and the lingering unknown. The entire situation was impossible except for the fact her mind suddenly flashed with a lost fragment of the two of them under the bay arbor.

Could she have seen it too and blocked it from her thoughts, or was she imagining it now because he had placed it there with his words?

Arleta's skin tingled, and she brushed imaginary foliage from herself. The sudden need to raise an emotional barrier overtook her. She'd done this with everyone in her life since her parents had died. Becoming too invested wasn't safe.

"And is this what you expected as your Fated?" Nervousness and a dash of wall-building sarcasm peppered her question. "A human? With no magic to offer you as a partner?"

His eyes raised to her once more. "No. And yes." Theo stepped in to close the gap between himself and Arleta. "There is plenty of magic in you. You *are* magic…for me." He reached up and touched her cheek, making Arleta's knees go weak and nearly buckle under her weight. "And I will be yours whether or not you want me, until I am no more."

Green and gold swirled in the air, entwining Theo and Arleta in its embrace. It took hold of Arleta, and every fiber in her being wanted his lips on hers. No matter what.

Her mind spun with a lifetime of dreams.

The past…

The future…

How their lives would turn out…

Together, always…

She wanted Theo to be hers.

And her soul told her it was so.

The two were inches apart when logic slipped away, and Arleta raised up on her toes to press her lips against his waiting mouth, to accept…

But before she got there doubt—reality—seized her and yanked Arleta back.

Theo should *not* travel this path with her.

She was a magicless human, and one with a propensity toward chaos.

Walls.

She was *not* his Fated. It was impossible because elves were *not* fated to humans.

He was confused.

This relationship would never work.

Especially not for *him*.

He was making a mistake.

*I can't let him in, even if it is true. In the end I will lose him and end up in pain.*

The thought broke the spell as if a cord had been severed.

Instinctively, Arleta cleared her throat and took two steps backward. "I can't do this."

The magic faded and vanished, dashing the remnants of what could have been. Arleta rushed to the main castle to go back to her room and figure out how in the stars she was even going to be able to get it together enough to compete in the finale, now only hours away.

Despite herself, she looked back at Theo, only to see Devdan rushing away in the opposite direction.

# 20

Barely catching her breath after what had just happened with Theo, Arleta made it to the top of the stairs of her wing before she collapsed into a heap. She had no idea how long she cried before the sound of shoes tapped their way toward her.

She looked up to find Shalina, the head judge elf, a vision of poise and control. She stood looking down at her, emotionless, for what seemed like an hour.

"We need to speak before the finale."

Her voice was soft, but Arleta could sense the danger in her authoritative tone.

Stunned to see the head judge, Arleta pointed toward her room. "Um. I was planning to rest before the competition starts." The words were barely audible. The truth was, Arleta knew full well that there would be no rest, but it was the best excuse she could think of at the moment.

"Now." The single word was all Shalina spoke while flinging her hand out, showing the way to their destination.

Arleta's heart pounded the entire walk to the head judge's office, echoed by the click of Shalina's hard-soled shoes on the stone floor.

Once they arrived, with a swoop worthy of the finest actor, the head judge yanked Arleta into her large office, lined with dusty books, and slammed the door. She wasted no time voicing her point.

"What in the stars are you doing with my son?"

Arleta was frozen to her spot on the edge of a blue floral rug. "I'm...I'm not doing anything with Theo." Her heart galloped in her chest.

"*Theo?*" Shalina spat, her lips curling in distaste. "My son's name is *Theodmon.*"

"I...I... We're friends," Arleta stammered. "He was kind enough to get me to the Baking Battle. We talked on the way. So, yes, we're friends."

But, despite the impossibility of it all, Arleta knew she wanted more. She just couldn't give more.

Shalina narrowed her steely eyes at Arleta. "No! You were overheard speaking to him about the Fated."

A lump of nervousness lodged itself in Arleta's throat, making breathing nearly impossible. "He mentioned it, yes."

The elf's ethereal features twisted, and in a flash, she was inches from Arleta. "You have no magic, and this is not the type of thing that is proper for you to be speaking about with *any* elf. The Fated are revered only between my people," Shalina hissed, confirming Arleta's nagging thoughts that elves and humans were not to be fated.

"I'm not the one who brought it up!" Arleta's protest rang

in the small room. Immediately, she regretted her words and wished she could stuff them back into her mouth, but instead they hung in the air like the reek of burned bread.

With an exasperated sigh, Shalina spun on her heel, her silver hair flung out like a fan behind her, and she stomped toward her grand oak desk. Nestled among the organized chaos on the top was a carved box. She spun it around with a flick of her wrist and flipped open the top.

Inside were gold coins.

A *lot* of them.

Arleta's eyes rounded at the sight. Involuntarily, she took a step back from the rug, her boots scraping on the stone floor.

"Is it money you want?" the elf growled, baring her perfectly aligned teeth. "Because I have plenty of gold I can offer you to go away and never look back. To leave my son alone and cease confusing him from his actual Fated."

The sight of the gold spun all of Arleta's goals in her mind. The bakery in Adenashire—it could be hers. She could leave this fantasy turned nightmare behind.

But it wasn't a nightmare. Theo had wormed his way into her mind, her heart, her soul. She knew he should not be there, but she *wanted* him there.

Arleta ripped her eyes from the riches. "I came here to compete in the Baking Battle. If I'm to walk away with any gold, I want to earn it," she announced, her fists clenched to her sides.

"*Ugh.*" Shalina flung open the drawer in the front of her desk and produced a small stack of papers. "Then why didn't you disclose you were a human when you checked in at registration?" She held the contract out to Arleta and pointed to a clause, but it was too far away for Arleta to read. Then the elf flipped to the line where Arleta's signature was.

"I…I didn't know that I needed to." Arleta's hands trembled. She knew she'd regret not reading the entire contract before she signed it. "There are no rules against those without magic competing."

"No," Shalina said, anger burning as a dangerous flame in her eyes, "but it must be known since we keep a neat record of who is competing each year."

Arleta gritted her teeth, fully aware she'd regret what she was about to say. "That's not why. You know very well there has never been one magicless in this competition."

"Is that so?" She casually glanced at the contract again. "It also states that all participants must inform us if anyone might have broken any contractual rules. Not doing so will prevent the participant from competing in any upcoming Baking Battles." Shalina's gaze moved back to Arleta. "Your roommate, she's a fennex, right? They have an incredible sense of smell, correct? And that dwarf who's involved herself in everyone's business, surely *she* knows a lot of what goes on around here?"

"They haven't done anything!" Arleta cried, her voice echoing. "Leave Doli and Jez out of this mess."

The elf held up the contract. "Their destiny seems to be up to you."

Arleta's eyes darted around the room in panic, feeling as if any dreams she'd had were crumbling around her.

"Leave, Arleta Starstone," Shalina said plainly. "There is a carriage waiting to take you back to Adenashire. All of your… *things* are in it."

She didn't have a choice.

"I want to say goodbye to my friends," Arleta protested, her words laced in desperation.

Shalina slammed the contract down on the desktop. "Go

now, or *they* go with you." She marched to the door and opened it to a stern-looking elf guard. "Take this woman to the carriage waiting for her downstairs."

With a swift push, she sent Arleta out into the corridor and slammed the door behind her.

Head hung, Arleta followed the guard down a hidden staircase and outside, where indeed a horse-drawn carriage waited. The elf driver held open the door, and Arleta mustered all her strength to step up and climb inside of the cab, where her satchel and something else awaited.

A sealed letter.

Just as the coach lurched forward and plopped Arleta into her seat, she grabbed the paper and opened it. As she did, her head spun with dizziness, and she shook it away. Her fingers trembled and she swallowed hard as she read the hastily scrawled words.

*I lied to you. Only elves can be fated to one another.*

*Theo*

Tears streamed down Arleta's face, tracing her cheeks as she clutched the letter from Theo and the carriage bumped down the road back to Adenashire. Her mind was hazy, trying to work out Theo's words. She knew they must be true, despite what had been said in the courtyard.

Everything about the Langheim Baking Battle had been a fairy tale turned tragedy, as if the spell had broken or a curse had been cast. At least if she left, she could protect Doli and Jez. They could go back home and be able to compete again next year. They would forget about her. Everyone would forget about her like a distant, terrible memory.

But her stomach twisted at the thought of never being able to say goodbye. She'd really never see them again. That was the worst part—knowing that there were so many people who cared about her and that she had to let them go.

Time moved slowly as they made their way down the road. Arleta did not know how long it had been since they'd left the castle, but it felt like hours.

Finally, elbows leaning out onto her knees with her face buried in her hands, Arleta heard the clopping of hooves sounding outside her carriage.

"Stop! Stop right now!" a muffled voice called from outside through the window.

Arleta recognized the voice immediately as Theo's, and she crumpled the letter in her hands. "Don't stop," she called to the driver, but he didn't seem able to hear her from inside, and so he brought the carriage to a gradual halt.

Without hesitation, Arleta threw open the door to Theo dismounting Nimbus. The horse eyed her and threw his head up and down multiple times, as if he had something to say, but of course she couldn't understand the gray-speckled animal.

"Why are you leaving?" The expression on Theo's face was pained and sweat beaded down the side of his face. "I found Doli, and she said you'd taken all your things? Neither she nor Jez knew where you were."

Arleta still held the crumpled letter in her hands, her grip tightening around it. "I'm going home. I never should have come to Langheim in the first place. It was a horrible mistake."

Theo eyed the driver and then brought his attention back to Arleta. "Come talk to me in private, please." The elf gestured off to the side, away from the carriage to a more secluded spot along the road.

But Arleta didn't move from the inside of the open door. Her eyes remained trained on the elf. "You sent me this, Theo." She thrust out the paper in his direction, her voice trembling with emotion.

His brows furrowed as he stared at the rumpled paper. "I sent you what?"

"*This.*" Arleta's voice wavered and tears burned the corners of her eyes again. She pulled her hand back onto her lap, trying hard to contain her feelings.

Theo stepped closer to the carriage and held out his hand. "May I see it?" he asked, his tone dripping with sincerity.

Hesitantly, Arleta produced the paper and placed it into Theo's outstretched palm. Quickly, the elf unwrapped the page and scanned it over. His eyes widened in bewilderment.

"I did *not* write this." His words were laced with disbelief. He gulped and quickly brought his attention back to Arleta. "I would *never* write something like this. And it's laced with magic to make you doubt yourself."

The second he mentioned magic, her head spun again and clouded. But even so, with him standing in front of her, part of Arleta knew his words were true. Everything Theo had done pointed in the complete opposite direction, but then the other part told her that her being here at the Baking Battle, competing, making friends, finding Theo, was some kind of painful, cosmic joke; a fiction she'd wake up from and go back to the mundane life she'd always led, always being late, barely making ends meet.

Having only herself to really rely on.

It was the only way.

The only safe, predictable way.

A low growl rumbled from Theo's throat, a sound she'd never heard him make before. "My mother wrote it. I'd recognize her writing anywhere. Then she tainted it with some kind of magic to make sure you believed it."

In a surge of frustration, Arleta snatched the letter from Theo's hand and flung it to the ground. "It doesn't matter. I'm going home."

She reached for the carriage door, but he caught the edge, not allowing her to close it.

"It *does* matter." The elf locked onto Arleta's gaze, and she couldn't look away. His chest heaved with anger and frustration. "What *else* did she tell you?"

Arleta's throat tightened, both wanting to tell him everything and nothing. "She offered me gold to leave," she confessed, not telling him all the details. She left out the part that the gold was also to leave *him*, not just the competition.

"What?" Theo's eyes went wide in shock as he briefly glanced into the carriage. "Did you take it?"

"Of course not," she said. "But it was enough for me to buy the building for my bakery. And then some."

Theo pinched at the bridge of his nose. "But you are still leaving?"

"She threatened to bar Doli and Jez from the Baking Battle next year." Arleta's tone was heavy with the predicament. "Then she brought out the contract I'd signed; there was this clause I'd missed. It was something about not revealing my bloodline. That I'm not a wizard. Since Doli and Jez knew I was human, they would be implicated—"

"I've looked over that contract before." Theo squinted at Arleta, skepticism in his gaze. "There is no such clause in it."

"I saw it with my own eyes," Arleta protested, frustration bubbling in her chest, because maybe she hadn't *actually* seen it. "There was no way I was going to risk Doli and Jez's chances of coming back."

"She's bluffing." Theo crossed his arms over his chest and gazed up at the clear blue sky, shaking his head.

Nimbus stomped his foot on the ground several times, kicking swirls of dust into the air as if in agreement.

"She doesn't *want* me here," Arleta spat back, "so I'm going home. This whole thing has been nothing but a disas—"

"Nothing but *what*?" Theo cut her off and stepped in closer, passionate fire in his eyes. "Because meeting you has *not* been a disaster for *me*. You being here has *not* been a disaster for the Baking Battle. There are *so many* people who are swooning over your bakes. Just you *being* here has changed this competition forever. You should have seen the last-minute invitation requests for the finale. We can't even accommodate all of them."

Arleta opened her mouth to speak, but Theo pressed on, determination fueling his words even more than before.

"It has *not* been a disaster for Doli. Even Jez complained she was worried about you, pacing back and forth all over the place trying to catch your scent."

Arleta caught her lip between her teeth. Her heart lifted just slightly. "They were both that worried?"

"We *all* were," Theo admitted as his hands found his pockets.

Arleta tentatively climbed out of the carriage, her feet touching the ground.

"I felt you leave." Theo's breath was ragged, and his eyes did not stray from her gaze.

Confusion clouded her features. "What do you mean?" Her

voice quavered as she kept her fingers clasped the edge of the door.

The muscles in Theo's face tensed as a vein pulsed on his left temple. "The air changed, like I couldn't breathe. And something in my heart knew you were gone. I rushed straight to the castle to find you."

"And then you came here," Arleta whispered, a fraction of hope lacing her words.

"*Of course* I did." Theo's voice turned raspy. "You know how I feel about you, Arleta. But that's not even really why I came." He searched the ground to avoid her gaze. "You *deserve* to be in the Baking Battle. You've earned your place." He steeled himself and returned to her gaze. "There seems to be a story that you keep telling yourself, and I understand; it has served you for some time. It *was* real. It kept you safe. But you've outgrown that tale, and now it's holding you back from becoming who you are really meant to be."

"And *who* am I meant to be?" Tears flowed onto her cheeks as emotion choked her voice. "I don't even know who that person is."

A small, tender smile graced Theo's lips. He picked up the false letter from the ground and pocketed it, then held out his hand to her. "That's for you to decide."

Arleta sighed as she fought against the waning magic from the letter. "I need to head back to the Baking Battle."

Nimbus snorted in agreement.

# 21

Nimbus galloped through the open castle gate, his hooves clopping on the stone of the entrance, ringing out in defiance. Theo leaped to the ground and quickly extended his hand to help Arleta dismount.

At the touch of his hand, electricity shot through her.

Devdan came out of seemingly nowhere, raking his hands through his graying hair. The middle-aged elf was the picture of anxiety. "Sir, we've been looking for you," he said to Theo, taking every effort to catch his breath before his gaze caught on Arleta. "Sir?"

Unflinching, Theo grabbed Arleta's hand and pulled her protectively to his side. "Take us to her," he demanded, and a thrill tingled in Arleta's chest at his sudden authority.

"Sir," Devdan warned, "your mother is preparing for the finale. Folks are arriving from all over the Northern Lands, and we don't quite know where to put everyone."

"I don't care what she's doing," Theo snapped and lifted his chin to Arleta. "She's missing one contestant. How can the Baking Battle even start?"

Devdan pinched his lips together. "She will not be pleased."

"I don't *care* what she likes or not. Take us to her immediately, or I will make an even bigger scene than I'm making right now, and in front of all those arriving folk."

Nimbus blew out his nose and stomped his hooves on the hard stone, as if demanding Devdan to listen.

The old Arleta still wanted Theo to stop with this nonsense. Part of her whispered she wasn't worthy of all this attention. But his firm hand on her arm kept her balanced, physically and mentally. Almost like a lifeline. What had happened was wrong, and she refused to be a part of letting injustice continue.

Sighing, Devdan turned on his heel and waved for Arleta and Theo to follow, leaving Nimbus to find his way to the castle stables.

The entire way to Shalina's office, Theo didn't let go of Arleta's waist.

She never wanted him to let go of her.

"She's inside." Devdan raised a brow as he held his hand out to the ornate wooden door.

Theo wasted no time in taking the handle, throwing open the door, and ushering Arleta inside. "Mother!"

Shalina stood behind her desk and tripped a step back. She looked like a cornered animal as Theo slammed the door behind him. The elf blinked in stunned silence while her eyes wavered back and forth between her son and Arleta in a mix of rage and shock.

"You lost someone," Theo said and gently nudged Arleta forward.

"She broke *the rules*," Shalina said through her teeth.

Arleta shrank back just a little and fought the urge to hide behind Theo, but managed, "I did not."

Immediately, Shalina's gaze locked on Arleta like a bird of prey.

"You didn't actually *show* me where the contract states I broke any rules." Gathering any courage she had, Arleta moved from Theo and closer to the desk, ignoring the pounding in her heart telling her to escape.

"You signed the contract," Shalina insisted.

Arleta steeled herself and rooted her feet to the floor. "Yes, I signed the contract, but you did not show me the clause in which any rules were broken. You lied."

Shalina's nostrils flared as the elf gripped the edges of the desk, her knuckles white.

"You know it's true, Mother," Theo finally spoke again and held up the letter. "You also wrote *this* to ensure Arleta would leave and then imbued it with magic to make sure your point got across."

"I was trying to protect you," Shalina said to her son, her angry protests turned to almost pleading.

The same growl as at the carriage came from Theo's throat once more. "You were attempting to protect *your* interests, not mine. I am quite an adult at this point and am free to make my own life choices." The elf shifted to stand at Arleta's side. "But we're not here for me. We are here for Arleta's spot in the competition."

Arleta's heart fluttered at his words, slowing a fraction as Theo gazed at her.

"You cannot be her Fated," Shalina insisted, not letting go of the topic. "You have overstepped your bounds, and your involvement with her is threatening the Baking Battle."

Arleta stomped her foot. "There have been no bounds stepped over."

Quickly, Theo added, "She's right. We've done nothing that would compromise your precious competition. We have not completed the bond."

Arleta's chest flushed at his words. *Bond?*

Theo took a step back, clarifying, as if he's said too much. "We might never. That is *her* choice."

"Elves are only fated to elves," Shalina insisted, and the statement drove itself into Arleta's mind.

Theo ignored her words. "You *will* reinstate her into the Baking Battle immediately."

That time, Shalina said nothing, watching them both with wary eyes.

"Or." Theo stormed up to the edge of the desk, his face set with determination. "Or I will reveal everything you have done to attempt to rid yourself of her. Some will agree with your choices. I know that. But others will not, and it will stain your precious contest. There will be infinitely more uproar than simply if a magicless won the Langheim Baking Battle." The elf dropped his shoulders. "And when this competition is done, you will resign as head judge."

"I will *not*," Shalina said in a stubborn whisper.

"You *will*," Theo retorted, his voice firm. "You are the one who has overstepped your bounds. Do whatever damage control you need to so as not to create a scandal. But tomorrow you will make an announcement that you need a break from the rigors of the planning and judging. Thiggul and Gaia are perfectly capable of taking the lead and finding a new third judge in the Northern Lands."

Shalina puffed up for a moment like a scolded child, her

face twisting as if to argue. But instead of uttering a word, her shoulders slumped, and she sank into her seat. She heaved a sigh that echoed in the otherwise silent room, then finally glanced at Arleta. "The finale begins in three hours. I'll inform them that you've returned to claim your spot."

Before anything else could be said, both Theo and Arleta had dashed out of the office, the door thudding closed behind them. The moment they were alone in the corridor, Arleta threw herself into the elf's arms, laughter bubbling from her lips as he spun her around.

"I knew you could do it," Theo said, setting her down gently.

She cleared her throat and stepped back, her cheeks flushed pink. "That was you."

Theo shook his head, the wide smile never leaving his face. "I only revealed the truth. You're doing this because of your talent. You deserve it."

Before Arleta could speak, he grabbed her hand and tugged her all the way to the Elyilon Wing, ending at room 206.

Arleta realized that she still had the key to the room in her pocket. She pushed it into the lock and turned. Inside was Doli, on her stomach, sobbing into Jez's bed, and the fennex hurriedly packing her things.

Jez glanced up and a rare smile crossed her lips, showing off her fangs. "What are you doing here?"

"I'm bawling my eyes out!" Doli exclaimed, so caught up in crying that she hadn't even looked up at Arleta yet. "What do you think, Jez?"

"Not you, dwarf. Arleta is back." Jez half chuckled, half growled in disbelief at Doli.

At that, Doli's head shot up, and her red and swollen eyes

grew what seemed to be two times their normal size. "Are you *back* back?"

Arleta's lips arched into a wide grin, and she held out her arms. "I'm back in the Baking Battle."

With a squeal of joy, Doli jumped to her feet and did a little dance right there on the top of the bed.

"Get *down*," Jez scolded, but her tone betrayed her affection.

Instead, Doli threw her arms around the fennex, who was next to the bed, and sobbed even louder. "Arleta's back!"

Both Arleta and Theo broke out in laughter as the fennex and dwarf tumbled to the ground in a messy heap.

"*Doli!*" Jez cried while Doli scrambled to her feet.

"I'm just so happy!" The dwarf left Jez on the ground with a half grin on her fennex face and ran over to Arleta and Theo, throwing her arms around both of them.

"Me too, Doli," Arleta admitted, her voice choking with emotion. "I hated leaving without saying goodbye." She lifted her eyes to Jez. "To both of you."

"We sort of missed you too," Jez said as she stood and checked her tail to make sure it was okay. "Now you need to get ready."

Theo stepped back from Doli's hug. "I need to go make sure everything is in order. I know I'm leaving you in good hands." He tipped his head to Arleta, his gaze lingering on her for a moment longer. "I'll see you soon."

"Yes. Soon," Arleta got out. Her voice was nearly breathless.

Theo hurried out the door and closed it behind him.

Doli threw her hands into the air the moment the door clicked as if to say something, but Arleta cut her off.

"I'm so sorry I wouldn't talk to you." Arleta bit her lip. "You got eliminated, and I made the entire thing about me when I should have been making sure you were okay."

Doli's eyes crinkled. "You're my friend who was hurting. I accept your apology." Her eyes danced with mischief. "Now, what in the stars is going on between you two?" The dwarf pointed to the door from which Theo had just left the room.

"Noth—" Arleta started.

"That's a load of horseshit," Jez said, plunking her bag onto her bed with a thump next to the part of the blanket stained with Doli's tears.

"What?" Arleta sputtered, a nervous flutter vibrating in her stomach.

Doli bumped her shoulder into Arleta's arm, a knowing smile tugging at her expression. "Well, it's not exactly how I would have put it but, yeah. That's a load."

Arleta eyed the two of them, not speaking and biting her lip until it stung.

Jez sauntered up to them, lowered herself onto Arleta's bed, and patted her hand as if to tell her to sit. "We have at least two hours before we need to get you down there for prep," Jez said, her voice unusually inquisitive.

Doli hopped up, eyes twinkling. "Yes, let's get it off your chest." She leaned in. "Tell us *everything*."

Forty-five minutes later, the story had stumbled out in a messy whirlwind of words and emotion. All the way from her parents' death, her life in Adenashire, the first time she saw Theo, the inn, getting her to the Battle, the *incident* in the garden, what Theo's mother had done, why she'd left and was back again.

The three friends found themselves flopped on the bed shoulder to shoulder, staring at the ceiling.

"All that," Jez groaned, "and you're still *just friends*?"

"Just friends," Arleta insisted, internally wanting it to be more, but she couldn't let that come into her realm of possibility. Not when then thought of ever losing him might be more painful than not having him at all.

Doli rolled over and propped herself up on her elbow. She smelled of cinnamon, ginger, and salty tears as she placed her free hand on Arleta's forearm. "You know you can let us in, right? There are people who like you just for you."

Arleta sighed, happiness tugging the corners of her lips. "And not just for my lemon bars?"

Her friends chuckled, and the sound was as sweet as sugar syrup.

"Well, lemon bars always help," Doli admitted.

Jez sat and pinched her lips together, her fluffy tail flicking from side to side. "Now let's go and kick Taenya's ass."

# 22

Arleta's knees shook as Doli and Jez led her down a less frequented staircase to avoid the crowds gathering at the castle for the finale. Along the way, Doli went on about something the entire way down, but Arleta could make very little of it out. And once they arrived, they found the entire lower level teeming with spectators from every corner of the Northern Lands.

There were elves, of course, dressed in their finest, but also minotaurs, halflings, dwarves, and so many other representatives. Arleta could hardly believe that, at least in part, they were all there for her. News of having a magicless in the Baking Battle had definitely spread across the land and apparently had brought enormous crowds to the finale.

After pushing through the crowd, they made their way toward the holding room, where most likely Taenya would be waiting. A meeting Arleta didn't exactly relish the thought of. In the arena was one thing. Being alone in a room with the elf was quite another. A knot of dread twisted in her stomach.

Arleta kept her eyes down, hoping no one would recognize her and she could simply get into the room unnoticed.

However, the stars had other plans.

"Arleta! Arleta!" two youthful voices chimed in unison, and Arleta brought her gaze up to find the source.

Before her were the twin fauns, Rhegea and Ronorae, whom she and Theo had met on the road before arriving in Langheim. They tugged their father along behind them, as well as a lady Arleta had not met yet.

With a friendly wave, Arleta smiled.

"This is our mother!" Ronorae announced as the family reached Arleta, Jez, and Doli.

The feminine faun gently dipped her head in a polite bow. "I'm Ginia, and I've heard nothing but stories about how you and the elf rescued them from their cart accident."

Dreap joined his wife. "Mostly from me," he joked, and she smacked him on the shoulder playfully. "Really, when the kids heard you were in the finale, we all knew we had to come."

Arleta blushed. "You'd do that?"

"Of course," the mother faun said. "This is the most exciting event in our lives in a long while."

"These are my friends from the Baking Battle," Arleta said and gestured to Doli and Jez. Then she leaned in to whisper, "And between us, they make amazing pastries too."

Doli had a wide smile overtaking her face, and Jez…was just Jez.

"So nice to meet you all." Doli thrust out her hand to the twins, who took the friendly gesture with gusto.

After the handshaking, Rhegea held out a parchment program to Arleta, along with a charcoal pencil they'd stowed in their pocket. "Will you sign it?"

Arleta graciously accepted the pencil and paper. She signed her name under the place that listed her participation, the charcoal softly scratching against the rough parchment texture.

"Thank you, thank you!" they both said, hopping up and down in unison.

Dreap patted Arleta on the shoulder. "Thank you for taking the time. We're going to let you all go now."

"*Aww*," the twins moaned.

"Let's go find the candy seller," their mother suggested, and any lingering frowns turned upside down.

Waving their goodbyes, the faun family disappeared into the throng of spectators.

With an air of pure delight, Doli threw her hands to her cheeks and looked at Arleta. "You have admirers."

Arleta chuckled, but immediately caught sight of two large, green figures. "Verdreth, Ervash!" she shouted without thought, eagerly waving them over.

The two orcs easily made their way through the crowd, and Arleta raced to embrace them both.

"I've missed you so much!" She threw her arms around Ervash's broad form first and then Verdreth.

"This is new," Ervash said, a hint of jest in his deep voice.

Arleta backed away from the two of them. "I'm so glad to see you here." There were so many things she wanted to tell them, about the adventures she'd had, the friends she made, but before she could get anything out, a gong sounded, followed by an announcement for spectators to take their seats.

Quickly she turned to Doli and Jez arriving at her side. "These are my fathers," she blurted. "Can you both sit with them to watch?"

"What...*what* did you say?" Verdreth barely got the words out and moisture immediately filled his eyes while he tugged Ervash closer.

"You heard me." Arleta hugged them again. "Now go get your seats before all the good ones fill up."

Doli and Jez flanked the two orcs, who had taken each other's hands, and showed them the way toward the seating.

The dwarf turned back to Arleta, her eyes blazing with confidence. "You've got this!"

Arleta smiled but blew out an audible, nervous breath as they left. The space was nearly cleared, and she made her way to the waiting room, where an elf stood guard outside.

"I'm Arleta Starstone." It was all she needed to say. The elf nodded and opened the door.

Sure enough, when Arleta entered the waiting area, Taenya was already there. But instead of meditating like she'd done before round one, she was pacing the room, beads of sweat falling down the sides of her face. Under her arm was a notebook, not unlike Jez's, its leather cover worn from use. Arleta had not seen the elf with it before.

Just the sight of her made breathing difficult for Arleta, like all the air had been sucked from the room.

"I thought you'd left?" The elf's voice cut through the stillness. Her hair was tied up in a tight, practical bun, and she wore a pair of black fitted pants and a matching shirt.

Arleta pushed the door shut behind her, her fingers trembling. "Um, that was a misunderstanding."

"Well, Shalina was angry." Taenya abruptly stopped walking

to sink into a chair up against the wall. Quickly, she pulled a pencil from her pocket and opened the notebook.

"I'm sure she was." Part of Arleta wanted to spew out the entire story, but she was pretty sure Taenya wouldn't care, and if she did, the chaotic nature of the situation would likely make her feel even more stressed than she already looked.

"You're lucky she didn't kick you out."

Arleta bit back the truth. She pulled out her pocket watch and glanced at the time. The competition would begin in less than half an hour. The muscles in her back tightened at the thought—so many people would be watching her every move.

She traced her finger around the glass of the clock face, drawing it all the way up to the top and stopping. "You know you don't have to do everything in life you're expected to do."

The words slipped from her mouth, as spontaneous as they were sincere. Arleta's gaze remained transfixed on the ticking clock hands, her voice filling the room with an echo of her own uncertainty.

Taenya scoffed, not looking up from her notebook. "And what do you know about expectations, human? We elves have a reputation to uphold."

Arleta's heart clenched. "I know that I have to work twice as hard to get half as far as elves or dwarves or anyone with magic for that matter. No one expects me to do that."

The elf glanced up from her notes, regarding Arleta with an expression of curiosity.

"The place I live, Adenashire… I've lived there my entire life, but I'm not sure I've really appreciated it until I came here. It's quiet most of the time, and yeah, I'd love to start the bakery on the corner I've always dreamed about. Get to share my 'little dash of magic' with more people."

"Your what?"

Arleta shrugged. "It's what I call the extras I add to my bakes. The sea salt tops on my chocolate chip cookies, different savory herbs in sweet desserts." She didn't really know why she was sharing all her secrets with Taenya, but maybe the elf needed someone to be real with her for once.

"Hmm" was all Taenya answered.

"Anyway," Arleta said, "Adenashire is far from perfect, but it holds people who want me to succeed."

"Like those two orcs out there?" Taenya asked, her voice holding a shard of hidden interest in her tone.

Her question made Arleta pause for a moment. Taenya had been watching her and who she was with. "Yeah. My fathers are amazing. Before this week, I kind of never admitted how amazing they really are. Sometimes it's the people that make a place a home."

"I don't have that," Taenya admitted and then tightened her jaw as if she wished she could take the words back.

"Maybe you just don't have it *yet*," Arleta offered, soft warmth in her words. "I used to believe the same about myself, but it was right in front of me all along."

Taenya scoffed and slammed her book shut with a quick snap. "Don't you try to get into my head. I have a life you're never going to understand. We're *not* alike."

Arleta tensed. "I wasn't trying to say we were."

Taenya scoffed and waved a dismissive hand. "Let's just get this damn thing over with."

As she said the words, the door leading into the arena creaked open, and Devdan appeared. His expression was blank of any emotion. The noise of the crowd for the finale seeped in behind him, interrupting the quiet of the room and breaking the friction of the competitors.

"It's time for you both to find your places," the elf said.

# 23

The arena had transformed into a glittering spectacle. The workstations, pared down to just two and placed side by side with only a few steps between them, seemed impossibly far away. Had the arena always been this big?

Arleta squinted up at some sort of fairy lights lighting up the space and then struggled to see if she could spot the orcs or her other friends in the audience, but it was too bright. All she could make out above the figures were the sparkling fairies flying excitedly over the packed audience, dropping something that brought thrilled cheers from the crowd. The sheer number of bodies was overwhelming, and a shiver traveled the length of her spine, but based on how many she'd glimpsed in the holding areas and corridors, she felt she should have been more prepared. Looking up at the stands, it seemed like thousands.

It may not have really been that many, but in Arleta's mind it felt that way. She wrapped her arms over her stomach for a second to quell the tide of nervous energy, but the gesture only amplified her growing anxiety and likely made her appear vulnerable, so she quickly dropped her hands to her side and straightened, trying her best to mimic Taenya's confidence.

Taenya, with a plastered-on smile, walked a few paces ahead of Arleta. Arleta was keenly aware the expression was a little too polished to be genuine. The elf held her arms in the air, giving off the same confident vibes as she had the first day of the competition. This was not the same person who'd been in the waiting room with Arleta a few moments before. Taenya was clearly confident in her baking ability, but in herself, her choices, her life? Arleta questioned that about the elf. Everything she'd seen pointed to the fact that the elf was unhappy.

Maybe she was reading too much into it, putting too much of herself into Taenya's experience, but everything in her gut told her that she was right.

And as for Taenya's future? This competition had been her identity for the last several years. Likely, if she won, she'd be invited to judge in the next year's competition. But from what she'd said in the waiting room, she didn't even want to be here. Would she want to come back of her own accord, or her brother's?

Arleta's neck tensed. But if she lost? By now everyone in the arena knew Arleta was magicless, and what if a two-time champion elf lost to her?

Would that even be possible?

She shook herself from her thoughts. This wasn't even her business or what she should focus on at the moment.

The sound of the crowd rushed back to her ears. The elf still had her hands in the air, playing to the crowd.

But they were chanting and cheering *Arleta's* name.

Arleta's stomach dropped to the floor just as Taenya took her place. The elf had dropped her hands to her sides, her stage smile replaced with a glare that was quickly masked.

Arleta gulped at her own station, her throat suddenly as dry as breadcrumbs, then she smiled and gave a small, forced wave to the audience as the cheers continued.

Luckily, the music began, and Arleta's attention immediately flipped to the small group of musicians off the side of the baking stage and then to Naexi Miraven. As the melody soared, the crowd finally hushed while the host entered the arena and stepped onto a small, round stage.

Arleta's eyes finally adjusted to the bright lights, and she could make out familiar faces in the crowd: the orcs, Jez and Doli, and Theo had joined them as well. Seeing the elf brought with it a strange sense of nervousness and calm. Doli raised up in her seat and waved enthusiastically and seemed to encourage Jez to give a single wave, followed by a pinched expression. In stark contrast to her friends, and not far away from them, was Taenya's brother, Vesstan. But instead of his focus on his sister, his attention lay buried in a piece of parchment, his indifferent demeanor suggesting it was much more important than what his sister was doing.

Arleta's eyes flipped back to her friends, who seemed more like family than Vesstan ever would be with Taenya.

Arleta forced herself to focus back to the present as a large table of cakes was wheeled out in front of the audience, fairies flying above it, creating small, brilliant fireworks like magic over the display as the crowd oohed and aahed.

The table was loaded with cakes that looked like they had sprung from a confectioner's dream. Cascading ripe and juicy fruits, piped chocolate, and fluffy white frosting adorned the cakes with exquisite decorations that looked almost too beautiful to eat. Although she hadn't heard the announcement, Arleta was pretty sure she'd be making a showstopper cake that day.

Arleta just kept a stiff smile on her face and tried to concentrate on Naexi, who was dressed in a long gown with flared sleeves with cupcakes embroidered on them. The elf used her hands to speak, so the cupcakes seemed to fly all over the place.

After the judges entered the arena to thunderous applause, Naexi revealed the challenge. This time there would be no limits on the ingredients. There were two of every choice. This round was focused on presenting the best bake possible without the pressure of ingredient scarcity. There were no tricks or roadblocks other than limited time, which seemed fair enough for even the most complicated bakes.

Now Arleta knew Taenya was more than a competent cake baker. In her initial signature offering in round one, she'd received the highest score of all the competitors for her multi-layered cake decorated with an elven forest. A sliver of doubt flickered at Arleta's mind, wondering if the choice to have the final round be cake was intentional, but she cast it aside. *She* knew how to make a damn good cake too, and with her "little dash of magic" box at her disposal, she had a very good chance at taking the grand prize.

Her shoulders rose with pride. Something had changed in her.

With the crowd cheering, the bell rang for the final round of the Baking Battle to start.

Quickly, Arleta dug through her secret ingredients box, pulling out a fragrant, perfect bunch of rosemary tied with twine. She set it aside and performed a quick inventory of her base cake ingredients.

Her mind crystallized with her baking plan.

A multilayered vanilla cake with cream cheese frosting generously filled with rosemary-infused blackberry jam. The top would be piled high with juicy, fresh blackberries.

The cake had been her father's favorite. Every year, minus the rosemary, her mother would make this cake to celebrate their wedding anniversary. Arleta clearly remembered standing at the kitchen counter on a chair and mixing the frosting. It took a lot of arm strength to get the frosting to the proper level of fluff, but once past a certain age, she was always determined to get it right—despite the muscle burn. Her arms tingled with nostalgia and readiness.

Her parents would be so proud of her. Not just for being in the top two of the Langheim Baking Battle, but for how deciding to make the journey had changed her in so many ways. Her heart warmed, but quickly went icy as she caught Taenya whooshing past her, her face hard and focused.

Arleta blocked the uncomfortable feeling in her chest from the sight of it, as well as the goings-on of the arena. She made her way to the pantries to gather her ingredients into a basket.

Blackberries.

Cream cheese.

With her breathing under control, she picked out the best of everything she could find. Out of the corner of her eye, she saw Taenya choosing red apples from a container and placing them into her basket.

But Arleta had no time to think about whatever Taenya was making. If she was going to win, she needed to stay focused on what *she* was going to make.

By rote, she brought out the bowls, ingredients, and saucepans, and began a meticulous dance with herself. This was a place she went often, even back in the cozy kitchen of her own home.

Baking had always been her safe space, before and after her parents had died.

Especially after her parents had died.

The oven was preheating while the fruit and sugar sat boiling on the stovetop. Arleta mixed the cake batter with a long wooden spoon in a large bowl in front of her. She felt the pull of the thick liquid and waited for just the right amount of resistance, telling her it was ready to pour into waiting, oiled pans.

Just after she placed the cake batter into the oven, she returned her attention to the blackberry jam, stirred it, and pushed the pan off the heat to cool.

A fairy was immediately flying over her head. "Need it cooled?"

Arleta bit her lip for a second and stirred the dark purple concoction. "Yes, please."

The fairy nodded and performed his magic, cooling and thickening the jam in seconds. Before he left, he flew a little closer and whispered, "You're my favorite this year." With that, and before Arleta could thank him, he flitted away toward the audience.

Arleta blushed slightly, but immediately refocused the positive energy and began working again. Her fingers curled around the wooden spoon as she whipped air into the fluffy frosting. Each stroke made her feel more determined, bringing with it a newfound sense of resolve.

Before she knew it, the cakes were out of the oven, fairy-cooled, and placed on the platter with several pieces of parchment underneath to keep the rotating serving platter clean.

As she began the assembly, Taenya caught her eye. She seemed to be ahead of the game, already putting the final touches on what looked to be a caramel apple cake taking form beneath her skilled hands.

Arleta smiled and went to work on her own labor of love, laying out each layer of cake, topping those with a generous brush of a simple vanilla syrup she'd made while waiting for her cakes to bake, then fresh jam, and finally the fluffy cream cheese frosting. The process was repeated until the cake had multiple layers of fragrant deliciousness.

Just like home. Exactly how she'd remembered it.

The remaining fresh blackberries garnished the top, mixed with just the right amount of jam to give them a beautiful sheen.

Finally, she gave her cake one last approving spin, then removed the parchment from the bottom.

It was perfect. *Exactly* the way she wanted it to be. Win or lose, the bake was a masterpiece of flavors and memories, just as she remembered them.

It was an embodiment of her journey thus far, the continued evolution of a little girl who used to stand on a chair in her mother's kitchen to reach the counter, all the way into the woman who now stood as one of the final two contestants of the Langheim Baking Battle.

# 24

The three judges approached the cloth-draped table where the two final impressive creations waited. Shalina hadn't looked at Arleta one time since the start of the judging.

Arleta tried to keep her attention trained ahead of her and off her friends up in the audience, but it was no use now that she had no baking to distract her.

Jez sat leaning forward with her elbows on her knees, her thick eyebrows nearly knitting *two* sweaters. Doli perched up on her knees in her seat, practically vibrating with excitement, while the orcs had their muscular arms around each other in a supportive stance.

And then there was Theo.

He had been the final encouragement for her to come to the Baking Battle. He may have had some ulterior motives, but she also was confident he had believed in her abilities. And just seeing him there made her heart do an uncomfortable little dance, so her eyes skimmed over to the now empty seat that had been filled by Taenya's apparently distracted brother before the start of the round, then landed back on her friends.

Afraid of catching their infectious nervousness, Arleta quickly cast her gaze to the ground in a futile attempt to keep her stomach from feeling worse than it already did.

The three judges circled the table, stopping at Taenya's entry like vultures sizing up a juicy morsel. The caramel apple cake's presentation was gorgeous. It boasted seven layers, and juicy, red-skinned apple slices were arranged in a circle on the outer edge of the cake's top. In the center, the thinnest of slices formed a delicate rose blossom. Gooey caramel drizzle trickled off the sides of the cake, somehow perfectly placed.

Quietly, the three leaned in together and whispered something Arleta could not hear.

A sidelong glance revealed Taenya was sweating, a tiny droplet slipping just past her pointed ear.

Gaia Thornage was the first to speak to the elf. "This is really lovely, Taenya, and it looks absolutely delicious. We're going to taste it now."

The audience hushed as Thiggul stepped to the table with his fork and knife and reached out to Taenya's creation. The dwarf cut the first slice, followed by the next two, and placed them on the waiting plates for the judges, who took them.

Each plunged their fork into the slices of cake and, almost in unison, took their first bite. At first, none of them gave any emotions away, and Arleta held her breath. But quickly Thiggul held his plate up in the air as if it were a trophy.

"This is *delicious*," he declared, a wide smile gracing his lips. "The cake is moist, baked to perfection. I thought the caramel drizzle might make the dessert too sweet, but not at all. I could eat two slices of this perfectly balanced cake, Taenya."

Taenya's shoulders dropped when, a moment before, they had nearly been at her ears. But there still were two more judges to speak.

Gaia tapped their fork on the side of their plate. "I couldn't agree more. The flavor is divine, and I could not ask for a better crumb."

Taenya breathed in deeply and quickly released the breath. "Thank you."

Of course, Shalina was the last to speak, and Arleta couldn't help but wonder if, with everything that had happened, Taenya's cake would always taste better to the head judge no matter what Arleta had crafted.

The elf judge savored a bite of the apple by itself, and then finally placed her fork on her plate. "I would proudly serve this at any gathering I hosted. This cake is nothing short of a masterpiece."

Taenya nodded and bit her upper lip. A slight smile worked its way at the corners of her mouth and her hands trembled as the praise seemed to sink in. It was obvious to Arleta that although the elf might not have wanted to be at the Baking Battle and deal with the stresses that came with it, she was proud of her work.

The elf glanced up to the audience, and Arleta followed her competitor's gaze to her brother's still empty seat. Her heart clenched.

"And next we have the blackberry jam cake, made by Arleta Starstone," Thiggul announced, drawing Arleta's attention back to her own judgment.

A few whoops came from the audience, and Arleta's eyes

went wide and looked in the sound's direction. It was from the twin fauns, who waved flags with golden cupcakes on them. Their mother quickly hushed her kids, but they kept waving the flags.

Gaia chuckled and raised their hand in the direction of the fauns. "I think it looks delicious as well, younglings."

This drew a ripple of laughter from the audience before Gaia's birdlike gaze softened and landed back on Arleta's creation.

Arleta's knees shook under her skirt while Gaia was the one to cut the cake and distribute the pieces. But as the griffiner did, Arleta found herself admiring the perfectly layered slices with a touch of awe.

The cake had turned out exactly how Arleta had wanted it. Multilayered with white frosting, pristine against the rich purple of the blackberry filling. The creamy frosting was smooth and tangy and not too sweet, a perfect balance to the fruit and vanilla cake flavors. On top was a perfectly placed pile of giant blackberries coated in a light layer of the jam and a mint sprig for garnish.

The three judges tasted the cake for what seemed like forever and gave Arleta's hands plenty of time to go clammy.

At that point, each of the judges said a few things, but Arleta only heard every couple of words. There were definitely good words in there: *creamy, perfect balance, delightful, fresh, tasted like spring.* Even Shalina had positive things to say before backing off and announcing that they would take a few minutes off to the side in private to complete the judging.

In the stillness of the hushed crowd, Arleta and Taenya simultaneously stepped back, as if the intensity of the moment demanded a mutual retreat of solidarity.

Minutes passed like hours, and Arleta finally glanced over at her elf competitor only to find Taenya's eyes already trained on her, seemingly filled with silent questions.

"You deserve it," Arleta quickly said.

Taenya narrowed her eyes. "I deserve what?"

"To have the life you want to lead, a place to call home," Arleta confessed, then quickly returned her attention to the already returning judges.

"If I could have the contestants step forward," Shalina announced. "We have decided on our winner."

Both Arleta and Taenya made their way to the judges.

"This was not a simple decision," Shalina announced while the audience hung on every word, "as both Taenya Carralei and Arleta Starstone both have some of the most incredible baking skills that these judges have ever seen. But today, one entry outshined the other." In her typical dramatic way, she let the suspense hang in the air for a heartbeat. "This year's winner of the centennial anniversary of the Langheim Baking Battle is… Taenya Carralei, three-time champion."

The elf's eyes became as big as the cake she had just baked, and she joined the judges to shake their hands. The crowd burst into applause, but there were likely a few of them that were more than a little disappointed.

Arleta gulped, but then moved to the side. She also noticed that her knees had stopped shaking.

The Baking Battle was complete. Arleta Starstone had *not* won.

And the reality was she barely felt disappointed about it.

A few minutes later, the eliminated contestants in the audience were invited to come down and sample the entries. Not long after that, Doli and Jez were at Arleta's side.

"Are you okay?" Doli grasped Arleta's hand while Jez hung back a bit, a slightly deeper than normal scowl on her face.

"I'm totally fine," Arleta assured her, drawing her friend into a warm hug.

Jez patted Arleta on the shoulder but eyed her friend strangely. "I'm going to get our cake." Before they could say anything, the fennex was off and in line.

"Well, there's no way her cake was better than yours," Doli huffed, her indignation clearly evident.

Arleta wrapped her arm around the dwarf's sturdy shoulders and chuckled softly. "I love how wonderfully biased you are."

Doli burst into tears and grabbed her friend around the waist and squeezed. By the time she'd finished, Jez was back with their sample plates and handed them to each of her friends.

The dwarf took the plate and wiped away her tears.

Arleta was the first to take a bite of the caramel apple cake. It really was amazing, like joy on a fall day wrapped in a sun-drenched caramel blanket.

Ever loyal Doli pushed Taenya's cake aside, not even tasting it. Instead, she took a big bite of the blackberry jam cake. "It's rewy gud," she said with her mouth full.

"I know." Arleta beamed. "I'm a great baker. Second place."

Doli scoffed and munched on the rest while Arleta looked around to find Taenya. While many people seemed to offer her congratulations, her brother was conspicuously absent, and the elf didn't have any friends in the competition.

But before Arleta could give that any further thought, she noticed Jez, who had skulked over to her baking station. With her plate still in hand, she gazed over the bowls and leftover ingredients waiting to be cleaned up.

In an unusually brisk move, Jez abandoned her plate and made a beeline for Arleta and Doli.

"What's up with you?" Doli asked as the fennex arrived.

"I need to talk with Arleta," Jez said, her voice curt. "In private."

"About what?" Doli said.

But Jez was already tugging her away, and the dwarf's question remained unanswered.

"Why don't you take some cake up to the orcs and Theo," Arleta called before Jez yanked her from the celebration and pulled her into the privacy of the hallway.

The change in atmosphere left Arleta's ears ringing. "What's wrong?" she started, her voice echoing in the corridor.

"You did that on *purpose!*" Jez hissed, leaning in closer while keeping her tight grip on Arleta's arm.

Arleta's stomach turned at the words, fearing the worst, that Jez suspected her motivations. "What did I do?" She tried to deflect, but it was a weak defense against Jez's unexpected onslaught.

The fennex's eyes narrowed, and she bared her fangs. "You allowed Taenya to win, that's what!"

Arleta stuffed her hands into her pocket. "I don't know what you're talking about."

Jez's nostrils flared and her tail lashed in agitation behind her. "I tasted your cake. You didn't use the rosemary in the jam. It was right there at your station, and the bunch was completely unused. You had it, I saw it. That was your 'magic' ingredient, and you *didn't use it!*"

The accusation left Arleta silent. The reality was that she *had* forgotten her herb infusion on purpose. She wasn't even going to try to convince Jez otherwise. When she had decided to skip the rosemary, she didn't truly know if it would cause her to lose, but she knew the choice to use herbs, or to mix savory with sweet, like the salt on her cookies, made her baking unique.

So it had been a risk, but she hadn't anticipated anyone else noticing it.

"After everything that's happened this week, Arleta," Jez said, her tail still sharp with irritation at her friend, "you just back off and offer her the prize for no reason when you could have won!"

The last word echoed in the hall.

Arleta gulped under the weight of Jez's scrutiny. In the past, it might have broken her, but she steeled herself and looked Jez in the eye. "That is how the cake was supposed to be, the way my mother made it. It was the right choice." Arleta paused for a second, holding her friend's gaze. "And I *did* win."

The fennex furrowed her brow in confusion and stepped back, her leather boots thudding against the stone. "Are you feeling okay? Was the oven too hot? Because you definitely did *not* win."

"I *did*," Arleta insisted, her voice carrying with unwavering conviction. "I'm headed back to Adenashire with a completely different outlook on life." Tears burned at the corners of her eyes. "I'm not there yet, but I'm on the way to learning who I am, to knowing I matter simply because I'm me. I have people in my life who don't care that I don't have magic. They care about me. They want me to succeed." She eyed her friend. "People like you."

Jez's face dropped with sudden understanding.

"And despite the looks of it, Taenya has no one," Arleta said. "Truth be told, she and I are evenly matched in the kitchen. I'm not going to deny that. Maybe I left it out on purpose to take away an edge this round, but I don't regret it." Arleta tightened her fists slightly. "And beating her, then gloating in her face that I have all of you *and* the title. No. So I'm glad she won. She's not the horrible elf everyone thinks she is. She has feelings too."

"And by doing that, you also gave up the prize money," Jez said, her fluffy tail now hanging and touching the ground. "How will you get your bakery? You're back where you started."

"No." Arleta shrugged, hope tugging at the corners of her lips. "That's going to work out. Not right away, but it will. And if it doesn't, something else will. I already have you all, and for now, it's enough."

The two stood there looking at each other for what seemed like an hour to Arleta until Jez outstretched her arms and brought her friend into a rare embrace. "As frustrating as it is, I'm definitely getting used to how annoying you are."

Arleta squeezed the fennex. "Back at you."

Heavy footsteps sounded behind them. "*There* you are," Verdreth said, and they both released the hug and turned to him. "We're all going to Theo's home to celebrate."

Theo. There was a topic in which Arleta did not feel nearly as confident.

❖

Forgoing a party at the castle, the group met up at Theo's cottage and were seated around a long, rustic table just to the side of his garden. On top of it was a feast of cured meats and fresh vegetables and fruits from his garden. Their aromas wafted into the air, a mix of spice and earth. Magic-fueled lights twinkled and made the place as enchanting as any ball held at the castle.

Theo, Ervash, Verdreth, Doli, and Jez sat laughing and deep in conversation while Arleta and Faylin were in the garden.

Faylin lounged atop the same bench Arleta and Theo had sat

on the last time she'd been there. Occasionally, his tufted ears would twitch when the laughter got a bit too loud. The lynx seemed to want to be at the party but still keep his distance.

Instead of sitting with the group, Arleta ambled through the rows of plants with a drink in her hand. She still didn't regret leaving the rosemary out of her jam. That said, she was already on her second glass of wine to stave off the knowledge that this would be her last night in Langheim.

Jez had promised not to tell what Arleta had done, and Doli had gotten too swept up in the excitement to ask why Jez had needed to speak with her.

Faylin's raspy voice met her ears. "You seem different from the last time you were here."

Arleta turned and found the forest lynx directly behind her. She flinched.

"Sorry," he apologized, his blue eyes reflecting a tinge of remorse under the light. "I forget not everyone is used to my silent approach. It took Theodmon some time to adjust as well."

Arleta relaxed and reached her hand out to a bunch of min-iature tomatoes growing directly to her side. "Different how?"

"Hum…" The cat thought for a moment, a purr rumbling in his throat while he extended his claws into the soil, then retracted them. "Some of your scents are more relaxed, while others are a tangle of knots."

Arleta chuckled. "Sounds about right."

"You don't wish to be Theodmon's mate?" The cat was as direct as a winter's wind, and Theo was right that felines didn't mince words—at least this one.

Her cheeks heated instantly. "He told you?"

"Not in so many words," the lynx said, half closing his eyes. "I've simply known Theodmon for a long time, and that elf has been searching for his Fated for all of it. Our connection is strong, so I sensed the change in him the night he first brought you to the cottage."

"I'm not his Fated, Faylin," Arleta said with a nervous chuckle.

Faylin sat, his tail swishing behind him against the soil. "He believes you are."

Arleta took a sip of her wine, the fruity notes dancing on her tongue. "Well, he's wrong, and it's not a simple matter of choice. And I certainly can't just pretend." She gazed up at the sky, not wanting to look him in the eye in case he'd catch the fact that her statement might only be to convince herself. "It has to be written in the stars or something."

"If you say so." The cat rose to his four paws. "You have every right to make your own choices. Though perhaps you are allowing fear of the unknown to guide your path instead of simply trusting that love is not up to the stars." Faylin turned and sauntered off without a response from Arleta. "I still like you," he said as he jumped back on the bench and laid down for what looked like another nap. "Even if you are as stubborn as they come."

Arleta blinked, her thoughts scattering until her senses returned.

She had changed. If Theo was truly her Fated, she would know it. She wouldn't have these doubts.

Would she?

As Doli's musical laughter met her ears, she turned back to the table filled with her friends.

"You have a bookstore?" the dwarf's animated voice rang out, directed at Verdreth. "How wonderful! I'd love to come and see it."

At the head of the table, Theo sat with a soft smile on his face, engaged in the conversation. Arleta couldn't help but be drawn back to the group.

She quickly glanced back at the lounging feline.

What if it were true that accepting that she was fated to the elf simply came down to a willingness to just say yes?

# 25

The next day, the plans had been settled. After multiple bottles of wine, they'd decided Doli would head back to Dundes Heights to gather her possessions and tell her family that she would embark on a new adventure of moving to Adenashire. Before Arleta had the chance to mention it might be a hasty decision, the orcs had agreed to rent her a room above Verdreth's cozy bookshop. The dwarf, although unsure of her exact plans in Adenashire, was determined to figure it all out. And, in all honesty, Arleta was happy to have her around for more time, no matter how long it would be for. Jez was still on the fence about her next move but was considering following Doli just to find out what might happen.

Verdreth and Ervash had wanted to take a few more days in Langheim for a getaway, and since Theo needed to pick up his cart at the Double Unicorn, he had volunteered to take Arleta all the way back to Adenashire. Plus, he generously offered to let the orcs stay at his cottage—with Faylin's permission, of course.

Before she left the castle, and with Faylin's words heavy on her mind, Arleta found her way to the library Doli had spoken of. The door was open, and inside she found row upon row of books in the large space. The high ceilings were lit by the warm morning light coming in from the enormous bay of windows at the edge of the room.

"May I help you?" an elf dressed in a pair of velvet pants and a fitted silk shirt asked as they came around a shelf of books labeled CREATURES OF THE NORTHERN LANDS.

Arleta winced. She had hoped to simply slip in and out unnoticed. "Um…" She smiled uncomfortably as the elf awaited her answer. "I'm about to leave and realized that I didn't get any information about the elven way of life."

The librarian pointed to their right. "There's an entire section on elven culture right there. You are free to browse but not to take anything."

Arleta nodded. "Thank you." She thought about specifically asking about the fated concept but couldn't get her mouth to form the words. And even if she had, the elf disappeared as quickly as they had appeared, leaving her alone again with the books.

Knowing she didn't have a lot of time before it would be time to leave, she walked over to the section and scanned over the titles engraved on the book's spines. Finally, one caught her eye: *Elves and Their Fated.*

Arleta's stomach fluttered at the sight of it, and she reached out for the book. Quickly, she opened to the contents and scanned the chapter titles. The Stars and Their Role in Fate… History of the Fated… She was looking for something that might quickly show that, in fact, an elf could be fated to someone other than another elf.

At the bottom of the list, she found it.

Fated Anomalies.

She quickly flipped to the chapter and scanned over the text and soon found what she was looking for.

*It is highly unusual for the gift of a Fated bond to be bestowed on anyone outside of the elven people. There have been only three known possible cases in the history of the woodland elves.*

*Possible.*

At the end of the sentence there was a reference to the back of the book, which Arleta quickly flipped to.

"Theo is looking for you," Jez said from behind her, and Arleta quickly slammed the book shut.

"Oh. Okay. I'm all ready." Arleta stuffed the book back into the empty slot on the shelf and turned to the fennex.

"You sure about that?" Jez asked, raising a brow.

"Yes." She hurried to her friend's side to go and gather her things and say goodbye to Doli.

❖

With both Theo and Arleta perched on top of Nimbus, the journey had been quiet. Arleta didn't quite know what to say to Theo, even with the information in the book *sort of* confirming there was a *possibility* of them actually being fated, though the chances were incredibly low. No matter how much she wanted him, it could hurt her in the end.

She knew that and knew she shouldn't even have gone to the library. That word, *possible*, had simply made her thoughts that much more clouded.

Nimbus walked more slowly than normal, as if he felt the weight of Arleta's choices.

"I imagine you'll be leaving soon after you drop me off?" Arleta asked.

Theo took his time before he answered. "I thought I might stick around for a bit. Stay at the inn. Faylin was fine with it if I was gone for a while, and I have someone who can care for the garden."

Arleta's stomach did a flip-flop.

"Unless you don't want me to stay," Theo added, his words hanging in the air.

"I think it's fine," Arleta said, her voice soft. "Doli will be coming next week, maybe Jez. Another familiar face will likely do them good. Maybe you can even lend a hand at the market again." She chuckled, but knew the market also meant she was going to have to deal with Mr. Figlet again.

"I'd like that, actually."

His words warmed her heart more than she wanted to admit.

They rode on for a few more miles before Arleta spoke again.

"I can't promise you anything more than friendship, Theo." The desire for more was there, but to step over that line? Arleta wasn't ready.

"I know." His answer was quick. "I accept that."

The hours went by, the distance blurring beneath Nimbus's steady but seemingly slowed hooves. By the time they reached the inn, it was somehow well past dinner, and stars twinkled in the sky. Arleta's eyes had grown droopy, and she shivered as the night air blew in chilly gusts against her skin. She started to realize how much the last week had really taken out of her both emotionally and physically. And, if she was honest with herself, she was still feeling the effects of too much wine the night before.

"I'm exhausted, and it's getting cold. Why don't we just stay the night here since there's no hurry to get me home," Arleta offered. "We'll just stay in the family quarters again. Hopefully, this time it will be a little quieter without the storm."

Theo agreed, and the two of them dismounted Nimbus. Before they entered, Theo led him into the barn for the night.

But when they got inside, the inn was not quiet. In fact, it might have been even more packed than the first time.

The two made it to the check-in counter, where the same dwarf as before waited. Quickly, Theo reminded him of the cart and paid for the rest of the storage.

"We'd also like to bunk in the family quarters again for the night," Theo added when the exchange was complete.

With a rueful shake of his head, the innkeeper's voice resounded over the familiar clamor. "I do apologize, sir. I remember the two of you bunking with the castors last time in the family bunks, but ye can either take the last single room, or I can't make accommodations. As ye can see"—his meaty hand performed a broad sweep of the reveling patrons—"we're full tonight on account of folks returning from the Baking Battle."

The entire scene felt slightly like déjà vu and yet was completely different.

Arleta's stomach clenched. The reality was she didn't mind spending the night in the same room as Theo—even *wanted* to—but the two of them could only remain friends. Despite what he had said to her, she knew in her heart he had a real Fated out there waiting for him, and she refused to take him from that. He'd been mistaken when he'd thought it was her.

As much as she had wanted it to be true, it could not be. She couldn't risk the pain of completely losing Theo if he were to find his actual Fated eventually.

Theo clenched his jaw and stared at the innkeeper for a few moments longer than was comfortable. "I could stay in the stalls with my horse, and..." He eyed Arleta, his brows furrowing slightly. "The lady should have the sanctuary of the room."

"That is yer choice," the dwarf drawled and plopped the room key into Theo's open palm.

"We don't have to stay," Arleta offered.

The elf spun to Arleta and held out the brass key. "There's no need to travel through the night. I'll see you in the morning."

Arleta held her breath, not taking the key. Guilt churned in her stomach for even considering letting Theo sleep in a barn. She couldn't take the room for herself.

Counter to Arleta's mounting apprehension, she took his forearm, and against her better judgment said, "You should stay in the room too. It's cold outside." Before he could answer, Arleta turned to the dwarf. "One room, but two beds, right?"

The innkeeper shook his head, and an amused smirk may or may not have briefly crossed his lips. "Nay. One bed."

Her stomach pinched. She wanted nothing more than to share a bed, and more, with Theo, and it wasn't as if he seemed to mind. The elf had gone as far as thinking they were fated.

Arleta gulped and said to Theo, "We're both grown-ups here. We can make this work."

After a few moments, Theo and Arleta trudged up the inn's rickety wooden stairs. Each groaning step wafted the musky smell of old cedar and dust into her nose. She was the first to get to the door and pushed the metal key into the keyhole and turned. When the creaky door opened, there in front of them was a bed lit by the lanterns in the hallway.

A small bed, and not much else.

Not even a window.

Her eyes widened at the sight, but she didn't let the churning in her stomach stop her from taking the needed steps into the room.

"Well, this is cozy," Arleta joked to lighten the mood, more for herself than Theo.

Theo rubbed his fingers together. Delicate wisps of green and yellow magic appeared over his palm, casting just the slightest ethereal light throughout the room.

Arleta veered left, and Theo went right around the daunting bed to a small lantern hooked on the wall. The spark of his magic lit the wick, and with it rehung, the lantern bathed the room in a tranquil, soft glow. As he closed the door, Arleta dropped her satchel on the floor and flopped on the bed.

"At least there's a chair," Theo said, still standing on the right side of the bed.

Arleta lifted her head. There was indeed a chair in the room's corner. A very *uncomfortable* ancient wooden one at that.

"I'll sleep there," Theo said and placed his bag down beside the seat. "It's only one night."

"*You* paid for the room." Arleta pushed herself up on her elbows, holding his gaze. "That means you should have the bed for the night." Soon after realizing that she'd already planted herself on it, her cheeks heated with embarrassment.

Theo eyed her. "No." With that, he plopped into the chair. It gave a groan of protest.

"That old thing will probably crumple in the middle of the night," Arleta chided. "We can both sleep in the bed. It's fine."

"I'm not sure if it's best," Theo said, gripping the arms of the chair as if for dear life.

"There's plenty of room." Arleta eyed the space next to her.

"And we're fully clothed, grown adults who should be able to handle getting a night's sleep in the same bed."

*Should* was the operative word.

But it sounded good enough, even if it were not the words her body wanted her to say. She scrambled to the top of the bed, pulled down the blanket, and slid under it. When comfortable, Arleta threw down the blanket on his side and patted it.

Theo grumbled and rose from the creaky chair. "You're sure about this?"

"I'm sure," Arleta said, steeling herself.

With that, he pulled down the covering and slid under, every move seemingly—and somewhat disappointingly—calculated as to not get too close. Before he completely settled in, Theo leaned forward with a puff of breath to blow out the lantern.

And the room went dark, save for the tiny sliver of light peeking from beneath the door.

Arleta lay there on her back with the warmth of Theo's body creeping in next to her. His scent that somehow that day was a mixture of cedar and vanilla settled in the back of her nose. She cleared her throat and turned away from him. Somehow her breath became slower and slower, and, despite everything, she drifted into slumber.

On the other side, her dreams took hold of her and brought her directly to a place where she'd been before. Arleta's breath hitched as she found herself in a flowy pink gown. Her palms moved up and down her thighs, taking in the soft velvet. She'd never felt anything more luxurious in her life. Overhead, the sky was caught in twilight, but with the Little Mouse burning bright above. Just as she had in Theo's garden, Arleta traced her finger in an invisible line to point out the trail of three stars forming the tail.

As her finger reached the end, it brought her gaze to the bay laurel arbor.

With Theo standing underneath.

Waiting.

◆

Arleta's eyes fluttered open as she lay in the soft, snug bed. For about one second flat she hadn't a care in the world, as if everything in the world was suddenly gentler, comfortable, right.

That was until she realized where she was and what she was doing, and the real world plowed into her mind.

Sometime in the middle of the night she'd rolled completely over onto Theo's side of the bed, which took effort, since the elf was entirely perched on its edge, likely as to not invade Arleta's space during their sleep.

Horrifyingly, she was practically spooning him, her arm snaked around his chest in a careless sprawl. The elf's breath flowed steadily in his deep sleep, completely undisturbed.

Arleta had told Theo that joining her on the bed was fine. She'd also never imagined in a hundred years that she'd end up on his side in such a compromising position.

What had she done in her sleep?

And suddenly, her dream of Theo hit her, as if her body wanted all the yeses.

"It was just a dream. That's it," Arleta muttered under her breath.

She stiffened and delicately unwrapped her arm from their warm tangle, slowly rolling back to her side of the bed without waking the miraculously still-sleeping elf.

Just as she was about halfway to her escape, he stirred,

yawned, and stretched. And gave zero indication that he knew only a second before that Arleta had nearly been on top of him.

"That was about the best night's sleep I've had in a long time." Theo's voice was thick with slumber as he sat up.

The room was still dim because of the lack of a window, the only light coming through the wide crack under the door. Arleta was glad for it since her ears and chest burned hot and likely bright red.

"Mm-hmm," Arleta mumbled, already at the far side of the bed with her body upright and her legs dangling over the floor. Quickly, she glanced back at the elf and gulped. There was still enough light not to miss the sculpted shape of his chest clearly visible under his billowy, linen shirt, and the lines of his square jaw.

Quickly, she tore her thirsty gaze away from those off-limits things and grappled for her bag to head back to Adenashire as soon as possible.

"We should get going," she managed, and he nodded.

But getting Theo out of her mind was going to prove harder than Arleta had hoped.

# 26

Two weeks had passed since Theo and Arleta had returned to Adenashire when a letter had arrived announcing that both Jez and Doli would be coming to town.

And their stay would be indefinite.

The pair had both confirmed they wanted something new, and, as Verdreth had promised, the place over his bookstore was available. In the days leading up to their arrival, Arleta and Theo had made sure the two-bedroom apartment was ready.

Fresh flowers and herbs sat next to the bedsides, and a platter of cookies and pastries Arleta had baked the night before—and well into the morning—waited in the small, shared kitchen of the upstairs apartment. Able to manage it with the extra silver she was earning at market now, since the news of her second-place win had spread, and a little extra from Theo's elven charm, she had taken several days off from selling just to greet her two friends on the road before arriving in the village.

Baking for the market could wait for a few days.

Arleta's feet could barely keep still before she had left her cottage to meet up with Theo that morning. On the way, the midafternoon sun blazed down on her head, but a slight breeze had picked up and cooled her body as she walked. Her heart fluttered with a mix of excitement and nervousness, but it wasn't only from the anticipation of seeing Jez and Doli. It was also from Theo's unwavering presence at her side.

Since their return, they had also settled into a delightful routine. Daily, before the market began, Theo would arrive at Arleta's doorstep and help her bring her goods to sell. Mr. Figlet had long past realized Theo was *only* Arleta's assistant, so the booth price had gone up some from the three silver Theo had been offered, but only to four. His excuse to Theo was that the first time had only been an "introductory price." Arleta's booths tended to be in better locations now as well, but likely only because even Mr. Figlet had to know that the market patrons were interested in the second-place winner of that year's Baking Battle.

In the evenings, Theo had come over for dinner out in the garden where the two of them had planted the iweocot pit she had pocketed and saved when they'd first arrived in Langheim. Sometimes he'd prepare her a quiet meal since she was usually too distracted by a new recipe to sell at the market. Other days, the orcs would invite them over for something delicious Ervash had created.

In all honesty, Arleta regretted the years she'd spent declining the orcs' offers to keep her fed. The two really were reveling in their newfound title of her fathers, and she was glad, since there was room enough in her heart for the memory of the parents she'd lost *and* the orcs she had found.

Not once had Theo brought up the topic of their fated connection, but she couldn't get it off her mind. At least according to Faylin, Theo genuinely believed that Arleta was his Fated. And maybe that was all it took if she wanted it too.

But if the lynx was wrong?

The thought was painful for Arleta.

What they had now worked.

She gazed up at Theo as he walked next to her in silence, and heat burned at her cheeks.

Because fated or not, maybe platonic did not work.

She'd begun dreaming about him, and although sometimes the dreams were mundane.

Some were...*not.*

In her dream version of meeting under the laurel arch, they had done considerably more than just *meet.*

But it was much deeper than that. Each day they spent together, Theo had become infinitely more attractive to her. On the surface he was handsome, there was no denying that fact, but it wasn't even what was on the outside for her anymore. It was all the little things. How on the way to the Baking Battle, he'd taken the time to calm her when she'd panicked about the loss of her herbs, how he believed in her and put her first.

"Is the plan still to take them to the Tricky Goat for dinner after Doli and Jez settle in?" Theo asked, snapping Arleta from her thoughts.

"Yes," she said, stuffing her hands into her skirt pockets. "Verdreth and Ervash are coming too."

"I'm glad," he said. "The four of us can also take Doli and Jez on a tour of the village."

"Mm-hmm," she managed, but really she wanted to talk about something else. About them. "Theo?"

He opened his mouth to speak, but the sound of hooves cut him off. A carriage was approaching on the road, with Doli half hanging out the window, waving excitedly, while a clawed hand hung on to the side of her blouse, keeping the dwarf from tumbling out onto the road.

"Arleta! Theo!" Doli cried with excitement before Jez tugged her back inside the carriage.

"If you fall out," Jez's voice scolded from inside the cab, "I'm not cleaning up the mess!"

"They're here," Arleta said, almost forgetting what she had just wanted to say to Theo. Maybe it was best, since she might have said the wrong thing, whatever the wrong thing was in that situation.

"Whoa," the driver said and pulled on the reins to slow his two horses. The high, neat pile of trunks on the top wobbled slightly but stayed in place due to the sturdy straps cinched around them.

The carriage had barely come to a stop when the door flew open, and Doli leaped to the ground, bounding toward them with her arms wide open. She was, of course, dressed in a frilly pink dress, complementing her rich skin and loose coiled hair.

Arleta couldn't help but mirror Doli's excitement and flung out her arms. The dwarf grabbed both Theo and Arleta and pulled them into a tight embrace.

"I'm so excited to be here!" Doli's voice was muffled since her face was wedged between both of her friends.

Arleta squeezed her back. "Not as excited as I am."

In a considerably calmer fashion, Jez stepped from the carriage with two bags, one in her right hand, the other slung over her shoulder. "Hey, is it okay if we walk from here? I'm tired of sitting."

Arleta nodded. She didn't mind the walk either.

The fennex gave Arleta a quick smile, ran her hand through her messy white hair, then told the driver to continue to their destination without them to drop off the rest of their luggage. Arleta assumed the trunks must have belonged to Doli.

When he was off, the four friends began their trek to Adenashire, and somehow were pulled into two groups. Doli was up ahead with Theo, talking up a storm—mostly Doli, of course, but Theo didn't seem to mind from his engaged expression.

"So, why'd you decide to come?" Arleta asked Jez. "The letter didn't really say. Did Doli talk you into it?"

Jez hiked her satchel strap higher onto her shoulder. "Nope," she said. "It was the same as entering the Battle. I came here for me. I actually like myself better around you all."

"Really?" Warmth filled Arleta's chest at the idea their friendship meant as much to Jez as it did to her.

"Really." Jez kept her gaze on Arleta for a second, but quickly looked off into the distance, her furry ear twitching in a display of nonchalance. "But don't get a big ego about it or anything. I still find you all *incredibly* annoying. Just better than my family back home."

"It's a burden you simply must bear," Arleta said with a straight face, but her tone was teasing.

"You understand fully," Jez said. "That's why I like you."

"Even with the smell?"

Jez raised her brow. "Speaking of smell." She slowed her gait. "What are you going to do about the elf?"

The levity Arleta had felt only a second before dissipated in an instant. "What do you mean? Does *he* smell?" But she knew exactly what the fennex meant.

Jez stopped, her intense gaze fixed on Arleta. "Don't be ridiculous. He's in love with you, and you are with him. The scent of it is so overwhelming it almost makes me want to go back home."

"Shh," Arleta hissed at Jez. "We're not talking about it."

"What? It's not a secret." Jez gestured for her to keep walking.

By this time, Adenashire was in sight, and Doli was still up ahead with Theo, bouncing on her toes as if to get a better view.

"Let's just go," Arleta said a little too loudly. "We're almost there."

Theo glanced back at her and smiled, then returned his attention to Doli.

Arleta tried to make a break for it, but Jez had already ensnared her shirt and held her in place. "He's all in, you know."

"Everyone keeps saying that." Arleta sighed and twisted from the fennex's grasp. She tried to keep her voice down, but her proclamation came out louder than she intended. "Maybe *I'm* not."

It was a lie, but one that felt necessary.

Jez's sand-colored cheeks flushed pink, and she dropped her hands to her side. "Of course. I just thought—" She straightened and looked Arleta directly in the eyes. "Doesn't matter what I thought. You have a right to your own choices. I won't bring it up again unless you ask me to. I'm sorry."

From the look on Jez's face and the nervous twitching of her tail, Arleta could tell she was sorry. Despite her own churning stomach, she took the fennex's elbow and pulled her in close. "I accept your apology. Now, why don't you tell me any news outside of my love life or Adenashire that you and Doli heard along the way?" She quickly glanced up and found Theo was only a few steps away from them, and the realization that he could have heard what she said tightened her throat.

Arleta managed a small smile at the elf, which he returned. Maybe he hadn't heard.

Jez cleared her throat. "She left."

"Who left?" Arleta caught Jez's eye.

"Taenya. She left Langheim before I went back south." The fennex's expression was serious. "She took the prize money and disappeared. It was the talk of the castle. Her brother was furious."

"Where'd she go?" Arleta was truly curious, and she was glad not to be talking about her relationship with Theo anymore.

"At least from what I heard, nobody knew," Jez said and picked up her pace. "But let's put all that behind us and help me figure out how I'm going to manage living with Doli *full-time*."

Just as she said it, Doli let out a loud, sweet laugh as if Theo had just told her the funniest joke in the realm.

Arleta patted Jez on the arm and scanned over Adenashire. "I think you're going to manage just fine all on your own."

# 27

The village had not woken up yet, for the most part, and there was no market that day, but relaxing had never been Arleta's strong suit. She'd gotten up early to take a walk and get a few things done before she met up with her friends for lunch at the Tricky Goat.

Although the above was an excuse.

A week and a day after Jez and Doli had arrived, Arleta was drawn by an invisible force inside her. She stopped in front of the still-vacant storefront. It was the same one she had long hoped to secure and convert into a cozy bakery if she had won the Baking Battle. Her fingers traced the surface of the window and rubbed away the thin film of dust from the glass so she could get a better view inside.

It needed a *lot* of work. The place had been a café, not a bakery, so it would need multiple adjustments, as well as repairs. But she saw past any flaws and could nearly smell the sweet pastries baking, seeing how she would display them in the window in front of her on fancy platters.

She stepped back onto the cobblestone street and gazed up at the unassuming taupe building. "Someday," Arleta said with a sigh, carrying both dreams and some regret.

As the word hung in the air, a gnome pulled up on a cart led by a shiny black miniature horse. He shot her a cheery grin and tipped his hat toward Arleta. She barely noticed his gesture as she stole one last longing glance at her dream before moving on. But a clattering sound came from behind her, so she turned back to the gnome, who was climbing down from the cart and unloading a ladder and a large wooden sign covered in brown paper from the back.

Curious, Arleta stepped to the side to allow him to work. Soon, with a pang, she realized what was about to happen.

He had set his ladder directly under the empty hooks where the old café sign had hung. When it was secured on the cobblestones, he gathered the sign from where he'd leaned it up against his cart, climbed the ladder's rungs, and hooked the mystery plaque into place.

Arleta's stomach sunk all the way past her feet into the earth below.

Someone had rented or bought the space she'd wanted for her bakery.

She wanted to ask the gnome if he knew anything about it, but her voice was trapped in her throat. She could only watch, as if from outside of her body, as her "someday" receded into the pile of lost dreams.

"New business coming to town?" The unexpected alto voice came from behind her. Arleta nearly jumped out of her skin. That voice was one she had not expected to hear again.

Arleta spun on her heel to the transformed figure of Taenya.

The elf's auburn hair, previously flowing well past her shoulders, was cropped just above her chin, and her clothes were loose. Something in her expression told Arleta that Taenya could finally breathe. Gone were the deep lines of stress around her eyes.

"Um, I don't know," Arleta managed, confused and hesitant. "I was just walking by and saw this." Her hands shook as she gestured toward the sign. "Why are you even in Adenashire?"

Behind them, the gnome fiddled with something in the back of his cart while the tiny horse threw her head up in the air several times.

"I moved here," Taenya said simply. "I'm buying a little house just outside town."

Arleta's stomach dropped further into the earth as the puzzle pieces came together. "What?" Her eyes darted back to the sign swinging in the breeze. "Is this...*your* shop?"

"I bought it," Taenya admitted and walked over to the ladder positioned under the sign.

Arleta stood there, speechless. Had she misjudged Taenya so terribly that the elf would actually come to Adenashire to rub the loss of the Baking Battle in her face?

The elf raised her hands and placed them on either side of the paper covering the sign. She pulled it most of the way down, revealing the carved words inscribed on the sign's surface:

A Little Dash of Magic Bake Shop

Arleta's knees went weak, and her head spun, but somehow she managed to stay upright. Those words, that phrase, it was how she described *her* bakes. How could Taenya go and steal it? It was as if the earth was shifting beneath her.

But then Taenya pulled the rest of the paper off. At the bottom of the sign were smaller words:

## MASTER BAKER: ARLETA STARSTONE

Quickly, Taenya scurried down from the ladder and produced several sheets of paper from her pocket. "It's in your name, the contract." She held it out to Arleta. "You deserved to win the Battle. I know that. This bakery is meant for you."

"I...I don't understand," Arleta sputtered.

"You don't need to. But at the end, when everyone had left, I tasted your cake. It should have won." The elf smiled. "So all of it, every last brick, it's yours. All yours," Taenya announced, sincerity in her eyes like nothing Arleta had never seen before. "There's even extra funds built into the contract for the upgrade. Only the best."

Arleta was stunned.

Taenya continued, "I didn't need the gold, and I didn't care about my title or life back in Langheim. What I really needed was a change of scenery. A fresh start. So I came here. Adenashire sounded nice when you talked about it. Like home." She gazed back at the sign. "Also, I came here to buy you this bakery. You gave me a gift and I wanted to return the favor."

"Uh...um," was all she could get out. Her mind had gone completely blank. Her thoughts felt scrambled, a puzzle where the pieces refused to fit together. So Arleta stood there, mouth agape like a fish out of water, teetering on the verge of falling over. "I gave *you* a gift?"

Taenya rushed to Arleta's side and grabbed her elbow to keep her from tumbling. "The courage to be me instead of someone else's version," she hurried to answer.

Arleta blinked in disbelief.

"Are you okay?" Taenya asked. "Did I do the wrong thing?"

"*No*," Arleta blurted out, surprising herself. It was as if her heart was speaking before her mind could process the shock. In a fluid motion, she threw her arms around the elf, and words spilled from her mouth. "I'd like this very much!"

Taenya patted Arleta on the back and broke from her. "I'm so glad. How about we meet up later and figure out the details?" Without waiting for Arleta's answer, she started to turn away.

Arleta gazed down at the contract for a moment. "But running a bakery is going to take so much work for one person!"

The elf turned back and chuckled. "Yes, it will. And I believe you are just the person to do it."

"What if you helped me?" Arleta got out.

The elf eyed her for a long moment. "Are you offering me a job?"

Arleta nodded multiple times. "If you want it. I don't want to assume you ever plan to pick up a whisk again."

Taenya tipped her head in surprise as tears welled at the corners of her green eyes. "Thank you. Yes. I actually do love baking; I just want it to be on my terms. I'd love a job."

"You know what?" Arleta stepped back and looked the crying elf in the eye while a ridiculous idea mulled its way around in her mind.

But something in her middle told her that she had judged Taenya correctly before. She could do it again.

"I don't just need an employee. I think I really want a business partner." She smiled. "Know anyone who might be reliable?"

# 28

Hours before dawn, Arleta stood in the heart of what would become her new dream bakery. Several weeks had gone by since Taenya had offered it to her, and the renovations had just begun. The air carried the scent of dust mingled with the earthy aroma of slightly wet pine since there was a small leak in the roof. The kitchen and dining area, a nearly forgotten space, had been the site of a halfling's attempt at a café some time before and was now showing signs of disrepair.

She knew she didn't need to be there that early every day, but so much of her wanted to see every bit of the transformation. Arleta gazed around the empty space, imagining working with the dough and fashioning the pastries that would be placed in the eventually clean window of A Little Dash of Magic Bake Shop to tempt patrons. Just the thought of it made her feel whole again and close to the parents she'd loved and lost. Regaining the years wasted thinking she had to go it alone. Now she had friends to help and support her. Really, she'd always had that in the orcs, but she was finally willing to accept that they were not going anywhere if they had any say in it.

The light from the magic-fueled lanterns Theo had installed flickered across the room, somehow already making it feel comforting despite all the work ahead.

*Theo.*

Arleta inhaled a deep breath at the thought of his name. The elf had been staying at the Tricky Goat Inn since the Baking Battle had ended, but he still lived quite silver free in her mind. The dreams of him had not stopped since she'd allowed them free rein. She relished the time she spent with him in the night world, but she had not admitted it to the elf because…well… friendship was safer. She could handle that with him.

In reality, it felt like some cosmic curse that would never end.

Although she knew it was only her fear holding her back, not the stars.

As she cast those thoughts aside for a moment, she heard the bell from the front door of the bakery. Probably Taenya, since she often came in early to continue the renovation as well. The door shut and the tread of boots made their way across the floor.

"Is that you, Taen—" Arleta called, but when the door to the kitchen opened, it was not her.

It was Theo, dressed and ready for the day.

"Oh, hello," Arleta stammered. Heat climbed her neck and she quickly worked to straighten her blouse and skirt. The lights flickered slightly again as the elf walked through the door. "You're up early. Here to help?"

Theo stuffed his hands into his pockets, weariness settling

into his eyes. "Nimbus and I are going to head back to Langheim. We're all packed and ready."

"What?" Arleta's chest tightened with panic. She struggled to find the right words. "I thought...I thought you'd be here longer."

The elf took another step into the room but hesitated, as if torn between the idea of staying and leaving. Theo's hands dug further into his pockets as he leaned against the doorframe. "I had planned that too, but it's just time."

Fear whirled in Arleta's chest. She didn't *want* Theo to leave. But she also knew that she couldn't make him stay, especially if she never admitted her feelings toward him: that she now believed they were fated too.

But what if she was wrong?

"What...what will you do back there?" The words barely came out.

"Go back to Faylin, work in the garden, avoid my mother." He shrugged, but a longing to say more lingered in his eyes.

Anxiety skittered in Arleta's chest at his words. They needed more time. *She* needed more time.

"And you can't stay longer here in Adenashire?" Her voice trembled as she took a hesitant step toward Theo. "Help open the bakery?"

Instinctually, he crossed his hands over his chest in a protective gesture. It barely covered the nervous magic that sparkled lightly on his fingers. Quickly, the elf tucked them farther under his arms, likely to avoid Arleta seeing it, but it was too late, as the sparks edged over his shirt. "And then after that?"

She knew what he was getting at. "You have an *elf* Fated waiting for you," Arleta said under her breath, but the excuse she knew was no longer true settled heavy in the air. "It's impossible."

Arleta had to give him one more chance to understand the predicament they were in—that *she* was in.

Despite all the others she'd managed, he was the last risk she just couldn't seem to take.

"There is no other, elf or otherwise, in my future. It's only you. So please don't tell me it's impossible for *me*." Theo bit his lip and raised his gaze to her. "However, if it is for you, I will accept that. But you must let me go if you do not believe us to be fated. No matter how much I want to stay, I can't."

The shock of the blunt statement caught in her throat and pushed Arleta farther back into the kitchen space. She tore her gaze from his face as her mind reeled with all the times she'd spent with Theo in the waking and sleeping world. It felt as if they'd spent a thousand lifetimes together in each other's arms. "And what of…you?"

"You *know* my feelings," Theo said, his voice vulnerable. "I love you, Arleta Starstone."

Arleta's chest heaved at the sound of her name on his lips. The ache of being without him tore at every muscle in her body.

He continued, "You are everything I will ever want. You *are* magic—*more* than magic. Yet, no matter how much my heart wants to remain at your side for the rest of our lives, I will deal with the destiny I have been given—a Fated who does not want me. And I will not hold you back by staying. Being with me or not is your choice. I cannot and would never attempt to make it for you."

Arleta's chest tingled with recognition. Theo *had* heard what she'd said about their relationship to Jez on the road outside of Adenashire and that had been the narrative he'd been living with until now.

Everything in her wanted to clarify how she felt about him, to keep him from leaving, but it still remained unsaid.

"So if you do not love me the way I love you, please tell me so *you* can move on." The magic that had been ebbing over his fingers spread out uncontrolled over Theo's entire body and floated into the room, lighting it as if there were ten times the lanterns there had been only a few moments before.

His words and the emotion flowed off him, consuming her, and if Arleta didn't say something, it would break her in two. The explanation caught in her throat, and she barely got out, "I can't."

"*Why?*" Theo's pupils dilated and he searched her face. "You must." His tone was begging. "I can't do this anymore."

"Because I can't lie to you!" she cried, and with that Arleta's feet moved her, closing the gap between them until there were only inches between their bodies. She could hold back no longer, despite her perceived risk to him or her own heart. Somehow, the words broke from their prison. "Or myself. I love you, Theodmon Brylar. I've seen you in my dreams—*so many* times—and I don't want to spend my waking life without you. It's torture to imagine otherwise. I want every part of you, and I want you to have me. We *are* fated, because I choose it."

And with her admittance of words and soul, the fated bond was sealed.

Arleta's body shuddered next to his. It was as if a magical cord had wrapped around her soul and bound the two of them together.

She couldn't imagine ever being without Theo.

His love was worth the risk.

*He* was worth the risk.

Theo gasped in long-awaited relief and wrapped his arms around Arleta. He pulled her to his waiting chest as the green and gold magic continued to pour from him, changed now from nervous to elated. The strands danced and twined as he ran his hands into her loose, dark hair and held the back of her head as if their lives depended on it.

Arleta raised up on her toes and gently placed her hands on either side of his tear-streaked face. She was finally ready to let go and find out who Arleta Starstone really was, to begin forever by breaking down all her walls. They had served a purpose to protect her once, but no longer did. Arleta was ready to pull the stones down one at a time with Theodmon Brylar at her side.

Her voice and heart filled with anticipation of so much more for herself than just the kiss, she whispered, "Meet me under the laurel. I've been waiting for you for so damn long."

"May I please kiss you now?" Theo's tone was filled with hope.

She smiled. "Yes. And for the rest of my days."

With that, Theo's warm lips were on Arleta's as they shared the passion of a lifetime, dreams, and endless possibilities.

# Epilogue

*Doli*

The carved wooden sign decorated with woodland animals holding cupcakes in the window read CLOSED, but the door would not be locked. Doli knew this. She huffed and puffed from her run through the streets of Adenashire so as not to be late, then reached for the brass handle and gave it a mighty tug.

Once inside, the dwarf flung the envelope into the air, the blue seal on the outside still unbroken, as she ran into A Little Dash of Magic Bake Shop. "I got a letter today," she said, out of breath.

She had been so late that she hadn't even had time to see who it was from.

The store was filled with the mouthwatering scents of bread, sugar, fruit, and herbs, accosting her senses, nearly making her forget what she was talking about or why she was there: the celebration of Arleta and Taenya's shop being open for one month, a milestone worthy of her favorite blue and yellow floral dress.

Jez, Theo, and Arleta sat tucked away at the booth in the corner in conversation, while Taenya stood and wiped the counter in rhythmic strokes. She smiled for a moment before any of them acknowledged her presence. Everything in her loved Adenashire. In the end, Jez was the one to follow Doli all the way to the village and to the rented rooms with her over Verdreth's bookshop, It's About Tome. She could have left anytime and gone back to the Southern Desert, and it spoke volumes that she hadn't.

Plus, she had taken the responsibility of greeting and bringing a basket of goodies to anyone new in town. She loved meeting new people and making them feel welcome.

Doli was glad her friends had decided to keep the booths and tables in the bakery, left over from the café that used to occupy the space. It gave them all a warm, cozy place to hang out together. Plus, the patrons loved it. Judging from the empty displays, most of the pastries had been sold out for the day, but several still waited on a steel platter, plenty for the crew to enjoy.

Jez groaned, breaking Doli's focus on the sweets as she slouched in her seat. "Are you going to open it?" Her furry ear twitched with the faux annoyance she always had for the perky dwarf. "Or just wave it around like a flag?"

Doli stopped at the end of the table and grasped the paper with two hands, eyeing the words in front her:

*To: Dolgrila Butterbuckle*
*c/o Adenashire*

*From: Gingrilin Butterbuckle*
*c/o Dundes Heights*

Doli gazed, transfixed, at the neat handwriting on the front of the envelope, her stomach flopping. "I don't know," she murmured, returning her gaze to her waiting friends. "It's from my mother."

Theo, with his arm draped lazily around Arleta's shoulders, held his free hand up in question. "I fully empathize with your predicament," he announced, his elfin eyes shining.

Arleta gave him a friendly body shove, rolling her eyes. "Your mother is taking positive steps. We can't expect all people to change immediately," she said before bringing her attention back to Doli. She noticed the dwarf admiring her necklace with a pendant of the "Little Mouse" constellation that Theo had made in Langheim especially for her. She softened her voice and asked, "Do you think you should open it?"

Taenya arrived with a tray of delicate teacups, each one hand-painted with golden blooms, and placed one in front of Jez, Theo, Arleta, and one more, likely for herself, since she knew by now that Doli never went anywhere without the cup affixed to her holster belt.

On cue, Doli released the teacup at her waist, placed it on the table next to the fennex, and sat, putting the envelope down and pushing it away. She immediately lay her hand over the top of the cup and before she lifted it, steam, smelling of vanilla, wafted through her fingers. Underneath was a creamy brown tea with three lumps of sugar added. Her favorite.

She turned to Jez just as Taenya reappeared back at the table with the silver platter of treats. "What kind would you like?" Doli asked the fennex.

"Rum?" Jez didn't even look at her while she chose a chocolate pastry twist from the plate with a sprinkle of fresh green herbs on the top, tearing off and stuffing an enormous chunk of it in her mouth.

With a theatrical scoff, Doli moved on to the other cups, already knowing everyone else's favorites. "I can't help you there."

"Fine, just tea," Jez conceded, and Doli immediately placed her hand over the cup and used her magic to fill it.

"So,"—Doli leaned into Arleta and Taenya to shift the conversation—"tell us about the first month." She already knew it had been a success, but wanted to hear about it again anyway, since that was what they were there to celebrate.

Taenya glanced at Arleta as if to give her the lead. The elf had undergone a remarkable transformation while in Adenashire, not only in appearance, with her once long hair now cropped at her chin, but in spirit. It had taken Doli a few days to accept Taenya being in the village, but since Arleta had been willing to trust her, the dwarf could give it a shot too. And the risk had been worth it.

As so many risks in life can be.

Arleta's lips arched into a smile. "It's been amazing. Tae and I, we just…we work really well together. It's amazing to have a person who I can bounce ideas off."

"No one is asking for discounts anymore?" Doli asked.

Arleta tipped her head. "At first they did, but I simply told them no. It's funny how sometimes when you stand up for yourself, people just accept it."

Jez dropped her chin. "Imagine that."

"The ones who don't like it, like Mr. Figlet, just shop elsewhere," Arleta said. "It's their loss."

"*And* we can switch off the early shifts," Taenya added, her shining eyes mirroring Arleta's smile.

Arleta clucked her tongue and pointed at the elf. "That too."

Theo pulled Arleta in close to him and gave her a congratulatory kiss on the cheek.

"Get a room," Jez quipped, a tired jest that felt ancient. However, a fangy grin played at her mouth as if she'd just coined the funniest joke in the realm, and seeing the fennex smile was a treat no matter how you looked at it.

But Doli watched as Arleta didn't miss a beat, and in one playful motion twisted her body toward her woodland elf. Before any counter jokes could be said, she planted an exuberant kiss on Theo's obviously surprised lips. When done, Arleta turned her face to Jez. "Oh, we have one. *And* use it often. Probably will again when this party is over. *Twice.*"

Theo's eyes grew large, and his cheeks went red, seemingly caught off guard that Arleta would up the ante from just the kiss. Sparks of green and gold magic ebbed off his hands, but he quickly recovered, folded them, and raised a brow directed at Arleta. He lowered his tone. "Shall we take our leave right now, my love?"

"Ack!" Jez threw her hands up in a show of defeat. "I fully regret bringing it up! Topic change!"

The hearty laughter that burst forth filled the shop with a kind of warmth not even a wood stove could match.

Jez also seemed to take the opportunity to search the table and find something new to talk about. She quickly snatched up the letter and held it in the air. "How about this?"

"Give me that!" Doli stretched her hand up for the paper, but Jez's arms were considerably longer than the dwarf's, so the action was futile.

"You *should* open the letter, Doli," Taenya said, taking a sip of her tea. "Don't put things off that can be done today. Believe me, I know."

"Fine," Doli said, pinching her fingers together, indicating for Jez to return it.

Jez twisted her lips in question at the dwarf's motives while she kept the letter in the air.

"I'll open it!" Doli said, exasperation coloring her words.

The fennex surrendered the letter, lowering it to the dwarf's level.

Doli took it, offering a resigned sigh. "I'm blaming you all if this goes south," she said in an uncharacteristically gloomy tone, then broke the seal.

With her teeth clenched, she pulled out the crisp paper, unfolded it, and read through her mother's familiar handwriting.

The rest of the table leaned in, looking as if they were holding their breath.

"Well," Theo said, finally broke the silence, "what does it say?"

Doli raised her brow in surprise. "My great-uncle died."

"Oh," Taenya said softly, sympathy in her tone.

The dwarf waved the letter as if to dismiss the concern. "I barely knew him. Maybe I met him once. But he left me something in his will."

"What did he leave you?" Arleta asked, taking a bite of an almond bear claw.

Doli placed the letter on the table and patted it. "I don't know, but apparently it will be delivered by messenger next week." Quickly, she lifted her cup in the air and, voice ringing, declared, "To unexpected surprises!"

Each clinked their cups of tea, smiling. Even Jez.

"To unexpected friends," Taenya added while beaming.

The words settled over the group of friends like a warm, cozy blanket on a wintry day.

❦

The honeyed glow of the lanterns inside A Little Dash of Magic Bake Shop flickered as the evening unfurled. The five unlikely friends—woodland elves, a dwarf, a fennex, and a human— talked and laughed for hours. None of them wanted to be the first to end the festivities.

Not more than half a year before, they had been strangers—at least in the waking world of the Northern Lands. But since then, and more than once, each of them had declared how much they loved each other and couldn't imagine life without the others in it.

They had formed a fellowship of bakers and magic.

And they had many more adventures together waiting out there in Adenashire.

# Bonus Chapter

## *Arleta, (Almost) Eight*

Arleta Starstone couldn't contain her (almost) eight-year-old self. In exactly two hours, she would leave seven behind and never return. She wore her new dress, a light-blue cotton with a tiny cream-colored flower print scattered on the fabric. The half sleeves had dainty ruffles along the hem.

The day was perfect: the sun shone overhead with only a smattering of puffy clouds in the spring sky. It was a perfect day to turn eight.

Completely giddy, she plucked a bundle of purple lavender stems along with white pansies from her parents' garden in the back of the cottage. That year, it was completely overflowing with vegetation. So much so that her parents were forever giving away the excess to the neighbors and their friends in Adenashire. Papa was familiar with most of the residents of the village because he owned the apothecary shop in town. People came around looking for small remedies that were unable to be solved by magic from the resident wizard healer.

Because, of course, magic was never the solution for *every* problem.

Mama was the most amazing baker. She made everything from cookies and cakes to scones and muffins...even though the stove in the house was quite rudimentary. She often dreamed out loud about a fancy cast-iron one she'd spotted at the local bakery. Mama was constantly experimenting, and succeeding, in creating unique flavors that Arleta couldn't get enough of. In fact, that very day Mama was inside preparing the ingredients for a very special cake, and Arleta had been salivating over the idea of the sweet for days.

"What are you doing, little kit?" A deep voice she recognized came from behind.

With a wide smile, Arleta turned to the large, dark-haired orc wearing round spectacles perched on the end of his wide nose. Verdreth was imposing just to look at. He was at least two heads taller than Papa, with green skin and rippling muscles he generally kept hidden under tidy button-up white shirts and cotton pants. His partner, Ervash, was a completely other story. In true orcish fashion, he often showed off his physique, unless it was snowing or a special occasion, then Verdreth encouraged him to put a shirt on.

But as massive as the orcs were compared to humans, particularly a seven-year-old girl (who was about to turn eight), their hearts were equally as big. The Starstones had moved into their cottage when Arleta was only one, and Ervash and Verdreth were the first to greet and welcome them to Adenashire. They had even brought a basket of delicious offerings from the local outdoor market full of honey, meat pies (because who has time to cook dinner when their family moves into a new home?), and pastries (which Arleta had since learned they had eaten half of what they had intended to give their new neighbors).

And ever since, they had been family.

"Picking flowers for my birthday cake!" Arleta held out her dirt-stained hands, holding the bouquet for the orc to admire.

Verdreth's eyes crinkled at the corner as he bent down, obscuring something in his large hand. "Those are very lovely."

Arleta looked down at the happy pansies. "I adore how they have little faces. You think they can talk?"

"Hum." The orc seemed to consider the idea. "Maybe there will be a day you'll meet an elf with plant magic, and they'll tell you."

Gazing down at the bouquet again, Arleta wondered what he was holding but giggled and said, "Not many elves are friends with humans."

The orc shrugged. "It's impossible to predict who the stars may bring into your life when you need them most. Sometimes the skies surprise us. Look at us."

"What's that you have in your hand?" Curiosity overtook her, and Arleta all but forgot what the orc had said concerning elves. She twisted her head to get a peek at the elusive package.

As if to play a game, Verdreth pretended to try to hide it again, although not very successfully. "I'm not sure what you're talking about, little kit." But he grinned, showing off his tusks, as if he knew exactly what she wanted.

"That!" She threw out her free hand and pointed to the brown-paper-wrapped parcel.

"This?" He held it up in the air, his eyes shining. "This is for an *eight-year-old* girl I believe lives around here." Verdreth looked around like he was searching for the mentioned girl.

Arleta's insides quivered with anticipation as she squeezed the flower stems a bit too tightly. "Me! I'm eight!" She paused for a blink. "Well, *almost*. In two hours!"

The orc slowly produced the simple package tied with cotton twine in a large floppy bow. "Is that so? Seems close enough for me." He also held out his free hand. "How about we trade for a moment?"

With gusto, Arleta thrust the flowers into his palm and grabbed the rectangular present. It felt solid, heavy. Like a good gift.

"Good morning, Verdreth." Papa's voice came from the walkway to the back of the cottage.

"It is. Isn't it, Declan?" the orc said. "You're home from the shop early."

As Arleta carefully removed the twine and unwrapped the present, her father walked up to them, his leather apothecary bag slung over his shoulder.

"Just had to go in and take care of a few things." The bearded human with kind hazel eyes gazed down at his daughter. "But it's a good day to celebrate."

With the tip of her tongue pinched beneath her teeth and lips, Arleta managed to rip off the last bit of paper, fully revealing the gift inside, a book titled *Baking All Over the Northern Lands*. A detailed illustration of an ornate cake decorated the front of the linen cover. She immediately flipped it open to reveal the pages within.

"A recipe book of my very own?" She could barely believe it. Her mother had a small library on the kitchen shelves, but none of them belonged to Arleta.

Verdreth grinned at Declan. "*Someone* told me baking was an interest of yours, and we just got in a few copies at the bookstore."

Beaming up at her father, she held out the thick tome to him. "Look, Papa!"

"I love it," Papa said.

"Oh, there you are." Mama came out the back door, her long chestnut hair, matching her daughter's, pulled into a low ponytail. She wiped her flour-dusted hands on her off-white, slightly stained apron. "I thought there were voices."

With joy beating in her heart, Arleta skipped over to her mother and held out the book with both hands. "See what Mr. Verdreth gave me for my birthday, Mama?"

"Oh, stars." Mama drew her hand to her heart. "How exciting."

"Can we make something from it together?" Arleta chirped.

Mama gave a wry grin. "Well, I had *thought* you'd first promised to help me make your coconut cake for tonight. But you seemed to have disappeared." Her tone was light while she raised her brows in jest. "I could have heard wrong."

Arleta's cheeks heated red. "I was getting the flowers for the decoration and got a little distracted."

The child was often distracted.

Her mother laughed and ran her fingers through Arleta's messy, loose hair. "My love, of course we can make something from the book. But for now we need to get those flowers." Her eyes twinkled as she moved her gaze beyond her daughter.

"Right here," Verdreth said with a tinge of levity from behind them.

Arleta twisted around to her father and the orc, both of whom had a single pansy tucked over their ears.

Everyone burst out laughing, and the sound was as sweet as any creation that might have been written inside the book Arleta still held in her hands.

"We'll see you and Ervash tonight?" Mama asked. "Six o'clock sharp. And there's coconut cake for dessert."

"Wouldn't miss our girl's eighth-year celebration, Nina." Verdreth gazed at Arleta and then handed Papa the remaining bouquet of pansies and lavender. "I'll leave you to the preparations. I may or may not have more presents to wrap." He waved goodbye and strutted to his cottage with the flower still on his ear.

When he was gone, Mama placed her arm around Arleta's shoulders, while Papa, sans his flower accessory, walked toward his wife and planted a soft kiss on her cheek.

"You're beautiful," he said. "As always."

Mama beamed.

Then he drew his kind gaze to his daughter. "And, birthday girl, what do you think if, after the party, we stay up late for stargazing? I heard the Little Mouse will be especially bright tonight." He whispered, as if in secret, "Don't tell Mama."

But Mama only grinned while Papa took one of the pansies from his hand and placed it over his daughter's ear.

The Little Mouse had always been their favorite constellation, and Arleta relished the special times she spent with her father studying the stars long past her bedtime.

"Perhaps I'll join you," Mama said.

Arleta bobbed her head up and down as she clutched her precious gift. "Yes, please!"

And even at (almost) eight, Arleta Starstone knew the true gifts in life were the people she shared it with every day.

# *The*
# LANGHEIM
# BAKING
# BATTLE
## *Recipes*

I hope you and those you love enjoy
these three magical recipes as much
as I enjoyed making them.

# Salted Brown Butter
## CHOCOLATE CHIP COOKIES

## Ingredients

- 1 cup unsalted butter (2 sticks)
- 1¼ cup all-purpose flour (150 grams)
- 1¼ cup bread flour* (150 grams)
- 1 teaspoon baking soda (6 grams)
- 1 teaspoon baking powder (4.8 grams)
- ¾ cup white sugar (151 grams)
- 1¼ cup packed brown sugar (260 grams)
- ¾ teaspoon salt (4.3 grams)
- 1 tablespoon vanilla (13 grams)
- 1 large whole egg, plus 1 egg yolk, room temperature
- 12 ounces semisweet chocolate chips (one standard bag) or chopped semisweet chocolate
- Flaky sea salt for topping

# Instructions

Place 12 tablespoons of butter in a medium skillet and melt over medium-high heat. Once melted, wait for 2–8 minutes (mine took 7.5 minutes) while stirring gently with a wooden spoon. The butter will give off a nutty smell and become a dark golden brown.

The moment the butter starts to brown, remove the skillet from the heat. Next, transfer the butter to either a large heat-resistant bowl or a stand mixer bowl.

Stir in the last 4 tablespoons of cold butter with the hot brown butter until combined.

Rest the butter and let it cool** in the refrigerator for 15 minutes.

While the butter is chilling, combine all-purpose flour, bread flour, baking soda, and baking powder in a medium bowl and set aside.

Once the browned butter has chilled, add white and brown sugar, salt, and vanilla to it. Then use a handheld or stand mixer to blend the ingredients together, starting at low speed and gradually increasing to medium to avoid splashing.

Add the egg and yolk and mix for 30 seconds until the mixture is smooth and combined. Let the mixture rest for 3 minutes and repeat the process of mixing for 30 seconds and resting for 3 minutes twice more.

Add the flour combination to the bowl and use the stand mixer or hand mixer on medium to mix just until combined (1 minute or less).

Mix chocolate chips or chopped chocolate into the dough using a spatula or spoon.

To make roughly 24 cookies, use a medium, 3-tablespoon scoop or a spoon to portion the dough, roll into a ball, then refrigerate for at least 30 minutes and up to 48 hours.

Preheat the oven to 350°F when ready to bake.

On a metal sheet pan lined with parchment paper, place 6 cookie balls per sheet, with 2–3 inches between them.

Add a pinch of flaky sea salt on every dough ball.

Place one cookie tray at a time on the center oven rack and bake for 14–17 minutes until golden brown with browned and set edges.

Remove from oven*** and allow to cool on wire rack.

It will be difficult to wait, but for the best results the cookies should be completely cooled before devouring.

# Notes

* The bread flour addition makes a chewier cookie (which

I love). In case you don't have bread flour, you can substitute an equal amount of all-purpose flour and still get good results.

** It is critical to let the browned butter cool. If not cooled, when added to the egg mixture, the eggs can scramble.

*** Right after taking the cookies out of the oven, tap the back of a heatproof spoon along any edges that went beyond a rounded shape to make them more uniform.

I highly recommend weighing the dry ingredients by using a food scale. This will ensure the correct ratios of ingredients, which can have a large impact on the finished product.

This recipe incorporates the *Cook's Illustrated* chocolate chip cookies recipe's technique of combining the melted butter with the wet ingredients.

# Lemon Bars
## *with*
## CARDAMOM SHORTBREAD CRUST

Cardamom is an interesting spice with an almost piney, perfume scent and taste. It gives a unique twist on lemon bars. If you don't have it or simply crave regular lemon bars, omit the cardamom. Either way you'll have a delicious treat.

## Ingredients

**FOR THE CRUST:**
- Cooking spray or butter for the bottom of metal pan
- 1 cup all-purpose flour (135 grams)
- ¼ cup granulated sugar (45 grams)
- ⅛ teaspoon salt
- 1½ tsp cardamom (omit for a plain shortbread crust)
- ½ tsp vanilla
- 2 tablespoons finely grated fresh lemon zest
- 7 tablespoons unsalted cold butter (90 grams)

**FOR THE FILLING:**
- 4 large eggs
- 1 cup granulated sugar (200 grams)
- ⅛ teaspoon salt
- ½ cup freshly squeezed lemon juice
- ¼ cup all-purpose flour (30 grams)

**FOR THE POWDERED SUGAR TOPPING:**
- 1 tsp cornstarch
- ½ cup powdered sugar

# Instructions

Prepare an 8x8 metal baking dish with butter or cooking spray. (Don't use glass because of the chilling step for the shortbread. Glass can shatter if put in a hot oven while it's cold.) Cut two pieces of parchment paper to fit the dish with 1–2 inches overhang. Arrange the parchment paper in a cross pattern. Set aside.

To make the shortbread crust, use a food processor with a blade attachment to mix the flour, sugar, salt, cardamom, vanilla, and lemon zest. Pulse several times. Add cold butter cubes to the mixture and pulse until the a coarse crumb texture is achieved.

Using your fingers, press the dough into an even layer in the prepared 8x8 metal baking pan. Then, place it in the refrigerator and chill for 15 minutes.

Preheat the oven to 325°F.

After cooling for 15 minutes, place the metal pan on the center oven rack and parbake the crust for 15–20 minutes until it turns light golden brown.

As the crust bakes, you can prepare the filling. Take a large bowl or the bowl of a stand mixer and add the eggs, sugar, and salt. Combine either by hand whisking or using the wire whip attachment to blend. Add lemon juice and flour, then combine.

Optional: To make the filling smoother, you can push it through a wire sieve with the back of a spoon.

Take out the partially baked crust from the oven and pour the lemon filling over it.

Place back in the oven and bake for 15–20 minutes or until the center of the filling is set. The edges of the bars should be light brown.

Place bars on a wire rack and allow to cool for 1 hour, then refrigerate for at least 2 more hours. By taking this extra chilling step, the bars can be cut with a clean edge.

After chilling, remove bars from the fridge and slice using a sharp knife. (Helpful hint: keep a cup of water close by when cutting the bars, clean the blade often, and dip the knife into the water.)

Combine cornstarch and powdered sugar. Adding cornstarch will stop powdered sugar from disappearing or weeping.

Transfer the cornstarch and powered sugar mixture into a wire sieve.

Place bars on a platter and sprinkle the powdered sugar on top.

# Note

Bars should either be consumed within 24 hours or covered and kept in the fridge for up to 3 days.

# Earl Grey
## CHERRY SCONES

## Ingredients

**FOR THE DOUGH:**
- 3 cups all-purpose flour (375 grams)
- ½ cup granulated sugar (100 grams)
- 1 tablespoon finely ground Earl Grey tea (about 4 bags)
- 1 teaspoon salt (5–6 grams)
- 1 tablespoon baking powder (14 grams)
- ⅔–¾ cup half-and-half, divided (start with ⅔ cup liquid total)
- 2 bags of Earl Grey tea (to steep in liquid)
- 10 tablespoons unsalted butter, frozen and grated (140 grams)
- 6 oz dried cherries (170 grams)
- 2 large eggs (room temperature)
- 2 teaspoons vanilla extract

**FOR THE GLAZE:**

- 1 cup powdered sugar
- ½ teaspoon vanilla
- 1–1½ tablespoons half-and-half

# Instructions

Line a baking sheet with parchment paper. Set aside.

Whisk together the flour, granulated sugar, ground tea (not the tea still in bags), salt, and baking powder in a large mixing bowl. Set aside.

Gently heat up 1/3 cup half-and-half in the microwave for about 30 seconds or in a small saucepan over medium heat until it's almost boiling but not quite.

Add 2 bags of Earl Grey tea and allow to steep in the half-and-half 5–10 minutes. When done, remove and dispose of bags and set half-and-half aside.

Use a box grater to grate 10 tablespoons of frozen butter.

Incorporate butter into the dry mixture, stirring and working it in slightly. The butter should easily incorporate and resemble uneven crumbs.

Add dried cherries and stir.

In a separate medium bowl, combine eggs, vanilla, 1/3 cup

tea-steeped half-and-half, and the remaining 1/3 cup plain half-and-half by whisking them together.

Combine the wet and dry ingredients and stir gently until the flour is moistened. (Add a tablespoon or two of half-and-half to the mix if it's too dry, until the dough is slightly sticky but not too wet.)

Place the dough onto wax paper that's been floured well and begin shaping it into a rectangle that's approximately 1–1.5 inches thick.

Fold the rectangle in half and reshape it into a rectangle that's 1–1.5 inches thick, repeating this process one more time.

Split the dough into two parts and transfer them to a baking sheet covered in parchment paper.

Take each piece and shape it into a round of about 6 inches, placing them next to each other.

Place the baking sheet with dough rounds into the freezer for 30 minutes.*

Preheat oven to 450°F.

Take out the scones from the freezer after 30 minutes and cut each round into 6 equal wedges using a sharp knife. Remember to clean the knife between cuts if the dough sticks.

Arrange the pieces on the baking sheet, leaving a 1-inch gap between them.

Brush each scone with half-and-half.

Bake the scones for 14–17 minutes until lightly brown. (Mine took 15 minutes.)

Remove from the oven and cool the scones completely.

Prepare the glaze. Combine powdered sugar, vanilla, and 1 tablespoon of half-and-half. Add one extra teaspoon of plain half-and-half at a time if the mixture is too dry. It should not be too thick or too thin.

Fill a zip-top bag with the glaze, then cut a small hole in one corner. When scones are completely cool, drizzle the glaze over each scone.

Scones that are uneaten can be stored for several days at room temperature in a zip-top bag or frozen for up to 3 months.

# Note:

\* If you intend to keep the scones in the freezer for over 30 minutes, I suggest cutting them into wedges before freezing. Avoid moving the wedges apart on the baking sheet until after freezing as they become easier to handle when frozen or partially frozen.

# About the Author

Baking magic into every page, J. Penner crafts cozy fantasy from her sun-kissed San Diego home. With a cat on her lap and a pen in her hand, she invites you into worlds as warm and comforting as a cup of tea.

Website: jpennerauthor.com
Facebook: jpennerauthor
Instagram: @jpennerauthor
TikTok: @jpennerauthor
Bluesky: @jpennerauthor.bsky.social

# WELCOME TO

# ADENASHIRE!

Spilling the tea has never been so cozy!
Look for these titles in J. Penner's
heartwarming Adenashire series.

## A Fellowship of
## Librarians & Dragons

In the quaint town of Adenashire, Doli Butterbuckle, a people-pleasing sunshine dwarf, is content with her simple tea magic and circle of friends. It's true she's never quite lived up to her family's expectations, but life is just fine. That is, until she inherits a dragon egg and turns to a charming gargoyle harboring a secret to help her…

# A Fellowship
# of Games & Fables

Jez, a grumpy fennex, wants nothing to do with the cold, snow, or bustling winter games descending on Adenashire. She'd rather curl up for a nap. But when a drunken boast lands her smack in the middle of the festivities and—even worse—fake dating her friend Taenya, she might just enjoy the season yet.

**"Filled with so much love, heart, and delicious baked goods—this cozy fantasy has secured its legacy in a genre dedicated to quiet moments of comfort."**
—Rebecca Thorne, *USA Today* bestselling author of *Can't Spell Treason Without Tea*, for *A Fellowship of Bakers & Magic*

For more info about Sourcebooks's books and authors, visit:
**sourcebooks.com**